ENSLAVED
THE DRUID CHRONICLES, BOOK 3

CHRISTINA PHILLIPS

PHOENIX 18 PUBLISHING

Enslaved
The Druid Chronicles, Book 3

Copyright © Christina Phillips 2013/2016

All rights reserved. This book is for your personal enjoyment only. No part of this book may be reproduced, scanned or distributed in any printed or electronic form without prior written permission from the author, except for the use of brief quotations in a book review. Thank you for respecting the hard work of this author.

This is a work of fiction. Names, characters, places and incidents either are the product of the author's imagination or are used fictitiously, and any resemblance to actual persons, living or dead, business establishments, events or locales is entirely coincidental.

Enslaved was previously published as *Betrayed* in 2013

ISBN: 978-0-6487568-2-8

Cover Art by Kim Killion of The Killion Group Inc

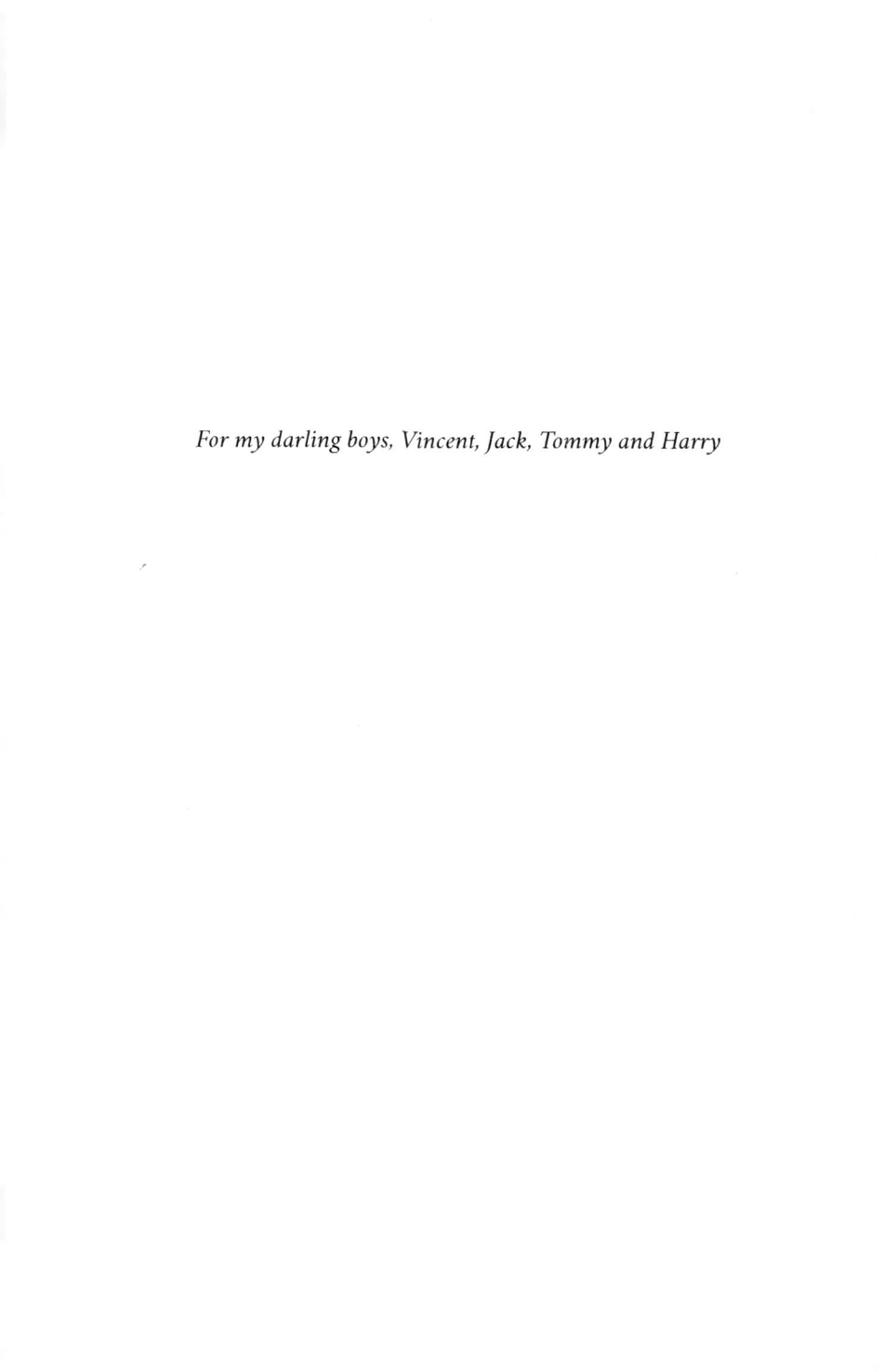

For my darling boys, Vincent, Jack, Tommy and Harry

CHAPTER 1

CYMRU, AD 51

"I'll find your daughter." Nimue unsheathed her dagger and glanced over to Caratacus, where he stood glaring at his warriors. It was obvious the Briton king wanted to stay and fight the barbarous Romans, yet equally clear if he did, he would be captured. "Where are you heading?"

"The land of the Brigantes," one of the warriors said. Nimue gave a brief nod, turned and ran farther into the mountain, to where she had last seen Caratacus' queen and daughter.

She knew of the land of the Brigantes, even if she had never been there. It was in the north, one of the few places left in Britain that had not succumbed to Roman rule.

Will my beloved Cymru succumb, now that the rebellion has failed?

She wouldn't think of it. *Couldn't* think of it. The notion of Romans swarming over her land chilled her blood and sickened her stomach. She tightened her grip on her dagger, crouched low behind concealing rocks and sent desperate prayers to her Goddess, Arianrhod.

Let me find the Briton queen before the enemy does.

Battle cries split the blood-drenched air, the clash of sword and shield echoed through the mountain passes and the earth vibrated with the relentless march of the Legions. Nimue pushed back her sweaty hair and glanced over her shoulder. For the moment, she was alone. She leaped to her feet, sprinted across the trampled grass to the small stand of trees where, beyond, she hoped the queen remained along with other non-fighting women in the secluded hollow.

"Choice is yours." The coarse Latin accent punched through Nimue's senses and she froze. She was too late. The Romans had discovered the hiding place. "You or your daughter."

Heart thudding high in her breast, Nimue edged toward the source of the voice. If there were only one or two legionaries, she might stand a chance. The queen was no warrior and the princess scarcely more than a child, but Nimue's aim with the arrow was unerring. Stealthily she sheathed her dagger and primed her bow. The trees thinned and relief scudded through her blood.

Only one filthy legionary loomed over the queen who shielded her terrified daughter with her body. As the legionary shoved the queen to the ground and prepared to mount her, Nimue let fly with her arrow and bared her teeth in satisfaction as the poisoned tip ripped into the heathen's vulnerable neck.

His strangled scream ended with a gurgle before she even reached the queen's side. There was no sign of the other women. Clearly they had fled as the battle approached.

"Where is the king?" The queen pushed herself to her feet and wound her arm around the princess. "We were about to follow the others farther up the mountain when that dog accosted us."

Thank the Goddess they hadn't left this hollow. Nimue would never have found them otherwise.

"I'm to take you to your king." She slung her bow over her shoulder and glanced around to ensure they were still alone. But they would not be alone for much longer. "If we make haste we might catch up with them before they leave the mountain."

"Is the battle over?" The princess, barely twelve summers old, looked at the fallen legionary and shivered.

Nimue reined in her impatience to leave this cursed mountain and turned to the girl to offer what comfort she could.

"No. The battle will never be over. Always remember that."

"The Druid speaks the truth." The queen smoothed her daughter's tangled hair back from her face. "Be brave for a little longer. When we rest, she can tend your wound."

Her wound? Only then did Nimue see the bloodied cloth tied around the girl's calf and another wave of impatience rolled through her. If only she possessed a sturdier frame, instead of the slender build she had inherited from her mother. While she was fast and agile on her feet and trained brutally to strengthen her muscles, she knew the princess was too big for her to carry any distance. She hoped the injury wouldn't slow them down.

"We don't have time to rest." Her voice was harsh, in an effort to convey how grave the situation was. "Come quickly, before the barbarians smother this mountain."

Without waiting for a response, or to see if her blunt words caused offense—they were not, after all, *her* queen or princess— she turned and led the way back through the trees. To her right, farther down the mountain, she saw the Romans' continued advance. No longer did they hold their shields over them in an impenetrable shell. There was no need. No Celt archers remained behind to rain death on their heads.

There was no time for sorrow, but still the acidic pain clenched deep inside. As she gestured for the queen and princess to crouch low and follow her, she recalled how certain she had been of her people's victory.

This battle should have been decisive. It should have crushed the enemy underfoot. Caratacus had persuaded them with his vision of triumph to leave the safety of their magical enclave and follow him to this quagmire of devastation.

They should never have left the enclave. They should have stayed and continued with the isolated attacks on the Legions. And she could have continued to unravel the mystery of the

Source of Annwyn. The power the great High Druid, Aeron, had harnessed from the cradle of the gods themselves with the help of Gwydion, the greatest of the Magician Gods. The magic Aeron had used, through the sacred bluestones, to conceal his clan of Druids from the invaders.

She ignored the labored breathing of the princess and the hushed encouragement of the queen to continue onward. Of course they had to continue onward. Just as she would continue onward with her quest.

Her fingers instinctively curled around the small leather pouch attached to her belt. After Aeron's heroic death, the immense bluestones that had protected his clan had shattered, catapulting precious shards across Cymru. From those shards, a second enclave had been created, a safe haven for the rebels in the midst of their enemy. And just before they had left their retreat, she'd stolen one of the shards and hidden it in her pouch.

This defeat would not deter her. The shards of bluestone had protected and hidden the rebels from the Romans sight, but they were a faint echo of the original magic. Not even the wisest of the Druids had been able to comprehend how it worked. Only that it did. But she would discover how Aeron had manipulated the Source to his will. When she completed her mission, she would return to the enclave and pursue the sacred knowledge. Gwydion would not assist her, a lowly acolyte. But, as mighty as he was, he was not the greatest of the gods. Her beloved Arianrhod, the powerful Moon Goddess, surpassed him in wisdom and knowledge. And Arianrhod would assist Nimue so she could follow Aeron's lead, and eliminate all Romans from the land of her foremothers.

She heard a stumble from behind her, a pained gasp, and then the queen gripped her shoulder and forced her to turn around.

"Druid, we must rest. My daughter is unable to travel any farther."

One glance at the princess confirmed the queen's words. The

girl was pale, sweaty and biting her lip in an effort not to make any sound of discomfort.

Nimue again silently cursed the fact that she didn't possess the brute warrior strength she craved. They would go no farther this day until she had treated the princess' wound.

"Quickly." She gestured toward a rocky outcrop. The shallow crevasse it overhung could be easily concealed with the strategic repositioning of a couple of small bushes. As the queen helped her daughter inside, Nimue dragged over a couple of rocks and wedged greenery between them. The camouflage would withstand a cursory glance. She hoped.

She crawled inside the makeshift shelter and made a quick examination of the gash on the princess' leg. It looked clean enough but continued to seep blood. And the girl certainly needed something for the pain.

What she really needed was to rest the leg, but since that was impossible, Nimue pulled her medicine bag over her head, dumped it on the ground and opened it. She could make a dressing for the wound to ensure it remained free of poison, and she could prepare a soothing tea with the last of her water to ease the pain.

She took a calming breath. There was no use railing against fate. They would not catch up with Caratacus now so she might as well accept the fact she would be taking the queen and her daughter to the land of the Brigantes herself.

"We will stay here until nightfall," she told them. "The moon will guide our way." She hadn't anticipated an overnight journey but the wise Arianrhod, Goddess of the Moon and weaver of the fates, would ensure their safety.

Swiftly, she prepared the pain-relieving tea. How shortsighted of her not to have filled her water skin before the battle began today.

"I need to find a stream."

"You're not leaving us?" The queen sounded incredulous.

"I'll be back directly." Nimue glanced at the princess, to ensure she had finished the potion. At least now the girl's discomfort would be dulled. She returned her attention to the queen. "Remain here. The Legions are advancing along another path." At least that had been her impression when she'd seen them in the distance. Besides, Arianrhod wouldn't have led them to this resting place if danger waited.

Without waiting for further argument, she unsheathed her dagger and cautiously left the shelter. Arianrhod was watching over her, but it was always wise to take precautions.

∼

EVENTUALLY, Nimue found a stream and as she filled the water skin, her dagger lying across her knees, she looked into the distance, where majestic mountains dominated the far horizon. No sound of battle reached her. No stink of blood or churned earth to give a hint of the devastation that she'd witnessed earlier.

She breathed in great lungfuls of the fresh mountain air, as if it might somehow cleanse the horror of her people's defeat from her soul. They would rise again. They would rid the enemy from their land. And they would—

An eerie chill trickled along her spine, causing the hair to rise on the back of her neck and arms. She leaped to her feet, dagger once again in her hand. But it wasn't a lone legionary who had caught her so unawares. It was a mounted Roman officer, in a flowing scarlet cloak, with his shield in one hand and sword in the other.

For a moment, all she could feel was the erratic thud of her heart in her ears, the uneven gasp of her breath in her throat. The sun dazzled her, glinting off the polished metal of his armor as he stared down at her, and obscurely, she noted his impressive biceps, his muscles flexing as he urged his horse forward.

Flee. The command whispered in her mind, faint and insubstantial. The treacherous rocks on her right, the fast flowing stream at her back and the steep bank on the far side didn't offer her a speedy escape. But somehow, she had to lead him farther away from the queen and princess. Except he had effectively trapped her by the edge of the stream.

Yet even as the weight of her responsibility tormented her conscience, she couldn't drag her fascinated gaze from the Roman. His face was hard, autocratic, unsmiling. The face of countless Romans, and yet like none she had ever seen before. His eyes were narrowed, his strong jaw shadowed. And the tip of his sword was a mere arm's length from her face.

"Surrender to the might of the Eagle," he said in the ancient Celtic language of her people. His voice was deep, sensuous, and dark embers stirred as if she faced a brave warrior of Cymru instead of a cowardly barbarian of Rome. "And you shall remain unharmed."

Her palm was sweaty around her dagger and she tightened her grip before it slipped from her grasp. She might not have a chance against this Roman but she would never surrender to him. And she would never willingly give up her weapons, either.

"I would sooner die fighting you," she said in Latin, just to show him she was no ignorant native of a fractured land. Her mother had taught her the language well. "Than surrender my freedom to your filthy Emperor."

She had no freedom under Rome. As soon as they discovered she was a Druid, her life would be forfeit. Crucifixion was terrifying enough, but it was the torture she would doubtless endure beforehand that shriveled her soul.

His black stallion whickered and pawed the ground, but the Roman didn't break eye contact nor did his sword waver.

"Brave words, little Celt." Still he spoke in her language, and disbelief unfurled through her breast at the tone of his voice. Did he find her challenge amusing? "But I don't fight women."

She ignored the threat of his sword and stepped forward, her dagger on clear display. He had no right to enter *her* land and then mock her prowess as a warrior. Just because she didn't possess the brute strength of a full-grown male didn't mean she lacked dexterity or speed. She glared up at him, wishing, obscurely, she could see the color of his eyes.

"Why? Are you afraid I may unman you?" Why was she trying to raise his ire? Wouldn't it make more sense to beg for freedom? Pretend to be a mere peasant, caught up in this revolt? Perhaps, then, he would allow her to escape without persecution?

Even as the thought teased her mind, she knew the silver bracelets on her wrists, the torque at her throat and jewels in her ears plainly branded her as anything but a peasant.

For one brief moment the corner of his lips quirked. Clearly he found her not only amusing, but highly entertaining.

"I believe I'm more than man enough for you, Celt." His voice was a seductive caress along the naked flesh of her arms.

What little breath she retained in her lungs evaporated, scorched by the heat his words ignited in her blood. The danger of his sword, the reality of her dagger, faded, insubstantial as a distant dream. All she could see was this Roman as he looked down his aristocratic nose at her, as though she were a delectable slave he wanted to purchase.

She failed to summon righteous fury at such a thought. She didn't have the strength. Because she needed all her wits to fight the overpowering urge to drag him from his horse and discover for herself whether he was man enough for her.

Goddess, what was she thinking? She tightened her grip on her dagger and stood her ground by sheer force of her Druidic will. He was a Roman. She would rather die here, impaled on his sword, than give in to such despicable desire.

For one sizzling moment, she imagined him impaling her, but it was not with his sword and it was not through her heart.

The ugly truth shamed the depths of her being, but it was the truth nevertheless. She wanted him.

She would cut out her tongue before she ever admitted such to another living soul.

"I believe I would need to be dead before you ever had the chance to find out." Her voice was husky, seductive, and the tightening of his jaw told her that, despite her resolve, she had failed to hide her illicit interest.

He didn't lean toward her. He was too proud, too sure of his own superiority and yet he filled her vision. As if nothing else on this mountain existed, and everything beyond was nothing but a bloodied nightmare.

"There would be little fun to be had if you were dead."

Her mouth dried, pulses hammered. It was inconceivable, unbelievable, but this Roman barbarian was flirting with her. He behaved as though they had met by chance in a marketplace, and not on the edges of a devastating battlefield.

A vague thought fluttered through the outer reaches of her mind. Why did he not attempt to disarm her? One thrust of his sword would end this confrontation. Yet still she couldn't back away from the danger. Still she couldn't drag her mesmerized gaze from his compelling face.

She fought the primitive need spiraling through her treacherous body.

"I didn't think Romans were so fastidious." Why did she continue this conversation? Was she truly so desperate to hear his voice once again?

"This Roman," his voice dropped lower, and liquid heat bathed her core, "prefers his women to possess a heartbeat. At the very least." *Unbearable*. She struggled against the need to press her thighs together and rub her aching breasts against this cursed invader's naked chest.

"And I prefer my men to possess a heart, at the very least." The words were out before she could stop them. As though she conversed with an equal, one worthy of her time. One worthy of her desire.

She scarcely managed to prevent squirming with shame. Except it wasn't shame that quivered through her breast or thundered against her skull. It was pure, unbridled lust.

"I possess a heart," he said. "As you will very soon discover when you lay naked in my arms." There was no mistake this time. He was mocking her. Yet she remained rooted to the ground, held by an invisible enchantment. And then he angled his body toward her. A slight movement, but a movement nevertheless. "All you have to do is surrender into my custody."

She could throw her dagger at his throat. Except she knew she would never have time to aim the deadly thrust before he killed her with his sword. And what would become of the queen and princess then?

"Beware, Roman." Far from sounding like a threat, she sounded as if she wished her words to caress. "Give me the slightest opportunity and I will carve your corrupt heart from your chest."

"That sounds…" He paused, considering the matter. "Stimulating."

Her own heart thudded against her ribs, as if it wished to make its own unorthodox escape from her chest. Her breath tangled in her throat and again the image of him impaling her with his foreign cock flooded her scalding senses.

She almost lost her tenuous grip on her dagger.

"I would never willingly share your bed." But who was she trying to convince? This Roman? Or herself?

This time his lips curved into a smile of pure decadence. "I will greatly enjoy changing your mind, Celt."

She tried to drag her gaze from his lips, but failed. How would they taste? How would they feel? When it came to pleasuring the flesh, how talented with his mouth was this arrogant invader?

"Then you are destined for grave disappointment." But the response was hollow because it was she who was destined for disappointment. The knowledge disgusted her as much as it confused her. How could she want a *Roman*? She had despised their race her entire life. She always would. This heat in her blood was nothing more than the aftereffects from the battle. It had nothing to do with the man who looked at her as if he'd like to strip her naked and intimately examine every flushed particle of flesh she possessed.

"I don't intend to be disappointed in this matter." He leaned a little farther over his horse, and yet still his sword did not waver. One false move and he could cut her down in an instant. "You will share my bed, and you will enjoy every mindless, ecstatic orgasm I claim from your writhing body."

Her chest contracted, as if he had reached inside her and squeezed the air from her lungs. His words conjured up a vision so intense, so vivid, she could feel his hands on her body. Could feel the tension screaming through her blood. Could see, on the edges of her sanity, dark fulfillment that would curse her soul forevermore.

She raised her arm, her dagger a poor defense against his Roman weapon. She didn't know what she intended. But in that instant as he looked at her, she saw the color of his eyes. A strange shade of blue, violet, unusual... entrancing. Before she could fully comprehend why she was moving toward him, a blinding pain wrenched through her shoulder, catapulting her backward to the ground. In that fleeting moment, as incomprehension weaved through her stunned senses, she saw the arrow embedded in her shoulder before her head cracked against something hard and the world turned black.

CHAPTER 2

*L*ucius Marius Tacitus saw the arrow impale the water sprite and saw her enchanting green eyes widen in shock, but before he managed to leap from his horse, she tumbled to the ground.

White fury lanced through his chest as he sheathed his sword and knelt by her side. She still breathed. But she was not conscious.

"Sir, are you harmed?" The mounted auxiliary rode to his side, his bow in his hand. Tacitus gave him a scathing glare.

"Harmed?" Derision dripped from the word. "By the hand of a *girl?*"

The foreign auxiliary glanced at the fallen Celt. "She'd drawn her dagger. I thought her about to attack you."

Tacitus' fist clenched. By the gods, he'd string that Gallian auxiliary up by his balls if this Celt died from her injuries.

"Whether she attacked or not, the danger was negligible." Gingerly he lifted her honey-colored braid. It was surprisingly heavy.

No blood seeped into the grass beneath her.

With odd reluctance, he released her hair and frowned into

her face. He knew he had never seen her before. He would never forget a face such as hers. And yet the eerie certainty that they had met in the past gnawed at the edges of his consciousness.

The auxiliary had dismounted and now stood by his side. "She's no peasant," he said, stating the obvious as though it were a great revelation. "She'll fetch a good price on the block."

Distaste for the Gallian mutated into cold loathing. Tacitus stood, towered over the other man, using not only his superior height and strength but also his rank and, gods curse it, his formidable heritage to intimidate.

Before the Gallian had time to do anything but stumble back in sudden alarm, another officer and several auxiliaries of the cavalry appeared. Tacitus transferred his glare to the tribune, Blandus, his own blood cousin, who had arrived with the Legion commanded by Ostorius Scapula the previous day.

Raw frustration ripped through his chest. When he'd encountered the Celt kneeling by the stream, his interest had been caught. When she whirled around, dagger in hand, he'd been enchanted by the vision of the fragile water sprite in warrior maiden mode. And when she answered him back as if she was his equal and not in imminent danger from her deadliest enemy, he'd been captivated.

There had been no doubt in his mind that this day would end with her in his bed.

"Tacitus." Blandus grinned, clearly well satisfied with the day's events. Until moments ago, Tacitus had been feeling good about the day too. Until that fucking stupid Gallian had interfered. "Wondered where you'd disappeared to." His gaze shifted to the ground, to where the Celt lay. "Not dead is she?"

"No." Tacitus forced the word between his teeth. A few moments longer was all he had needed to secure her surrender. Then he could have protected her as a casualty of war. Now if she survived, she risked the fate of all captured insurgents.

And looking as she did, her fate would not be crucifixion.

Blandus dismounted and strolled toward the fallen woman. "Gods, she's a beauty." He crouched down to get a closer look. Tacitus only just prevented himself from shoving his cousin onto his arse. "Clean her up, get rid of the blood and filth." Blandus reached out and brushed tendrils of her hair from her face. If any other man had dared to touch her so, Tacitus would smash his fist into their face. But Blandus was his cousin, and this woman —*this girl*—did not even belong to him to warrant such protection.

"And the arrow." Tacitus' voice was scathing. "Or didn't you notice that?"

Blandus grunted. "Whoever is responsible for that should be gutted." His hand curved over her uninjured shoulder and along her arm, before cradling her breasts.

Tacitus crouched on the other side of the Celt and glowered at Blandus. "She's not a fucking horse. Take your hands off her."

Blandus shot him a salacious grin before sliding his fingers across her belly toward the apex of her thighs. Tacitus knocked his hand away. It turned his stomach to see Blandus treat her as if she wasn't even human.

"I see the way your mind is working." Blandus' voice was low, although dark amusement glinted in his eyes. "She's damaged goods. We could get her for a bargain if we offered to attend her injuries ourselves. And I've no doubt we could make a good profit on resale by the time we tired of her."

Tacitus looked back at her face and a jolt shot through him. Her eyes were open, staring up at him, but they were glazed as though she could not truly see him. Without thinking, he cupped her jaw and rubbed his thumb across her cheek. As much as he wished to take issue with his cousin's offensive remarks if he didn't get this Celt back to civilization soon, the chances were high she wouldn't survive the night.

With a deep breath, he gripped the arrow in her shoulder and snapped the shaft. She gasped and then her eyes rolled back and she descended once more into oblivion.

"Ten lashes?" Blandus said as Tacitus gently lifted the Celt into his arms. He hoped she remained unconscious until the physician managed to remove the rest of the arrow from her shoulder.

"What?" He glared at Blandus. The girl weighed next to nothing. So light, she could easily be a water sprite. What the fuck had she been doing, wandering alone in the aftermath of battle? She had wielded a dagger, but there had been no danger to his life. She was too small, too fragile to cause harm to anyone, let alone a warrior.

Blandus nodded at the girl. "The one who damaged her. Ten lashes?"

Tacitus stood, his attention on the pale face of his Celt. "He's from your Legion. Your responsibility."

Blandus jerked his head in confirmation, then reached out for the girl. It took a moment for Tacitus to realize his cousin was merely offering assistance while he mounted his horse. With grim reluctance he handed his charge over and then lifted her limp body and positioned her against his armored chest.

One arm wrapped around her, he angled his jaw in an attempt to keep her head upright. Her hair was soft against his throat and the faint scent of wild berries teased his senses.

He gritted his teeth and urged his horse forward. The Celt was soft and vulnerable and unconscious. It was depraved that he still found her not only intriguing but impossibly desirable.

Blandus drew alongside. "We'll have to make our intentions known directly," he said. "Even injured, this one will attract plenty of attention. I for one don't want to lose out to your beloved commander."

Tacitus shot his cousin a black glare. His commander was Blandus' uncle, although no blood relation to Tacitus. He was, however, a lifelong friend of Tacitus' father.

The thought of the commander touching this Celt was repugnant. But too easily imagined. The older man had an insatiable penchant for young girls, especially those with blonde hair. Already Tacitus could see the lust in the commander's eyes. There was no doubt that, if he saw her, he would buy her before she even reached the market.

Blandus made a sound of impatience. "She's an enemy of Rome, Tacitus. She was captured in battle. Her fate is sealed. Now are you interested or not?"

Tacitus tightened his hold around the Celt. Her breasts pressed against his bare arm, full and tempting, and the extent of her vulnerability was acid through his gut.

In the eyes of his countrymen, she was already a slave. It was inevitable and another wave of fury against the Gallian scalded his blood. She could have remained free. He would have ensured she remained free.

Now all he could do was ensure she remained out of the clutches of his commander.

"I'm interested." The words seared his throat and he glared ahead, not able to trust himself to look at his cousin in case he followed with physical violence. It wouldn't help the situation and it wasn't as if Blandus was to blame.

Blandus punched his arm and Tacitus shot him a grim look. His cousin, who knew as much about him as anyone, and more than most, had an odd expression on his face. He knew of Tacitus' reluctance—*of course he fucking knew*—but Tacitus was aware he still found it hard to comprehend.

"You need to get over this aversion." Blandus' voice was low, for Tacitus' ears only. "It's unnatural. I'm not saying you have to fuck every female slave you own but gods, Tacitus. It's better than solitary relief."

"I'm more than capable of finding women to serve my needs." That had never been a problem. The only difficulty he had was taking a slave. Despite how many his father had offered him from the age of fourteen.

"True. But you won't always have that opportunity. It's not as if you'd have to take any of them against their will. Some of them are more than eager to share their master's bed."

"Shut up, Blandus." Irritation spiked through him that he couldn't gallop away from his cousin. The terrain was too uncertain and he didn't want to risk injuring the Celt any more than she had been already. "Tell me. What would you do if one of your slave girls refused your advances? Reward her with a few coins, a pretty ribbon for her hair? Or relegate her to the foulest tasks on your estate?"

From the corner of his eye he saw Blandus recoil, clearly offended. And even through the fog that clouded his mind, Tacitus knew his accusation was unfounded.

Blandus might enjoy the favors of slave girls, but he never took what was not willingly offered. The trouble was, Blandus couldn't appreciate the irony. How could a slave ever truly have the choice?

"It's as well I know you," Blandus said. "I trust you don't speak of such things in general conversation. Your loyalty to Rome would be in serious danger of being questioned."

Tacitus grunted. "The Emperor has my loyalty." He imagined the Celt being shipped off to Rome and instinctively pulled her closer. Her exotic beauty would ensure she was bought for pleasure. They had spoken for only a few moments but he doubted she'd hold her tongue when faced with the prospect of slavery. She could end up beaten, branded. Forced to work in the fields. And end up being used by any man who so much as looked at her.

Two legionaries emerged up ahead and with an impatient hiss, Tacitus reined in his mount. They were from his Legion, and addressed him as their senior officer.

"Sir, we believe we've found Caratacus' queen and daughter. The Primus is with them now."

He forced his mind away from his Celt's bleak future. A future he had no intention of her ever enduring.

"Good." He turned to Blandus. "Would you take my stead? I'll continue back with our captive."

Blandus gave a sharp nod, but his eyes gleamed with appreciation. He had instantly caught Tacitus' meaning. The argument was over.

"Secure a good enough price," Blandus said as he prepared to follow the legionaries, "and when we're done, I'll sell my share back to you at cost. Then you can salve your conscience by granting her manumission." He paused for a moment. "If they allow you such favor."

TACITUS TOOK her to the makeshift valetudinarium in the camp situated at the base of the mountain, not far from the river. But it was only a temporary camp, swiftly constructed before they'd marched on the enemy that morning. As soon as circumstances allowed, they would return to their permanent garrison, to the southeast of Cambria.

Once they returned to the garrison, the slave traders would arrive, and those captured during this battle would be sold.

He shouldered his way into the medical tent. Until they had breached the Celts' roughly constructed ramparts, Romans had fallen beneath the missiles rained upon them. But once the ramparts had been demolished, his countrymen's superior training and equipment had decimated the enemy without mercy. Tacitus knew that, considering the scale of the battle, Roman casualties hadn't been harsh but enough needed treatment for their injuries that would ensure an unconscious Celt wouldn't be seen until the morning.

"Marcellus." He caught sight of the physician he sought. The man he'd known from childhood and the only one here he would trust with the Celt.

Marcellus, only a year older than Tacitus, strolled over, wiping his hands on a cloth. He eyed the girl with interest.

"Since when do Tribunes bring in the injured?"

Tacitus ignored the taunt. "She hit her head on a rock after the arrow impaled her."

Marcellus studied her face. "Leave her over there." He jerked his thumb to the left, where a regimented line of the injured lay on pallets. "We'll get to her shortly."

"No. You'll treat her now."

Marcellus finally tore his gaze from the girl's face and looked at Tacitus.

"Why? Is she someone of import?"

"Yes. She's mine." But not officially.

Marcellus raised his eyebrows. "Your slave?" He sounded skeptical.

"Yes." They both knew it was a lie. But Tacitus would pay well for the special treatment. They both knew that too.

"If you say so." Marcellus indicated that Tacitus should follow him. "The conditions here are primitive but I'll do my best." He opened a flap in the side of the tent that led into what Tacitus assumed had to be an operating room. Except it wasn't a room, it was another fucking tent.

With reluctance, he laid the Celt on the operating table, positioning her on a pile of cloths to reduce unnecessary pressure on her injured shoulder. Then he folded his arms and swept a condemning glance around. Primitive was putting it mildly. Barbaric was the term he'd use to describe the conditions.

Marcellus hitched open the flap and Tacitus heard him order for assistance, instruments and whatever else he needed. Then the physician turned back to him.

"You can go now," Marcellus said. He went to the Celt's side and sliced through the sleeveless leather waist tunic she wore over her pale green woolen gown. The leather had stopped the arrow from going right through her shoulder, which was a relief. Had she not been wearing the short tunic, her injury would be far worse. "I'll send a messenger to inform you of the outcome."

"I'm staying."

Marcellus looked up, a frown darkening his brow. "This is my area of expertise, Tacitus. I don't want or need you here."

An auxiliary medic entered, bringing the requisites Marcellus had ordered. Tacitus' lip curled. Did Marcellus really think he'd leave his vulnerable water sprite alone with two men?

"Just get on with it."

Marcellus swore under his breath, but obviously decided this was a battle he was doomed to lose. He turned back to his patient and began to peel her stained gown over her breast.

"What the fuck are you doing?" Tacitus snatched the material and pulled it roughly over her breast. And tried not to think about the tantalizing glimpse of pale, luscious flesh or rosy nipple Marcellus had so callously exposed to view.

Marcellus jabbed his scalpel in Tacitus' face.

"Shut up or get out." He sounded irritated. "I'm a physician. I've seen naked women before without experiencing the animalistic urge to rut with them. Now do you want me to try to save this *slave* of yours or not?"

Tacitus gritted his teeth, clenched his fists and refolded his arms.

And managed to keep his mouth shut for the rest of the procedure.

CHAPTER 3

Nimue was back in the forest of her childhood, in the sacred oak grove, watching her mother give sacrifice to the most powerful Goddess of them all.

She looked up into the night sky. The full moon, as bright as if it were illuminated by a thousand candles, dominated her vision and awe filled her soul at the breathtaking beauty.

Arianrhod, let me be worthy.

Her mother beckoned Nimue to join her in the center of the glade where all the women of their clan waited. Heart pounding with a combination of fear and pride, Nimue obeyed. Instantly, the other women encircled her and removed her gown until she was as naked as them.

They raised their arms, chanted the ancient rites to their foremothers and gave thanks for the Goddess' blessing upon Nimue.

Today, her first moon time had occurred. A great blessing indeed, to take the first step on the path of womanhood when the full moon glowed in a cloudless sky. A sign that Nimue had, without doubt, been accepted and chosen by the Goddess she adored.

This was the happiest day of her life. The proudest moment

she had yet experienced. But something—something was wrong. Something had happened that had taken this moment and shattered it, destroyed it, tarnished its beauty and wonder forevermore.

Something that had changed the course of her life and twisted the future she had always believed her birthright. *Just as surely as my destined path has been irrevocably altered today.*

Jagged pain lanced through her body and the sacred grove shimmered, as if it had been plunged into a bottomless pool of glimmering water. She struggled for air, clawing through the grasping tendrils of fog that wrapped around her. For one tangled moment, she thought she saw a tough warrior above her, his hypnotic eyes gazing at her intently, trying to infuse her with additional strength.

Without knowing why, she tried to reach for him but her limbs were heavy and uncoordinated. Desperately she thrashed her head from side to side, trying to escape from unseen restraints. Then, from the dark corners in her mind, a shadow walked unerringly toward her. And then it was no longer a shadow as, from nowhere, a shaft of sunlight surrounded the figure. Disbelief speared through her as, without knowing how she knew, she recognized him as one of the most powerful gods of her people.

Gwydion, warrior magician, in all his youthful glory, smiled down at her. Terror froze her to the spot, but the god did not appear to mind her lack of reverence.

What does Gwydion want with me? She had always given him due reverence when she worshipped the gods of Annwyn on their sacred days. But he had never shown her any preference before. She had never experienced any special affinity with him, the Greatest of the Enchanters. To her knowledge, Gwydion had never bestowed his benevolence on a female Druid nor taken one as his blessed acolyte. That he had appeared to her now was utterly terrifying.

"Nimue, acolyte of my sister goddess Arianrhod, you are truly a chosen one." His voice echoed in her mind, vibrating with power. She fell to her knees, holding her head, fearful her mind might collapse under the unwanted invasion. "The High Druid Aeron comes to you. *Return what you have taken.*"

Nimue forced her eyes open and peered up at the magnificent, glowing god. He extended his hand toward her, uncurled his fingers and showed her what he held.

Mesmerized, she stared at his palm. He held the shard of sacred bluestone she had taken from the magical enclave.

NIMUE WONDERED at the lethargy that clung to her limbs and clouded her mind. A dull throbbing encased her shoulder and arm and her head was oddly light, as though it did not quite belong to her body.

Where am I? Scarlet and black flickered across her vision and it was simply too much effort to open her eyes.

And then a pinprick of awareness glowed in the welcoming embrace of oblivion.

I have to protect the Briton queen. The memory was jagged, bright as a Druid's blade, and sliced through her languor with a deadly knowledge. *Goddess, where's the queen?*

Unease stirred as fragmented recollections jarred her mind before coalescing into one shocking, indisputable fact.

She had been captured.

White fury steamed through her blood, once again obliterating the physical pain. Her body didn't want to cooperate, but she dragged open her eyes. And saw the face of the one who had caught her so unforgivably unawares.

Her tongue felt swollen, her throat parched. But she focused on him, drawing on what little reserves she possessed and finally, while he continued to frown down at her in apparent incomprehension, she managed to locate her voice.

"Spineless Roman." The words were little more than a wheeze, but she knew he heard. Knew he understood. Because his frown intensified and he looked as if he might take issue with her accusation. But she hadn't finished yet. "How dare you drug me?" She hitched in a harsh gasp of air. "I'll kill you for dishonoring me so."

He continued to glare down at her. "Why has she awoken? Can she feel anything?"

She reached for his throat, but only her right arm appeared to belong to her, and even that did not fully obey her commands. Instead, the Roman took her hand in his, and if he had been anyone else, his touch might have been considered comforting.

"She's not fully conscious." The other voice sounded unconcerned. "She won't recall a thing, Tacitus."

The Roman's large hand still held hers. A maelstrom of pain and humiliation disoriented her senses. But still she was aware of the strange tingle that attacked her trapped fingers.

A muted sense of alarm washed through her. She attempted to pull from his clasp, but all she managed to achieve was for him to tighten his grip. But it wasn't his arrogant possessiveness that caused her pulses to flutter or her heart to hammer against her ribs. It was the realization that his touch did not repel her.

Raw panic kicked deep in her gut, sloughing off the lingering remnants of whatever foreign drugs they had forced into her body. *What else have they forced into my body?* While she had been oblivious, how many of the enemy had raped her?

"Can't you give her more?" Tacitus shot Marcellus a black glare. "She's having a seizure."

"No, she isn't. She's slipping back into unconsciousness. All she needs is some rest and then she's all yours."

"Filthy…coward," the Celt gasped, her glazed eyes locked with his. "Taking me when I could not…couldn't defend myself…"

"Go back to sleep." He didn't know if she could hear him or not. Despite Marcellus' assurances that she spoke through the opium and neither understood the words she uttered or would recall them afterward, he had his doubts. She appeared lucid enough.

"Slice your balls from your maggot infested crotch… Putrefy your…rancid cock…"

With his free hand, he brushed her hair back from her face. Her eyes were losing focus and her nails were no longer gouging into his hand. There was no longer any doubt in his mind.

She spoke through the poppy. Not because her coarse language did not befit her evident status. But because had she been fully aware of her surroundings she would never have uttered such threats to her perceived captor.

For all she knew, it would be suicide.

"How soon can she be moved?" He had only a tent in this temporary camp but at least it was private. And he could set a legionary on guard to ensure her continued safety. Here, in the valetudinarium, he could ensure no such thing.

"Not before morning."

Tacitus finally dragged his gaze from the Celt's unnaturally pale face and looked at his friend.

"She's not staying in here overnight." And he needed to get to the quaestorium. There was no doubt in his mind he could negotiate the purchase of this Celt with the administrator. With his connections and the price he was prepared to offer, along with the fact the slave in question was injured and therefore damaged goods, the administrator would have no cause to refuse.

Only then would she be safe from the fate that awaited every other female slave rounded up this day.

She would also be safe from his cousin. And his commander.

"I don't run a brothel." Irritation soured Marcellus' words. "Any man found abusing one of my patients goes under the lash."

Not if the abuser was a fellow officer. But it was irrelevant. She was not going to stay here overnight.

"I need to report in." But not until he'd settled this matter. Only when the Celt legally belonged to him would he report to the commander of his Legion.

"I'm sure you do." It was obvious Marcellus knew exactly what Tacitus had in mind. "And in the meantime you expect me to ensure your concubine remains inviolate."

"She's not my concubine." The words were a growl. Because if she hadn't been injured, if he had persuaded her to surrender into his protection, he had the feeling he might well have made her his concubine for the duration of their affair.

Of course he would. It would have been the only way to ensure no other man took what he had already claimed.

Marcellus stared at him. "You risk opening the wound if you have her tonight."

Tacitus had no intention of having her tonight. Irked that Marcellus felt the need to even state such an obvious warning he merely maintained eye contact until the other man shrugged in obvious irritation.

"Go and conduct your business. I'll ensure it's known the slave belongs to you, and should any harm befall her, the mighty Lucius Marius Tacitus will not allow it to go unpunished."

The words were caustic but the pledge satisfactory. With one last fleeting glance at his Celt, Tacitus left the tent to face the unsavory task of buying her.

CHAPTER 4

Nimue hitched in a harsh breath and blackness engulfed her. A dream. *A memory.* A vision?

Already the details were fading, becoming obscure and fluttering through her mind like petals in a summer breeze. Strong arms held her against a solid chest and now she became aware of moving.

She was being carried. Instantly her eyes flew open, only to be confronted by an expanse of white tunic stretched across impressive shoulders. *The Roman.* Jumbled images cascaded across her mind. They had spoken by the stream. She had been shot. And then…

Then what? The uncanny sensation of urgency, of needing to accomplish something of utmost importance gnawed the edges of her mind. She could almost recall and yet the details eluded her. And what was worse, she almost did not care. Her senses were pleasantly numbed.

She shifted and tried to see his face, but his hold on her was so secure she could scarcely move at all.

"Be still." His deep voice rumbled in his chest and caused

tremors to flutter deep in her womb. "We're almost at my quarters. Then you can rest."

"Rest." Her voice sounded strange to her ears. Only then did she realize his hand grazed the curve of her breast as he held her against his body. She should have been enraged. But instead, heat radiated from the contact, spreading across her skin and tightening her nipple until the ache consumed her entire body.

She groaned, eyelids fluttering. She wanted his hand cradling her breast, his thumb circling her throbbing nipple. It was more than a want. It was an overriding need.

Her left arm was immobilized, and so she dragged her right arm up from where it nestled between the length of her body and the Roman's. Goddess, if she didn't know better, she would imagine he was a fearless warrior. For surely only a warrior could possess a body so irresistibly hard and sculpted.

She flattened her knuckles against the soft linen of his tunic, uncaring of the fabric. Wanting only to caress the heat of his naked flesh. Vaguely she wondered at his lack of armor. Not that it mattered. She didn't want his armor coming between them.

With a sigh, she nuzzled her face against his shoulder and ripples of lust rolled low in her belly. Pleasurable and somehow illicit although she couldn't quite fathom why that should be so.

"Will you be resting with me?" Her voice still sounded odd, as if her tongue could not quite articulate the words. The back of her hand grazed his throat and she felt him swallow, the action impossibly arousing.

"No."

Languidly she brushed her fingers over the uncompromising line of his jaw. He was rough, and chafed her skin. Entranced, she rubbed her hand along his jaw again, and again the roughness caused tingles of desire to dance through her blood.

"Why not?" If only she could see his face properly. From recollection, his face was worth looking at. She was sure his body was too.

"Because I'm on duty." For a fleeting moment, he glanced down at her, and the blatant lust glowing in his eyes caused raw need to bloom deep between her thighs.

Her lips parted, but it didn't help her deprived lungs because every jagged breath held a subtle hint of foreign spices that fogged her reason and heightened her desire. Tendrils of fire wove through her blood, curled around her nipples and flickered with sensuous intent through her quivering sheath. He wouldn't chose duty above her when she craved for his touch on her burning skin. When she ached to be filled by his tongue and his cock.

The image pounded against her temples and again she moaned. She imagined him spreading her thighs and impaling his length inside her wet folds. If he didn't take her soon she would shatter from unfulfilled need.

"Are you in pain?" Once again he was looking straight ahead. She turned her wrist and dug her nails into his face, and satisfaction spiked when once again his gaze clashed with hers.

"Yes."

His gaze didn't waver. "When you're settled, I will administer more opium."

Opium. The word drifted through her mind, but failed to grasp hold. It was unimportant. All that mattered was that this hard, rough-jawed warrior stripped her naked and took her until the raw, primitive need hammering through her veins was sated.

"When we're settled," she dragged in a rasping breath as he paused, "*you* will administer to me."

Jaw rigid, Tacitus entered his tent. The flap remained opened to give him light, but unfortunately, it also ensured little privacy. Not that the legionary stationed outside would dare breathe a word of what he might overhear, but right now that didn't give Tacitus much comfort.

"I'm going to lay you down." But instead of following through, he remained staring at her upturned face, at her drug-hazed eyes and her seductive smile. Her left arm, wrapped in a sling, rested across her waist. Her right hand, that had been pressed between their bodies, now cradled his jaw and her tempting body curved against him, as if she didn't find him repulsive in the least.

His cock thickened, balls tightened. Gods, how easy it would be to lay her down and take what she so unknowingly offered. He knew her inhibitions were lowered and no longer did she see him as her enemy. She saw only a man she wanted.

A man the opium wanted.

Breath hissed between his clenched teeth. It was the opium talking. He knew that. But he couldn't drag his gaze from her. Couldn't summon the strength to sever their connection.

The tip of her tongue slid over her lips. He ached to taste those lips, to plunder her mouth, to thrust so deep inside her welcoming cleft she screamed out his name.

She didn't even know his name.

"Yes." Her voice was a breathy whisper. "And then I can watch you strip. I long to see your naked body, to hold your cock and cradle your balls in the palm of my hand."

Her drug-induced promises incinerated his senses. Gods, no woman had ever uttered such words to him. No woman would have dared. Even this one would not, had she been in full possession of her mind.

But still they thundered through his blood. Pounded against his temples. The image was carved into his brain, of her on her knees, holding him. Cradling him. *Scrutinizing him.*

It was headier than the most expensive aphrodisiac from the East. *Headier than opium?* The thought barely registered. Because all that registered was the woman in his arms, offering herself to him.

CHAPTER 5

Still holding her in his arms Tacitus lowered his head toward her, no longer caring of the open tent flap, the proximity of the legionary or the fact he was still on duty. All he could see, all he could feel was the woman nestled so seductively against his chest, her breasts pressed against him while her palm caressed his jaw.

Her lips parted and her breath was sweet, like incense. Blood pounded, pulses hammered yet with rigid restraint, he brushed the most chaste of kisses across those tempting lips.

So soft. So full of promise. So deliciously responsive. She lifted her head and instead of breaking contact, he captured her lips once again. Nothing chaste about this kiss. Their mouths clung together as if nothing else in the world existed.

She wound her hand around the nape of his neck. Her fingers speared through his hair, scraping across the base of his skull. Desire spiked through his groin, her touch as potent as if she had grasped his cock, and restraint splintered.

He slid his tongue inside her open mouth and she sucked on him, sudden and hard and unbelievably shocking. He withdrew, a slow slide against her wet flesh then thrust into her again, teasing the roof of her mouth, and claimed the strangled moans that vibrated from her throat.

Fingernails dug into his scalp, primitive and wild. His hand closed over the mound of her breast, filling his palm. Her nipple was hard through the material of her gown, and with a primal growl, he rubbed the tips of his fingers over the erect nub. Backward and forward. Increasing the pressure. She squirmed in his arms, her muffled moans of pleasure stoking his need.

He needed to lay her down. Rip off her gown. Explore her writhing body.

The exhilarating vision of her laying naked on his bed hammered in his mind. She was willing. She did not know she was a slave. He could fuck her, make her come, give her such pleasure that when she discovered the truth she wouldn't feel as if she had been used at all.

Her sweet taste slid insidiously into his senses, heady and somehow illicit. The tips of their tongues touched, and it was mindlessly erotic.

Somehow, he stumbled to the bed. Curse this primitive camp. He wanted his own bed, but this makeshift one would have to do. Carefully he lowered her, his mouth still claiming hers—or was she claiming his?—and as he laid her down the light diminished.

He scarcely noticed. Tearing his mouth from her, he panted down into her face, relishing the jagged gasps of her breath, the way her fingers dug into the back of his neck, the way her breasts heaved beneath her soft gown.

The way her left arm was immobilized in a sling.

For a moment he stared, uncomprehending. She was injured and he had been about to *fuck her?*

"Roman." The word was scarcely above a whisper, and wrapped around his reeling senses like a seductive embrace of purest silk. Her right hand slid from his neck, over his shoulder and along his arm. It was a light caress and yet as arousing as if she slid her naked body along him instead.

Gods. What was he thinking? Marcellus had warned him not to have her tonight. She was injured. She was under the influence of opium.

She was his slave.

He couldn't move. He remained kneeling on the floor beside her as her hand curled around his wrist. The light was oddly dimmed and yet he could see her delicate features and the fragile outline of her enticing body. And still he could not find the strength of will to stand up and leave.

"Are you man enough for me, Roman?" Her words were heated, provocative. A blatant challenge. "I've never had a barbarian before." She smiled, as if that thought gave her great amusement and he battled against the renewed lust that thundered through his blood at her taunts.

"You will lie here and rest." It was an order. Any other woman —any other man—would have instantly quailed. But this Celt, this slave—*who didn't even know she was a slave*—merely offered him another sultry smile and pulled on his hand.

He didn't resist.

She dragged his hand between her thighs and pressed him against her slick core. Air hissed between his clenched teeth as her feminine dampness caressed his fingers, as she rolled her hips and a breathy sigh escaped her lips.

"Don't you want me, Roman?" She increased pressure on his hand and of their own volition his fingers pushed against her soft gown, seeking and finding the wet opening of her welcoming pussy.

Primal need thudded through his veins and tightened his rock-hard balls. This was madness. Feverishly his fingers bunched up her gown, exposing her thighs, until he gripped the material and wrenched it up to her waist.

Honey-blonde curls crowned her glistening lips, her flesh plump and pink and deliriously tantalizing. Mesmerized by the sheer eroticism of how she angled her hips toward him and by her evocative scent that caused his cock to thicken, he couldn't remember why taking her was such a bad idea.

He trailed the tips of his fingers over her stomach and then lower, teasing her soft curls. She sighed in evident pleasure and collapsed back onto the pallet as if she no longer possessed the strength to entice him. But he needed no additional enticement. Everything he needed was here, between her spread thighs.

She was wet and hot. His finger slid along her cleft, her soft folds promising a wild, unforgettable ride. Breath rasped along his throat, need pounded through his groin, sanity sank beyond the fiery horizon.

She was willing. She was ready. *And she was his.*

The final thought pounded with primitive possessiveness through his mind, through his soul. She was his and no other man had the right to touch her. No other man had the right to look at her naked body, breathe her heady scent, or hear her gasps of impending climax. Somehow, he dragged his gaze from her desire-swollen lips, up the length of her prone body, expecting to see her watching him.

Her head had fallen back onto the pallet. Her eyes were closed, her lips slightly parted. For a moment, he couldn't comprehend the evidence before him, but her sudden lack of response was clear enough.

She had fallen asleep.

Disbelief hammered through his veins, but it was muted by the lust that still thundered in his blood. She was asleep, and he was so hard he feared he might rupture.

His fingers curled into a fist against her silken slit. Just moments longer and he would have been inside her. The thought of being clasped by her tight sheath, of her legs wrapped around his waist, of her fingernails scraping along his naked back caused streaks of agonized pleasure to burn his cock.

But she was unconscious.

He reared back, his breath harsh against his clenched teeth.

By the gods, he was no better than his commander. *No better than my father*. Bitter disgust curdled his gut and he jerked her gown back over her thighs. Removing temptation from his vision.

Except the image of her seductive nakedness was branded inside his brain.

He flexed his fingers, and her arousal drifted in the air. Mocking his restraint. He struggled against the overpowering urge to grip his cock and find some measure of solitary satisfaction. Yet the thought of doing so while his Celt lay oblivious, felt wrong. Even if he didn't touch her while he brought himself to climax, he couldn't shake the feeling that to pleasure himself while she remained unaware was vulgar. As if his act of self-gratification would somehow defile her.

Fuck the gods. He lurched to his feet and glared at her peaceful face. He was cursed with a conscience few of his peers possessed and until this moment, it had never unduly concerned him.

But now, because of his convictions, he couldn't wake his own slave. Couldn't take what his body demanded. Couldn't— *wouldn't*. Was there even a difference? He was so fucking hard he couldn't even think straight.

He grabbed a blanket and dropped it over her, not trusting himself to touch her in case his tenuous control shattered. Then he wheeled around and saw the tent flap had been closed.

His mood darkened further and he wrenched it open and marched outside. The legionary didn't glance in his direction. Just as well. The way he felt right now, eye contact would be an excellent excuse for a fight.

"No one enters." He sounded rabid.

"Sir." The legionary remained looking straight ahead. But how much had he seen before the bastard had closed the tent flap?

How dare he close the tent flap? Yet if he hadn't, his Celt would have been on public display to any man who passed by.

The thought fed his rage. Pressure throbbed against his temples; his balls were on fire.

For one heart-thundering moment, he considered returning to his Celt and taking what, by law, was his.

He turned, secured the tent, slung the legionary one last black glare before marching off. He needed to report to his commander and discover if it was, indeed, Caratacus' queen and daughter who had been found.

But duty was the last thing on his mind. Because all his mind could conjure up was the image of his half naked Celt writhing beneath his questing fingers.

∼

"Tacitus." The commander waved his hand in an imperious gesture for Tacitus to approach. The social meeting was being held outside the commander's tent, to take advantage of the lingering twilight. "Come, sit down. We've been waiting for you."

Blandus was already there, seated on a chair beside a table covered in unrolled documents. Tacitus sat. At least now his cursed erection had begun to diminish. It was still fucking uncomfortable, though.

The commander sat and slung him an amused glance. Tacitus could see nothing amusing in the situation. But since it was impossible for the commander to guess the extent of or reason for Tacitus' current frustration, clearly he was missing something vital.

"No need to look so ferocious," the commander said as he sat down and jerked his head so they could be served refreshments. "I agree this is barbaric and not what you're used to. However, we'll just have to conduct ourselves as if we were in the bathhouse."

A session in the bathhouse was very appealing. A good massage might well go some way to relieving the tension.

Then again, it might not, considering the reason for his tension.

He attempted to relax his features. Then decided it was too much effort.

"Is the woman Caratacus' queen?" He picked up his goblet and drank the contents in one long swallow. Then signaled for a refill.

"She is." Blandus sprawled back in his chair and looked smug. "A well-equipped bag of medicinal herbs and strange concoctions was found with them. Apparently they had been traveling with a healer who'd gone to collect water to tend the princess' injuries."

Tacitus only just prevented himself from choking on his wine. Was his Celt a healer? Had she been traveling with Caratacus' queen and daughter?

No. It was sheer coincidence that he had found her by a stream so close to where the queen had been discovered.

"Has the healer been found?" He kept his tone casual, but the glint in Blandus' eyes told him that his cousin was fully aware of the interest behind the question.

"Apparently not."

"I see."

It would be best if the connection—not that he believed there was a connection—between his Celt and the healer was not made. Although it made no difference now, since she was already his slave and couldn't be punished without his approval. He didn't want any unsavory suspicion to fall on her.

"Today," Blandus said, "has been very satisfactory altogether."

Tacitus grunted. He was feeling far from satisfied. "Good."

"An excellent day's work." The commander sounded as satisfied as his nephew. "We'll ship his queen and daughter back to Rome. It won't take long to hunt down Caratacus now his band of rebels have been scattered and captured."

"And finally," Blandus said, "the tribes of Cambria will bow before the Eagle. The outcome of this day is going to make our careers, Tacitus."

"Do we know where Caratacus went to ground?"

"Ostorius Scapula believes his only recourse is to travel into the barbarous north." The commander glanced at one of the documents on the table, a cartography of the local area. "I'm in agreement. Our client kingdoms in Britannia are loyal to Rome. He'll find no powerful allies there."

"However, due to the unpredictable behavior of the natives," Blandus said, "it appears the remainder of my term in service will be spent in close proximity to you, uncle." He shot Tacitus a grin that had nothing to do with their two Legions now being stationed in the same far-flung outpost of the Empire. "I hope your garrison contains all the necessary luxuries for life."

"Tacitus has never complained, and if ever a man indulged his son more than my brother has you, it's Gemellus."

Tacitus ignored the jibe. It was scarcely a secret that his father had all but given up on siring a son before Tacitus' birth. His numerous half-sisters attested to the fact as to how vigorously his father had worked in that area of his life.

The consequence being—his father denied him nothing that was in his power to give.

"In that case I won't petition the Emperor to be relocated to a less hostile province." Blandus shot a second lascivious grin in Tacitus' direction. "I'm sure Tacitus and I can find some enjoyable amusement with which to entertain ourselves. It's been a while since we've had the opportunity."

Tacitus felt a scowl threatening. Blandus would discover soon enough that Tacitus had bought the Celt solely in his own name. His cousin would be pissed. No doubt about it.

Tough.

"You'll find plenty of that kind of entertainment, Blandus." The commander then turned to Tacitus. "I heard a rumor this evening that I can scarcely believe. Did you buy one of the female slaves that were rounded up from the aftermath?"

Tacitus' fingers clenched around his goblet. He had been hoping his commander had not become aware of that fact yet. But of course he would know. It was his duty to know everything that went on in his Legion.

"I captured her after she was injured. *After* the battle." He wondered if it was worth emphasizing that the Celt had been about to surrender, but then decided that would create yet more complications. "I bought her so she could recuperate in comfort."

He heard Blandus give a smothered snort, but ignored him. The commander, who had been staring at him in barely concealed astonishment, relaxed back in his chair and laughed, as if Tacitus had just shared a witty jest.

"That explains it. I knew you wouldn't have purchased a young girl because you wanted to fuck her. Not your way, is it?" He grinned, and for a moment reminded Tacitus of how Blandus would look in another twenty-five years.

And then he thought of the last time he'd seen his Celt. Of how close he had come to taking her while she slept. The thought caused disgust to churn his blood and finally his cursed erection fully deflated.

The commander was still talking. For an obscure reason he now appeared to consider the Celt little more than a child. "Do you intend to have her trained in your kitchen when she is well?"

Have her work in his kitchen? She would likely try to poison him given half a chance.

"I haven't decided yet." His voice was stiff. The commander didn't appear to take offense.

"You'll have to give her something to do to occupy her days. An idle slave is a liability, Tacitus. We all know that." He stood, rolled his shoulders and frowned into the distance. "I'd better inspect the slaves captured today. Ensure they're being held in adequate conditions."

As the Commander strolled off, Blandus raised a skeptical eyebrow.

"Ensure there are no beautiful blonde girls there, he means." Blandus turned to Tacitus. "Fortunately, our blonde beauty is safely ensconced in your tent." Then he laughed. "Wait until he discovers our slave is no innocent child. And I do believe she can be as idle as she pleases during the day. She'll certainly be kept busy enough at night."

Blandus' words shouldn't have irritated him, and yet they did.

"Have you forgotten? She's just had an arrow removed from her shoulder." And still he had almost taken her. Even after Marcellus had warned him against such a thing.

"Of course I don't wish to inflict any more pain on her." Blandus looked taken aback, as if Tacitus' feral growl had been unwarranted. "But surely we can all enjoy ourselves until such time as she's ready. By the way, how much do I owe you?"

Tacitus stood and glared down at his cousin. "Nothing." He said the word with relish and watched Blandus frown with incomprehension. "She belongs to me. Not us. And I have no intention of sharing."

With that, he marched off, in full awareness of the infuriated glower his cousin aimed at his retreating back.

CHAPTER 6

Nimue's entire body ached. The pain from her head thudded in tandem with the throb in her shoulder, which pulsed in time with every beat of her heart. Gritting her teeth, she forced open her eyes. The light was diffused and disoriented her. She wasn't outside. *Where am I?*

It felt as if she was lying on a bed. Gingerly she turned her head and saw shadowy outlines of huge caskets and a couple of chairs. Sluggish memories crawled from the depths of her mind and panic clutched her chest, making it hard to breathe.

What had happened to the Briton queen and her daughter? She was responsible for their safety. Responsible for returning them to Caratacus. And she had allowed herself to be captured by the enemy.

The Roman. The arrow. Fragmented recollections stabbed through her brain, elusive and terrifying because of their very obscurity.

Had the Romans discovered the queen's hiding place? Or were she and the princess still waiting for the return of Nimue? Goddess, what of the princess' injury? The pain reliever she had administered would last only a few hours.

She shifted on the straw mattress and then froze as another thought ripped through her mind.

Was I brutalized? Her body hurt, but was that due to having been shot or because of what had been done to her while she'd been unconscious?

Jagged breaths clutched her breast. She had to remain calm. She had to remain in control. But the panic escalated, and the horror of what she might have endured—what she might continue to endure—hammered through her senses.

She forced her hand along the length of her body. It was a relief to discover that, at least, she wasn't naked. Her breasts did not hurt. Her belly was uninjured. Tentatively she pressed her fingers between her thighs and for a fleeting moment incoherent images flashed through her mind.

Relief streaked through her. Her sex was not tender, her thighs were not sore. To the best of her knowledge, she hadn't been raped.

Yet something teased the outer edges of her consciousness. An elusive sensation of touch, of need. Of rampant desire threaded through with nebulous promises of passion-drenched satisfaction.

Her fingers pressed against her lips and instantly the face of the Roman filled her vision. She could feel his mouth on hers, feel his tongue invading her, and Goddess save her, she remembered kissing him back with such wild abandon that heat flooded her body at the memory.

But then what? Everything was dark. As if nothing further *had* happened.

Stealthily, she pushed herself upright with her uninjured arm. She wouldn't think about her wounded shoulder right now. She couldn't afford to. Later she would attend to it, and could only hope the Romans hadn't mutilated her beyond repair.

A large shadow on the ground next to her caught her attention. Her heart jerked in her chest. It was the Roman. Lying on the ground. Asleep.

For a moment she stared, bemused. Why was this arrogant Roman on the ground while she had his bed? It made no sense. Because it suggested he had considered her comfort before his own.

And then another, equally bizarre thought filled her head. Why hadn't he shared the bed? Why hadn't he taken her when he'd had the chance?

Because she certainly wouldn't give him the chance now that she was in full possession of her senses.

Slowly she eased back the blanket that had covered her and held her breath as she slid her legs to the edge of the makeshift bed. Perhaps she could escape while the Roman slept. Return to the queen's hiding place and resume the journey into the land of the Brigantes.

"Where do you think you're going?" The voice was low, but power throbbed in every syllable. The hairs on her arms shivered in reaction to it. Although the Roman remained unmoving, he was obviously fully alert.

"I'm going to stretch my muscles." Her legs felt wobbly, her left arm stiff, and she needed fresh air to clear the lingering cobwebs from her mind. But as much as she wanted to push herself upright and stalk from this enclosure, she had no desire to humiliate herself by staggering on unsteady legs.

"Are you in pain?" He sat up, and he was far too close. His masculine scent drifted in a tantalizing caress across her senses and her nipples hardened in response. She licked her dry lips, craved water for her parched throat and hoped he couldn't hear the accelerated thud of her heart.

"No." Her voice was a croak. She would die before she admitted to experiencing any pain. An uneasy flutter of memory nudged at her. Had he asked her that question before? Had she responded *differently* before?

"Do you need assistance?" His entire attention was focused on her. He pointed no weapon at her face but she was reminded of when he had come upon her by the mountain stream.

Now, as then, she was trapped.

"Certainly not." She infused as much pride into her words as possible. "It was my shoulder your cowardly countryman shot, not my leg." Thank Goddess. Had her leg been wounded her chances of escape would be greatly reduced.

"Rest assured," the Roman said, not taking his gaze from her, "he is not my countryman."

"He fought on the side of Rome. You're all the same to me." And because she had the overwhelming compulsion to remain sitting, to remain talking to him, she curled her fingers into the edge of the mattress and took a deep breath.

She would not exchange idle conversation with a Roman soldier. An *officer*. She had to regain her strength, discover where she'd been taken and make plans to return to the queen.

A horrifying thought slammed through her mind. *Suppose the queen and her daughter had been captured?* She couldn't leave, until she'd found out. But how was she supposed to find out when she could scarcely ask outright without arousing suspicion that she was the Druid they'd been traveling with?

My medicine bag. She'd left it behind. The thought of her personal possessions being scrutinized by the enemy was abhorrent. A violation. All they needed to do was examine the intricate embroidery on her bag, where Arianrhod in her sacred image of an owl was depicted. It would take little effort to compare it to the engravings on her silver bracelets and torque to discover the indisputable connection to the Moon Goddess.

If the enemy *was* in possession of her medicine bag would they draw the inevitable conclusion that she was the Druid they, most certainly, now sought?

Instinctively her fingers went to her throat, but her torque was missing. Perhaps it had been stolen for its beauty and value.

Yet her bracelets remained on her wrists. Again the panic twisted through her stomach and she risked shooting the Roman another glance. He continued to watch her, and in the dim light, she could not decipher his expression at all.

If they had made the connection already, she would be in chains. She would be at the mercy of their barbaric torturers, and the arrow would have been wrenched from her shoulder with the intention of causing as much damage as possible.

They hadn't made the connection. *Yet*. Perhaps they wouldn't, for what did Romans know of her culture or the gods her people worshipped? They saw only land to conquer and precious metal to claim. Perhaps the silver had already been melted down, and sold.

She smothered the shaft of pain that speared through her chest. The torque had been her mother's, but it was only a torque. And even if the Romans took everything she possessed, they would never own her memories.

Her memories were engraved into her very soul.

"The physician removed your torque before he operated." The Roman opened a leather pouch that had been on the ground beside him. "He didn't want any constriction around your throat."

Bemused, she stared at her torque on the palm of his hand. He was returning it to her? Did he not know how valuable it was?

But then, if it was plunder he wanted, he could have stripped the bracelets and earrings from her while she slept.

He had not. Nor had he brutalized her. Finally, the question she should have thought of instantly slid through her mind.

What *did* this Roman want with her?

Half suspecting this was a trick, she picked up her torque between finger and thumb, careful not to touch his hand. Since fixing it around her throat required two hands, and she had no intention of asking for his assistance, she held it on her lap.

Perhaps it was no trick. The queen and princess were still

safe, her medicine bag hadn't been found and no sharp-eyed Roman had seen the similarity between the embroidery and engravings.

It was time to discover the fate this Roman had in mind for her.

"So, am I free to go now?" She managed to give him a haughty look, although in this dim light she wasn't sure whether he noticed or not.

"You wouldn't get very far." He glanced at her injured shoulder. "You need to recuperate."

A flicker of comprehension dawned.

"Is this your place of healing?" She tried not to feel awe that the Romans treated their injured enemies so well. Celts didn't go to such lengths to ensure captured Romans recovered from their wounds. Not that Romans generally allowed themselves to be captured, but that was scarcely the point.

Had a wounded Roman ever been captured in battle, he would be sacrificed to the gods amid much rejoicing.

"These are my private quarters."

"You're a healer?" Such a thing had never occurred to her. She had thought him a foreign warrior, and nothing else.

"No." Was it her imagination or was that a trace of amusement in his voice? "I'm a Tribunus Laticlavius. You're here so I can ensure your safety."

His rank meant nothing to her, except that he was an officer in his Legion and, as such, was responsible for the rape of her homeland. Once again, the thought hovered in her mind that she was exchanging idle conversation with her deadliest enemy. And yet somehow she couldn't help herself.

As she hadn't been able to help herself back at the mountain stream. And look what had happened to her because of it.

"I don't need the protection of a Roman." *But why does he feel the need to ensure my safety?* If all he wanted was to use her, he could have done that already. There had been no need for him to go to the trouble of healing her wound. With shaming reluctance, she pushed herself to her feet, praying desperately her muscles would support her. But as she had feared, her legs buckled, her torque tumbled to the ground and she knew she was going to collapse back onto the bed.

Her injured pride scarcely had time to manifest before the Roman was by her side, one arm around her waist, supporting her weight. As his strong fingers curled around her hip, as his muscular body pressed intimately against hers, lightning streaked across the shadows in her mind. And she recalled in vivid, mortifying detail how she had tried to seduce him last night.

CHAPTER 7

Tacitus felt her entire body stiffen in clear affront as he held her upright. Unfortunately, her reaction to his touch did nothing to diminish the erection he'd woken with.

He tightened his grip on her. Although her mind had obviously recovered from the effects of the opium, her body hadn't. And he had to stop thinking about her body. It made no difference how she tensed her muscles in outward denial. Lust sizzled between them, in every uneven breath she took, every resentful glance she gave him. Her thigh pressed against him and his chest crushed the warm swell of her breast. His arm supported the small of her back and curve of her waist and his fingers cradled her hip. Defeat thudded through his mind. He could scarcely think of anything *but* her body.

"Unhand me." She sounded infuriated. "How dare you maul me like an animal."

He let out a measured breath, and attempted to convince himself that her words of condemnation hadn't fueled his lust further.

"I'm not mauling you." He'd done a lot more than *maul* her in his erotic fantasies during the night. "I'm preventing you from falling. Sit down until you've regained your balance." He hooked his ankle around the leg of a chair and jerked it toward him.

"Don't order me around." She glared at him as if he'd just ordered her to strip naked. Gods. That was the wrong thing to have thought. He forcibly sat her on the chair and then stepped back before he was tempted to force her to do anything else.

She was still in absolute ignorance of her new status. Was it possible he could prevent her from finding out? If she didn't know she was a slave, she wouldn't behave like a slave. And if, tonight, she wanted him without benefit of the drugs, he could have her.

Because, in her mind, she retained the choice.

There were so many drawbacks to that plan that it wasn't even worth seriously considering. And yet he considered it. Because it was the only way he could envisage them consummating the mutual desire that had ignited between them by the spring.

"Suggesting you sit before you fall is hardly an order."

Her hand clenched against her thigh. "If you hadn't brought me here against my will, I wouldn't be in *danger* of falling."

"And if I'd left you on the mountain, you would have been rounded up with all the other rebels."

He didn't need to elaborate. The way she ground her teeth together and slung him another condemning glare made it obvious she knew exactly what he was talking about.

But she didn't appear to make the connection that, despite not being in the prisoners' tent, she had been enslaved as surely as the rest.

She would not be a slave for long. He could free her before she even knew, and he could make her his official concubine. Her lack of reverence for his social status would ensure the remainder of his term in this gods forsaken province would be entertaining, to say the least.

Her glare slid from his face and traveled down. Renewed lust scorched through his groin when she paused, her eyes riveting on his erection as if she could not help herself.

He didn't have to look down to know his tunic hid nothing of the extent of his arousal. And knowing she looked, that she continued to look, caused his shaft to thicken further.

"You need not think," her voice was husky and his cock jerked with appreciation. "I have any intention of continuing what you started last night when I was full of your heathen, hallucinatory drugs."

He stepped toward her. And recalled her seductive promise of holding him in the palm of her hand.

"Are you certain of that?" He ached to take her in his arms. For her to wrap her legs around him. But he kept his distance by sheer force of will. *She* had to come to *him*.

"Of course I'm certain." She sounded offended that he could even suggest such a thing. "You took advantage of my vulnerable state. It won't happen again."

"I didn't take advantage." But he nearly had. "Rape isn't something I find enticing."

She opened her mouth as if she was about to disagree, and then narrowed her eyes instead. Obviously his words weren't what she had anticipated.

"I did not suggest you raped me." Her voice was haughty. "I know full well you didn't violate me. I'm merely telling you that you won't find me so—*responsive* to your loathsome touch now. I'm no longer in thrall to your foreign drug."

Despite the lust hammering through his veins, he grinned. The look of disbelief on her face only served to heighten both his amusement and his desire.

Extraordinary.

"You find my touch loathsome?"

"Utterly." Her fingers twitched against her thigh. She either wanted to grip his cock as she had promised, or scratch out his eyes.

He knew which he'd prefer.

"So the only way to lower your inhibitions is when you're under the influence of an aphrodisiac?"

Her lips parted in clear annoyance to his accusation. But as he fixed his gaze on those luscious lips, he thought only of how they would feel wrapped around his cock. Gods. She was so close to him. He could feel her erratic breath through his tunic, caressing his shaft.

Such fucking agony. He strangled the groan in his throat, fisted his hands by his sides and tightened the muscles in his thighs.

None of it helped.

"An aphrodisiac?" She spat the words at him. "How dare you suggest I have *inhibitions*?" She sounded as though he had flung the worst insult imaginable at her. It was enough for him to drag his attention from her lips and his cock to focus fully on her face. Even in this light, he could see the flush on her cheeks and the way her eyes sparkled in obvious affront at his comment.

"Of course you have inhibitions." Gods, how intensely exhilarating it was to have such an unorthodox conversation with a woman. He had never imagined such a thing before. "You're a woman."

She leaned forward in her chair, her eyes never leaving his, apparently unaware that her mouth all but grazed the head of his engorged cock. *So close…*

"I do *not* have inhibitions." She heaved herself to her feet, her immobilized arm dragging up his erection with agonizing disregard. "I've no need for aphrodisiacs when I'm with a man I *want* to fuck."

He'd had plenty of girls and women in the past, both plebeians and nobles. They had been enthusiastic lovers, agreeable companions and not one of them had ever suggested by look or word that they found his presence distasteful. On the contrary, they made it plain they desired his attentions.

Until this Celt, he'd never had to do much more than smile at an available woman to indicate his interest and without fail, he'd always received encouragement in return.

"And you don't want to fuck me?" The top of her head barely grazed his shoulder, and she glared up at him as if she wanted to tear the flesh from his bones. But her breath was erratic and the scent of feminine arousal drifted in the charged air, thickening his blood and twisting through his gut.

She could say what she liked. Her body told the truth.

"The very thought of it nauseates me."

Her words were insults. Her breathless delivery an erotic caress. It was hard to draw breath, to think straight; to keep his hands from cradling her face and silencing her with his mouth.

"What really nauseates you is the fear you'd enjoy it."

Her eyes widened, her lips parted and her tempting breasts heaved, straining against the delicate wool of her ruined gown. She was in need of a bath and her hair was messy with loose tendrils curling over her cheeks and shoulders. There was no reason why he should find her so irresistible in her disheveled state. Yet he found her as sexy and fuckable now as he had when they had met by the mountain stream.

"With a *Roman*?" She flicked her gaze over him, and once again lingered on his cock. Would she really protest if he just took her now? He'd never been so fucking hard before. "I hate Romans." Her eyes were fixed on his groin. Her words of condemnation weaved through him like a potent aphrodisiac. "I *despise* them and everything they stand for."

He couldn't help himself. He reached out and grasped her untidy braid, letting it slide along the palm of his hand. She didn't gasp in outrage, didn't jerk her head or push his arm away. She simply stood there, and slowly dragged her gaze up his body until their eyes meshed.

"Yet you still desire *this* Roman." It wasn't a question. He could see the answer in her eyes. He didn't need her to like him. What did it matter if she despised him?

All he wanted from her was her willing compliance.

Her breath hitched, as she attempted to drag air into her lungs.

"I'm not a bitch in heat." The tip of her tongue moistened the seam of her lips. He recalled the feel of her tongue inside his mouth, demanding, exploring. *Uninhibited*. "I don't need to act on every desire that attacks me."

He wound her braid around his hand. Imagined unbinding her hair and spearing his fingers through the honey-gold tresses.

"So you admit that you do desire me?" Satisfaction hummed through his blood, threaded through his voice. He tightened his grip on her hair. "What else do we need between us, Celt?"

Her eyes were dark, seductive, the green almost obliterated. Her hand pressed against his chest, against his heart, but it wasn't a defensive gesture. It was as if she couldn't help herself.

"Respect." The word was little more than a whisper, but the unmistakable thread of despair pierced through his pounding lust. He released her hair, cupped her face and stroked his thumb across her silken cheek.

It hadn't occurred to him she might fear such a thing. She was not, after all, a gently bred Roman girl. Celtic women took lovers whenever they pleased. Even their chieftain class did not, to his knowledge, demand that their women remain virgins until their wedding night.

Somehow, this unexpected fissure of vulnerability caused an odd sensation deep in his chest.

Perhaps this Celt wasn't as experienced as he'd imagined. He found that notion pleasing. More than pleasing. He found it excessively arousing.

With his free hand, he tenderly stroked errant curls from her face. She had a sharp tongue but it was nothing but a shield to hide her relative innocence.

"When you belong to me," he whispered, "I will still respect you."

She continued to gaze at him for endless moments, as though she did not quite understand his meaning. Then her hand slid from his chest and her eyes widened in comprehension.

"When I *belong* to you?" She sounded incredulous. "I don't care for *your* respect, arrogant Roman. I speak of mutual respect between a man and a woman but more than that—I speak of the respect I have for myself." She tossed her head, to dislodge his hands, and he was so stunned by her response that he released her without protest. "Not that I expect you to understand that, since *Romans* don't know the meaning of the word."

She glared at him, as proud as if she was the Emperor's daughter and as indignant as if he had grievously offended her honor. When all he had intended was to comfort her with his words.

"It's you who appears not to understand the concept of respect." Or self-preservation. But although he knew that, with another, her belligerent attitude could cost her life, right now he was more irked that she clearly did not care a fig about possessing his respect.

"I respect those who have earned it." Her voice was scathing, but still her breath was short. Her breasts rose and fell with erratic distraction. He battled against the primitive urge to pin her to the mattress and ride her until she screamed with orgasmic delirium.

At the mountain stream, he'd been enchanted by her forthright manner. It was refreshing to meet someone—especially a desirable woman—who didn't defer to his rank or social standing.

But she was pushing the boundaries. If she behaved in such a disrespectful manner in public, or insulted another officer, they would think nothing of wrenching her tongue from her mouth.

If she didn't learn a modicum of obedience or, at least, a sliver of common sense, he'd have no alternative but to keep her in utmost seclusion.

He wound his hand around her throat. A gentle grasp, only to remind her how vulnerable she was. Her pulse fluttered against his thumb, an erotic counterpoint to his own hammering heartbeat.

"If you want to survive in this world, you had best learn to hide your disdain for your conquerors."

She didn't break eye contact. Didn't try to wrench his hand from her throat. It was as if she possessed no fear of him at all.

Instead, she jabbed her finger into his chest with unbelievable lack of deference. "You will never be my conqueror."

He leaned in close until their lips all but touched, and offered her a grim smile. "I already am."

CHAPTER 8

Nimue attempted to convince herself the flutterings in her stomach, the tightness in her chest and inability to think clearly was because she had been injured. But her swollen pussy, her trembling clit and the unmistakable dampness between her thighs told the true tale.

No matter how this Roman's arrogance should inflame her fury, his words only inflamed her despicable lust.

His hand encircled her throat. She had no illusion that if he so desired he could snap her neck as easily as he might a bird's. Yet, irrationally, it wasn't fear that flooded her body and tampered with her mind.

How much easier would it be for her sanity, if she feared this Roman as she should.

Her hand flattened against his chest, against his hard muscles and a tremor raced from the tips of her fingers, along her arm and shimmered across her exposed cleavage. She longed to pull his tunic from his body, run her hand over his naked flesh and feast upon the glory of his cock.

There was no doubt it would be glorious. Even through his tunic, she had been mesmerized by its tempting promise.

Despite all her convictions, her body softened, and no matter how she clenched her inner muscles it did nothing to stop the frantic need pulsing in her blood. His mouth was so close to hers. His gaze, intense. And the tips of his fingers scorched the vulnerable column of her throat.

It was hard to remember why she was so furious with him, why she should resist the fiery attraction that sizzled between them.

"No man owns me." It sounded like an invitation to prove her wrong. Goddess, were her senses still enslaved to the foreign drug? But she knew they weren't. And yet she couldn't summon the strength to shove him aside.

"No *other* man owns you." His voice was raw, his words primitive. She tried for indignation and failed. Because a despicable part of her still craved this man.

Slowly her hand slid up to his shoulder. His powerful muscles flexed beneath her questing fingers, sending primal need shuddering through her blood. All the reasons why this was so wrong splintered and scattered to the winds. Because right now all she could think was how it would feel to be held in his arms, crushed against his body and succumb to the flames licking the slick folds of her pussy.

"Tacitus. You decent?" The disembodied voice shattered the sensual cocoon as effectively as if she had been plunged into an icy mountain stream. She jerked her hand from the Roman's shoulder and sent him the blackest glare she could dredge up from her disgusted soul.

He—Tacitus?—scowled down at her as if the interruption could not have come at a worse time. She tilted her head very slightly to the side, an unspoken demand, and he slowly, with obvious reluctance, released her throat from his imprisoning grip.

He stalked to the side of the enclosure—now that she was fully awake she could see it was a tent—and ripped open the flap.

Sunlight streamed in, and Nimue squinted as a huge dark shadow entered.

"Marcellus." Tacitus sounded rabid. "It's not like you to make house calls on your patients."

The other Roman grinned. "With what you paid me, my friend, the extra service is all inclusive."

Nimue shot Tacitus a startled glance. He had paid for her treatment? Why would he do that? It was one thing to ensure her injury was tended to, even though she couldn't fathom his motives. But it hadn't occurred to her that he had paid a healer to administer to her wound.

Her unease spiked and suspicion raked through her. So he had paid for her treatment. He'd better not assume she owed him anything in return. Irritably she twisted one of her bracelets around her immobilized wrist. It was obvious her personal wealth was of little interest to him, otherwise he would have stripped the jewelry from her while she slept. But it was all she had to offer in payment since her dagger had vanished and her bow— *Goddess, I left my bow with the queen.*

Her mission slammed through her brain, obliterating the irritation beneath a wave of crippling guilt. She had to focus. Had to discover the fate of the queen. And who better to sound out for information than this healer?

"She appears to be recovering." Tacitus sounded as if the prognosis did not especially please him, and Nimue's pledge to think only of the queen and princess, and not about a certain Roman officer, fractured.

Who was he, to tell the healer whether she was recovering or not?

"My shoulder," she said in Latin, in case the other Roman was ignorant of her language. "What exactly did you do after removing the arrowhead?"

Both men turned to stare at her, as though she had suddenly grown wings or sprouted a second head. She stiffened her spine and stared right back. She was the injured one here. Why did they look so astonished that she wished to know the extent of damage they'd caused her?

The healer, Marcellus, looked at Tacitus as if requesting permission that he might speak directly to her. But that made no sense. She'd heard many rumors about life under the Romans, but she had never come across anything that suggested a man could not speak freely with an unattached, non-Roman woman.

Tacitus, in the process of lighting a lantern, gave the barest jerk of his head, apparently bestowing such permission. Unease compressed Nimue's gut. She had tried not to face the obvious, but clearly she was this Roman's prisoner. And because of his rank, he had somehow managed to keep her from wherever prisoners were usually kept.

The resentment bubbled, dark and corroding. Until yesterday, she had never seriously considered she might be captured by the enemy. Killed by them, certainly. But her mind had shied short of actual capture, because capture equaled torture and ultimate crucifixion because of her heritage.

But only if they discovered her heritage.

Her head began to ache.

"I cleaned the wound and stitched it." The healer smiled at her in what she could only assume he believed to be a reassuring manner. She ignored it.

"What did you clean it with?" As yet, although her shoulder hurt it didn't feel as if it was putrefying from the inside out. She could only hope these barbarians knew more medical aid than rumor suggested.

"Vinegar."

Startled by the knowledge this Roman used the same method for cleansing wounds as her own people, she was momentarily silenced. Perhaps her shoulder would make a full recovery, after all.

"Now," Marcellus said, once again glancing at Tacitus. "Do I have permission to inspect my handiwork?"

"You do," she said quickly, before Tacitus could respond. He merely glowered at her and folded his arms, and before she could stop herself, she glanced at his groin.

Oh yes. He was still massively aroused and she hoped he was in grave discomfort because of it.

She certainly was.

The treacherous thought slid through her mind, and she gritted her teeth. It didn't help knowing that, had Marcellus not arrived when he had, she would likely have succumbed to the lust surging through her veins.

The thought was revolting. Even if her cursed body disagreed.

"Please, sit." The healer indicated the chair she had recently vacated and since he had asked, and not commanded, she sat. He examined the back of her head and then proceeded to remove the sling and unbind her arm. As he reached her shoulder she held her breath, and despite all her training her stomach pitched with nerves at what she might see once the last dressing was removed.

Romans were butchers. Everyone knew that. Perhaps, despite her best intentions, something on her face showed her fear because Tacitus suddenly loomed over them.

"There's no need to look." His frown had intensified. "Avert your eyes."

Despite his demanding tone, he sounded concerned. Did he imagine she might faint at the sight of her mutilated flesh? She offered him a pained smile.

"There's every need to look, Tacitus. How else will I see what damage I've sustained?"

Tacitus stared as if she had just uttered something completely incomprehensible. Even Marcellus paused in his ministrations and looked at her as though he couldn't decide whether he was shocked or wanted to laugh.

"What?" She transferred her glare from Marcellus back to

Tacitus before once again looking at her shoulder as the healer removed the dressing.

"Nothing," Marcellus said, and from the tone of his voice, it appeared amusement had won over shock. "Isn't that right, *Tacitus*?"

Tacitus grunted, whether in agreement or not she couldn't decipher. Why they should think it so extraordinary she had deduced his name from their conversation she couldn't imagine. If that *was* the reason.

Her breath escaped in a relieved gasp. The wound was not fiery red or weeping yellow pus. It was a surprisingly small puncture between her collarbone and armpit and the stitches astonishingly neat. She leaned down and sniffed. And smelt only the faintest tinge of astringent.

"Curse the gods." Tacitus glared at her shoulder as if it mortally offended him. "Fucking Gallian."

"Who has been punished for his lack of foresight."

Was she imagining that slight censure in the healer's voice?

Carefully she prodded her shoulder. The arrow hadn't penetrated right through, thank Goddess, otherwise her arm would be useless for moons. It appeared the sleeveless leather shirt, which her mother had always insisted she wore in battle, had saved her from far more serious an injury.

Her mother. Whenever she thought of her, a shaft of pain speared through Nimue's heart. A wretched maelstrom of strangled love, despairing guilt and an overwhelming sense of loss and betrayal.

"Are you in much discomfort?" Marcellus pulled up the other chair and sat, his attention fully on her. "I can administer more opium if you require."

And risk losing her senses once again?

"I don't require any more of your drugs." But even as she spoke, a flicker of intangible awareness vibrated through her soul.

I need the opium.

The thought pierced her brain and she instantly tried to smother it. She didn't want the drug. She would have to be dead or at the very least unconscious before she'd allow them to fill her with their heathen potions again.

Yet the feeling persisted. She needed the opium.

"At least—not at this moment." Goddess, what had possessed her to say that? She clamped her teeth together before any other unwary word escaped.

"I still have the opium you gave me yesterday," Tacitus said. "She didn't need any during the night."

"Good." Marcellus sounded faintly surprised, as if he had expected her to welcome his brain-numbing potions with open arms. Skeletal fingers trailed from the base of her skull and along the length of her spine. And once again, the overwhelming compunction to demand more opium pounded in her mind.

What was wrong with her? The more she craved it, the more she would resist. She would never be able to discover the fate of the queen and escape this Roman if her mind was forever fogged by erotic dreams and...

And something else, something of utmost importance; something she could almost recall if only the veil in her mind would lift.

The healer redressed her wound, all the while telling her how she had to rest her arm and not put undue strain on her shoulder. She didn't bother telling him she had no intention of allowing her muscles to become soft and useless by such coddling. Was this the advice he gave his Roman patients?

Her irritated thoughts reminded her of something she shouldn't have forgotten in the first place.

"Have you tended many Celtic casualties?" She hoped her voice didn't betray the urgency of her question. "Women and children?"

Marcellus glanced up at her, a guarded look in his eyes.

"There were not—"

"Have you finished?" Tacitus' impatient voice cut through the healer's and Marcellus straightened. Nimue pressed her lips together as the moment of possible illumination shattered before her eyes.

"Yes. The wound is healing satisfactorily. There's no hint of corruption. But don't hesitate to come and see me again if you're at all concerned."

Nimue pushed herself to her feet. The healer's words offered her no comfort because what had he been about to say? That there had been no other Celtic casualties? Because all the Romans had left were fatalities?

Did that mean all the children who had been hiding in the mountains had been slaughtered by the enemy, or that they had escaped into the surrounding forests?

"You've treated no injured children?"

"Be silent." Tacitus rounded on her with such ferocity she actually recoiled. Was he speaking to *her*? No one had ever spoken to her in such a manner before. No one would *dare* speak to her in such a manner. But in the fleeting moment that her senses reeled, Tacitus virtually ejected Marcellus from the tent. "Repeat nothing."

Far from looking offended, Marcellus shot her a calculating glance before tossing Tacitus a grin.

"There's nothing to repeat, my friend. But may Fortuna smile upon you because by Mars, I believe you're going to need her."

CHAPTER 9

*T*acitus scowled at his friend's retreating back before ensuring that the legionary guarding the tent was far enough away so as not to have overheard the conversation.

Then he yanked down the flap and turned to face his Celt.

She was looking at him as if he was a plague-ridden leper.

"And why shouldn't I know of my countrymen's fate?" Her voice was haughty. "Would you be silent in my place?"

He'd expected her to rant in fury at his command, not coldly question him. He wasn't used to people questioning his commands and, for the life of him, he couldn't recall a single instance when a woman had.

There was a time and place to be entertained by this barbaric Celt's behavior and now, when he needed to be by his commander's side, was neither.

"I'm not in your place, and the likelihood of my ever being so is remote." He wrenched off his tunic and tossed it onto the pallet he'd tried to sleep on last night. "Therefore your question is redundant."

When she didn't immediately respond he shot her an irritated glance and saw how she stared, riveted, at his erect cock. The look on her face was a heady combination of shocked disbelief and blatant lust.

He gritted his teeth and grabbed his clean tunic that lay across the top of his casket. He was in need of a fuck, a bath and a long, relaxing massage but the most he could look forward to today was, most likely, supervising the dismantling of this camp.

"My questions," her voice was husky and only when the linen covered him did she drag her gaze up to his face, "are deserving of answers." The tip of her tongue moistened her lips. "You have no right to deny me such knowledge."

In the process of swinging his cloak over his shoulders, he slung her a disbelieving glance. True, he didn't want her to behave like a slave. But gods, did she really have no idea when she should hold her tongue? No woman of his acquaintance was so insistent on having the last word once a man had made himself clear.

"I don't have time to pander to your whims." He fixed his fibula to his shoulder. "Remain here. I'll have food sent to you, and water so you can wash." Cursed inconvenient none of his personal servants were here. But back at the garrison, he could ensure she was looked after properly in his absence.

She let out a surprisingly loud hiss.

"You're doing it again. Stop giving me orders. And if you refuse to answer my questions then tell me that. Don't pretend my concerns are mere *whims*." She spat the word as if it offended her.

It probably did.

He realized he was staring at her when, slave or not, he should be telling her—once again—to be silent.

Only this time she didn't need to remain silent for her safety. This time she needed to be silent because...

Because she talked too much. He'd never met a woman who talked as much as she did. At least, not one that talked of such things that continually irked and astounded him.

It had been different by the mountain stream when sexual awareness had sizzled in the air and he'd been so certain of having her. It had been blatantly erotic, early this morn, when she had openly defied him. Yet even then she'd continued to push beyond acceptable boundaries and she was doing it again.

"I refuse to answer your questions." He waited for her exclamation of outrage, but it didn't come. She just glowered at him. His balls ached, his cock throbbed and frustration thundered through his veins. "For your own safety you'll remain here. If you're hungry, you will eat the food I provide. And if you have any *self-respect*," he emphasized the words with heavy sarcasm, "you'll use the water to wash the filth from your body."

He watched the mortified blush spread over her cheeks, as if she understood the full intent of his barbed remark. His scowl deepened when a stab of regret pierced his conscience. Gods, as if it mattered whether he had injured her feelings or not, so long as she cleaned herself up?

"And if I am to remain here, how am I to relieve myself?" Despite the way he had just intentionally insulted her, pride spiked her words. Somehow that made him feel even worse.

It took him a moment to understand her meaning. And then he was the one who felt heat crawling up his face.

By the gods. He'd never spoken of such intimacies before. It wasn't something he wished to experience again, either.

He had no intention of allowing her to use the latrines. Not even if he accompanied her to ensure no other legionary entered while she was…relieving herself.

"I'll have a bucket brought for you."

"A *bucket?*" She sounded as if she had never heard of such an item. Except the look of horrified disgust on her face assured him she knew exactly what a bucket was and the thought of using it filled her with revulsion.

"I'll return later." He turned to leave, then hesitated. "If you need anything, ask the legionary on duty outside." He'd give instructions that the Celt's wishes were to be relayed to him instantly. "But don't attempt to engage him in conversation."

"Why would I want to engage a filthy Roman in conversation?" Her voice was belligerent and there was a proud tilt to her chin. But as she folded her arms, her hand cradled the elbow of her injured arm and that single gesture tore through his chest.

In spite of her brave words, she was a vulnerable woman. Little more than a girl. Although she was here with him, although she belonged to him, this was not how he had imagined it when he'd come across her on the mountain.

But this was the reality. When she was in a more accommodating frame of mind—when they were back at the garrison and he'd had time to make the necessary arrangements—he'd tell her she was his concubine. And he could wipe the unsavory fact that he had purchased her from his mind.

"No reason." He preferred she spoke to no one. Then no one could inadvertently betray her status. His mind lingered on his recent thoughts and although he was perilously close to being late for his meeting with the commander he couldn't help himself. "How old are you?"

For a moment, he didn't think she was going to answer. Then she let out a long sigh.

"This is my twenty-second summer."

He barely hid his surprise. She was older than he'd imagined, scarcely two years younger than he was.

"Well?" She sounded irked by his continued silence. "How old are *you*, Tacitus?"

For the second time that morning, her use of his personal name stunned him. Of course, once she was his concubine he intended she would call him that, but it was a privilege not something anyone could refer to him by.

Certainly not a slave. It was a wonder Marcellus hadn't remarked upon it.

"You have me at a disadvantage." There was no reason to

make an issue of it. No one would know but Marcellus, and his friend would repeat nothing of what had occurred during the course of his *house call*. "I don't yet know your name."

"Oh." She sounded scathing. "I believe we're even, Roman, since I know your name and you know my age."

Why couldn't she answer a simple, civilized question? And why was he standing here conversing with her when his commander waited?

"If you prefer I can give you a new name. A Roman name." Not that he truly intended to. It was too closely entwined with ownership and slavery. "I've no intention of referring to you as *Celt* for the remainder of our liaison."

Her lips thinned in clear annoyance. Whether it was the threat of him renaming her or the fact he intended for them to enjoy a liaison, he wasn't sure.

"You may address me as Nimue." She sounded as though she conferred a great honor.

"Nimue." It was an unusual name, like nothing he had heard before. But since Nimue herself was like no other woman he'd ever encountered, her name suited her perfectly. "I like it."

If he expected a positive response to his remark, he should have known better. She shrugged her good shoulder and gave him a look that suggested he had just crawled from beneath a steaming pile of manure.

"It's the only name I'll answer to."

And then, as if she were an empress and he a lowly plebeian, she turned her back on him.

~

TACITUS WAS STILL SEETHING with unrequited lust and justifiable fury at Nimue's insolence when he arrived at his commander's tent. His temper didn't improve when he saw Blandus was already there.

Why the fuck wasn't he with his own commander?

"We're leaving today," the commander said without preamble. "Inform the centurions."

"Very well." Tacitus glanced at his cousin. "Shouldn't you be with Ostorius Scapula?"

"Already received my orders for the day." Blandus fingered the hilt of his sword. "Two of our cohorts are to remain behind and scour the countryside for any stragglers. I doubt they'll find Caratacus but who can say? We picked up one of his brothers at first light this morning."

Tacitus jerked his head. "If that's all, I'll give the Primus his orders." He needed to work off some of this excess energy. Keep his mind occupied so Nimue's haughty face didn't incessantly intrude.

Gods. He'd not envisaged she would be so hard to please once she'd regained her senses. All he needed was for her to accept the desire that burned between them. Why was that so hard? He knew, as surely as he knew he had only three more months left to serve in the Legions, that once he'd had her, this frenzied need in his blood would abate.

Then he could enjoy her barbed tongue and seductive body at nights, and forget about her during the days.

"So, Tacitus..." Blandus' smile didn't reach his eyes. "Is the reason you're so late this morning due to that delectable little slave you purchased yesterday?"

"What, the child?" The commander glanced up from the scrolls he was scrutinizing to frown at Tacitus.

"Hardly a child, my esteemed uncle." Blandus gave a mirthless laugh. "She certainly tempted my noble cousin to forsake his mighty principles. Although the glower on your face, Tacitus, suggests she wasn't as accommodating as you supposed."

"The Celt," for some reason he didn't feel disposed to tell Blandus her name, "is still recovering from her injury."

"She was shot in the shoulder, not between her thighs. I'm

sure she's more than able to spread her legs with suitable encouragement."

"And that," Tacitus said, hanging onto his temper by the slenderest of threads, "is something only I will ever know."

"By Mars." Amusement lurked in the commander's tone. "Aren't you boys too old to be fighting over your female entertainment?"

"There's nothing to fight over." Tacitus flexed his fingers and maintained eye contact with his now-scowling cousin. "The woman is mine. No discussion."

The commander slapped him on the shoulder. "She must be quite something, Tacitus. I look forward to making her acquaintance."

CHAPTER 10

Using the bucket had been one of the most degrading experiences of Nimue's life, but that was before a hated auxiliary of the enemy arrived to remove the offending object. She stood, rigid with mortification, as two more auxiliaries brought in a small tub and more buckets of hot water.

None of the auxiliaries said a word to her. They didn't even make eye contact. She might have been invisible for all the notice they took of her. When she was once again alone she released a ragged breath and using one finger pulled open a crack in the flap of the tent.

A legionary was stationed outside. Other tents were opposite and the entire area was a seething hive of activity. Beyond, in the distance, was the mountain where her people had been so disastrously led by the Briton king's vision of victory.

She had no chance of slipping out unnoticed. And even if she did, where would she go? She still hadn't discovered whether or not the queen had been captured.

Hugging her aching arm she glared with resentment at the buckets of water and assortment of what she could only imagine were cleansing lotions. It was humiliating enough to face the fact she was a prisoner, without having the additional fact thrown in her face that she *stank*.

The childish desire to tip the cursed water over the floor assailed her. Except she was certain such action wouldn't gain her access to a stream. She was torn between the desire to feel clean again and acidic indignation at having a Roman bark orders at her as if she were a stray dog. Her glance snagged on the large casket she'd noticed earlier that morn and upon which an auxiliary had left a plate of strange, foreign food.

Her heart hammered in sudden excitement. Perhaps Tacitus had stowed her dagger there? She felt naked, horribly vulnerable without it, and although she was under no illusion that her dagger could grant her safe passage from this heathen camp, at least it would afford her a sense of personal security.

The casket was locked. Of course it would be. She scrutinized the lock and a grim smile twisted her lips. This mechanism was familiar to her. Her mother had owned a Roman crafted casket with such a lock. But not only that. Her mother had taught her how to open such locks without benefit of a Roman key.

She slid her earring out of her lobe, straightened the silver spike as best she could and inserted it into the keyhole. Several painstaking moments later, the mechanism clicked open.

She dropped her earring onto her lap and picked up the plate. After she placed it back on the ground, she attempted to lift the solid timber lid with one hand. It was too heavy from that angle. She pushed herself to her feet. It was only her shoulder that was injured, yet it affected her entire body.

She braced her thigh against the side of the casket and this time when she tried to lift the lid, it swung open. A timber box lay on top of purple-striped linen, filled with silver and gold brooches. They were encrusted with precious gems, and looked similar to the one Tacitus had used on his cloak just now. She glanced over her shoulder, but the tent flap was still secured. She had to hurry. There was no telling how soon the Roman might return. The last thing she wanted was for him to discover her rifling through his possessions.

Holding her breath, she knelt, slid her hand into the side of the casket and spread her fingers. She could feel nothing but soft linen. Perhaps her dagger was hidden beneath the layers of clothing instead of down the side of the casket. She lifted the top garment.

Her fingers stilled and she stared, unbelieving, at her medicine bag.

Arianrhod save me. All her desperate hopes that somehow the queen and princess remained safely hidden fled.

They were not safe. They had been captured. How else would her bag be here? She'd left it with them when she'd gone to find water. Her fingers crushed the embroidered handles as indecision seared her breast.

Where were they? In another Roman officer's tent? Was that the way Romans secured their valuable prisoners?

But while Caratacus' queen was certainly valuable, of what value was *she*? As a Druid they might, possibly, want to postpone her execution until they returned to the Roman fortification. That way they could ensure a significant crowd might watch her torturous death by crucifixion. But she was certain they didn't know of her heritage. If they did, they wouldn't have wasted their time by treating her injury.

With difficulty, she unhooked her fingers from her bag. It was clear it had been emptied of all its contents. And it was equally clear of what value Tacitus placed on her.

He wanted to fuck her. It was as simple as that. Why he hadn't already, she could not quite comprehend, especially after her discovery that he'd paid for her treatment. But it didn't change what she knew.

Biting her lip she continued to search through the casket, but it was a halfhearted effort since she knew she wouldn't find her dagger. The only items that might be used as weapons were the pins in the brooches. She took one final look at her bag, traced her finger over the embroidered image of the owl and then covered it with the linen and closed the lid.

She leaned back against the casket, feeling desperately fatigued. Even if a chance presented itself, she couldn't escape. She'd have to stay until she had worked out a plan of rescue.

And for that, she first needed to discover where the queen and princess were being held.

Wearily, she looked back at the steaming water. Part of her wanted to flaunt her bloodied and filthy state at Tacitus. But another part, entwined with feminine pride and her perilously fragile *self-respect*, balked at the notion.

Gritting her teeth, she shuffled on her knees across the ground, rescuing her torque on the way. Her belt was laying on a chair—removed from her while she was unconscious—and with some difficulty she managed to squeeze the torque into one of the leather pouches attached to it. Tacitus might have stolen her dagger but he hadn't appeared to have taken any other personal possession. Somehow, the knowledge irked her.

Laboriously, she cleansed her body as best she could and then started on her hair. It became progressively harder to breathe, as if all the air was being sucked out of the tent, and her heart pounded an erratic staccato against her ribs.

She screwed her eyes shut, then opened them. But the light continued to diminish, as though she entered an avenue of massive oaks that hid the sun from view. Her vision spun and stomach pitched and, with a detached sense of disbelief, she felt tears prick her eyes.

But she never cried. She hadn't even cried when her mother...

The thought hovered, unformed, yet it haunted the darkest recesses of her mind. She wouldn't think of her mother. Not now. But even as she struggled to focus, to finish rinsing her hair, the darkness swallowed up the interior of the tent and invaded her senses and with a sigh of exhaustion, she sank into oblivion.

It was the seventh hour before Tacitus had time to check on his Celt. Since leaving her five hours ago, his anger had mellowed and, while it was highly unorthodox, he decided to share the late midday meal with her. She'd likely be hungry again. It had been four hours since he'd instructed food to be sent to her.

As he marched back to his quarters, an auxiliary following laden down with the more appetizing rations on offer, he hoped she was in a more agreeable mood. Even as the thought formed, amusement flashed through him. Who else of his acquaintance would consider, let alone hope, that his slave's mood might be agreeable?

The legionary snapped to attention at his approach and pulled back the flap of the tent. Tacitus entered and instead of being greeted by caustic words or even a frosty silence, Nimue lay crumpled on the ground next to the bathtub.

And she was naked.

With a livid curse, he unclasped his fibula, swung the cloak from his shoulders and covered her chilled body.

"Get out." He shot the auxiliary a deadly glare, and the man placed the basket of food on the casket and left as if nothing was untoward. As soon as he was alone, Tacitus knelt by Nimue's side. If anyone had dared touched her, he would have them flogged to within an inch of their miserable existence. For one torturous moment, the face of his commander flashed into his brain. But the commander would never take what belonged to another. "Nimue, can you hear me?"

She shivered, and snuggled farther into his cloak as if the warmth comforted her. Her hair was unbound, tangled about her face, and disappeared beneath his cloak. But in that brief moment before he'd covered her, he'd seen how it curled in glorious abandonment to her waist.

He reached for her, before recalling her injury. With difficulty, he maneuvered her into his arms without placing undue pressure on her shoulder. Only as he lifted her did he catch sight of the untouched plate of food lying on the ground next to his casket.

No wonder she'd fainted. She hadn't eaten.

Carefully, he lowered her to the bed. Her eyelashes flickered and she looked up at him and in that unguarded moment, he recognized a rare glimpse of utter trust.

It stabbed through his chest, as tangible as a dagger.

"Tacitus." Her voice was husky from sleep, undeniably alluring. He knew he should rise from his knees, sit on the edge of the bed, but somehow he couldn't bring himself to risk the possibility of shattering this moment.

No one would ever know that he knelt by her side.

He offered her a drink from his own water skin and she gulped inelegantly, clearly parched. "You didn't eat." It was a gentle admonishment. Yet she had washed. And by so doing, had exhausted her fragile resources.

He should have returned earlier. How long had she lain on the ground, unaware and exposed?

A slow frown crinkled her brow, as she attempted to process his words.

"I don't know what happened." Her frown intensified, and he saw the precise moment when her vulnerability hit her and wariness replaced the trust. He tried not to care. What did it matter? And yet, somehow, it did. "There must be a residue of your heathen drug still in my blood."

It was possible, but he doubted it. "How are you feeling now?" Gods, he sounded like a physician. His father would be rendered speechless if he knew his beloved son spoke in such a manner to a woman so far beneath his social status.

Then again, Tacitus' actions in such matters had often reduced his father to speechlessness.

Nimue's frown mutated into a scowl and she struggled to sit

up. He didn't offer to assist, since first he was certain she would refuse and secondly it was entertaining to watch her trying to keep his cloak wrapped around her while she wriggled into position.

"I've never been so incapacitated." She sounded distressed, although she still glared at him. "It's humiliating."

"It will soon pass." If her blood had poisoned, she would already be showing the symptoms. "I regret you were shot, as if you were an enemy. It should never have occurred."

Her glare faded and she looked confused.

"But I *am* your enemy. I only wonder that you didn't strike me down yourself."

Her fingers peeked from between the folds of his cloak. He covered them with his hand in a blatant gesture of possessiveness. She didn't protest.

"I told you." He didn't bother hiding his amusement. "I don't fight women. You posed no threat to me or the Empire. Why would I strike you down?"

"Had our positions been reversed I would have had no hesitation in striking *you* down." She sounded irritated.

How enchanting she believed herself capable of felling a warrior. The conversation reminded him of the one they'd shared at the stream, before he'd had no choice but to make her his slave.

"I'd like to see you try." He knew some Celtic women fought alongside their men-folk but they were built like men themselves. Or so he had heard. Personally, he'd not faced any in battle and for that he was relieved. The thought of killing a woman, even a woman who thought herself as good as a man, horrified him.

"You would not have time to see." Nimue's eyes darkened before his gaze. "If I struck, you'd be dead before you realized what had happened."

Gently he pulled her hand from the folds of his cloak. She

didn't resist. Still holding onto her, he traced the fingers of his other hand along her slender forearm. Her skin was smooth, warm and gave a tantalizing glimpse of how the rest of her body would feel beneath his questing touch.

"This isn't the arm of a woman who wields a sword." He thought of his noble Roman-born mother; of her admirable womanly skills. "Although your prowess with the loom is doubtless exemplary."

She stared at him as if she hadn't the faintest idea what he was talking about. Did Celt women not take pride in their weaving abilities, as did the noblewomen of Rome? Nimue's gown had been of the finest quality and she was no peasant, yet she appeared not to realize he'd just paid her a high compliment.

"I don't possess a sword." Her gaze dropped to watch as he toyed with her silver bracelets. They were all intricately engraved, but one in particular drew his attention. It showed the passage of the moon during the course of a monthly cycle, and interspersed between each lunar image was a detailed engraving of an owl. For a reason he couldn't fathom, it appeared oddly familiar. "What have you done with my dagger?"

He abandoned her bracelets and once again caught her mesmeric gaze.

"You have no need for your dagger." Just because he knew she couldn't kill him didn't mean he wasn't fully aware she could cause him severe injury if she attacked him while he slept. He'd secured it with his own weapons. "I'll protect you against any who might wish you harm."

"Noble Roman." There was a hint of mockery but her fingers slid between his, and he wondered if she was even aware of her action. "Who will protect me from *you*?"

His finger slid up her delicately defined biceps, and he knuckled his cloak aside. Her slender neck, unmarred shoulder and arm and delectable breast tempted his reason and it was a struggle to recall that, beneath the left side of his cloak, she had been shot.

"Do you need protecting from me?" He trailed his fingers across her collarbone. Her breath whispered from between her parted lips but she didn't attempt to push him away. "Do you fear I will harm you, Nimue?"

"I don't fear you." She said the words as if she didn't even have to think about them. As if the notion he might hurt her had never seriously crossed her mind. The knowledge that she trusted him to that degree, even if it was a trust she hadn't acknowledged to herself, caused an odd glow to ignite deep inside his chest.

His fingers traced across the creamy swell of her breast and she hitched in an uneven breath. Heart thudding, he circled her erect nipple and imagined sucking the tempting bud until she gasped with mindless need.

"I want to see your naked body, Nimue." He tried to repress the raw need hammering through his blood but only partially succeeded. He knew she was injured. He would be mindful. But gods, he needed relief.

"You can already see it, Roman." Was that a hint of amusement in her tone? She hadn't blushed at his words, nor had she affected outrage. He tightened his grip on her hand, and rolled her exquisite nipple between his finger and thumb. Her lips parted and the tip of her tongue peeked out. As if in deliberate provocation.

"Not well enough." He loosened his grip on her hand and bracketed her wrist, slowly sliding his palm up her arm, over her firm biceps, across her shoulder and down the smooth contour of her back. "I want to suck on your nipples until you writhe in delight, tease your clitoris with my tongue and thrust my cock so deep inside you that you scream for mercy."

∽

Nimue fought against the seductive images Tacitus' promises evoked. But his fingers, teasing her sensitive nipple, caused ripples of lust from the tip of her breast to the core of her being. And between her thighs she was tender, wet and Goddess help her, starving for his touch.

Had he been any other man, she wouldn't be fighting this savage attraction that was unlike anything she'd experienced before. But he was a *Roman*. He would always be a Roman and if she succumbed to the dark desire pounding through her blood how could she live with herself afterward?

"I would never scream for mercy." Her voice was raw, her words breathless. She could deny she wanted him but he would need to be dead not to see she lied. "No matter what torture you inflict upon me."

And the worst torture of all was that he would cease touching her treacherous flesh. That was the truth. The secret shame she would die before ever revealing. The knowledge that she enjoyed his touch, *craved* his touch, and wanted him more than she had ever wanted a man before.

"Is this torture?" His breath drifted across her lips. When had he leaned so close to her? "I would inflict nothing but pleasure upon your body. Do you doubt me?"

No, she did not doubt him at all. His hand cradled the curve of her buttock, as if he had every right to hold her so intimately. And instead of outrage at his possessive manner she wanted more.

Unable to help herself she flattened her hand against his chest. He wasn't wearing armor, only a tunic with a wide purple stripe and she could feel the strong thud of his heart vibrating through her fingers.

She wanted him naked too. The thought crippled her, but it made no difference. He was polluting her senses as surely as his healer's heathen drug had.

Her fingers fisted, crushing his linen, and the unyielding

expanse of muscle beneath her hand caused ripples of delight to chase across her exposed skin. This morn, she had been mesmerized by the tantalizing glimpse of his naked body. Had been unable to tear her fascinated gaze from his magnificent cock.

All that masculine perfection was now within her grasp. She could have him. Sate her need. Rid this fever from her blood.

And then she could devote her entire concentration on...

Her mission. The Briton queen.

Relief washed through her. She could live with that decision. It was a strategic decision, one that would clear her mind, calm her body and, simultaneously, lower both Tacitus' suspicion and obsessive desire for her.

There was one thing she needed to know.

"Afterward, will you let me go?"

His eyes darkened and his hands tightened over her bottom and breast. She dragged in a constricted breath and struggled to concentrate. Goddess, the sooner they both achieved orgasm the better. Only then would she be able to endure his touch without constantly fantasizing how it would feel to have him inside her.

"Let you go?" He was so close to her his lips brushed hers. A tantalizing whisper of a touch that promised so much. "No, Nimue. I have no intention of letting you go yet."

CHAPTER 11

Nimue attempted to dredge up disappointment that Tacitus had no intention of releasing her the moment after she'd had him, but failed.

Besides, she didn't want him to discard her instantly. If she was ejected from his camp, how much harder would it be to find the queen? Especially with her injured shoulder. She needed a few more days with this Roman, just to regain her former strength.

His plans for her suited her. She could enjoy his body without guilt that she was betraying her people.

Because she was doing this *for* her people. But still a sliver of guilt ate through her heart. Should she really feel such lust and anticipation at having her enemy? Shouldn't her mind and body recoil at what she intended to do?

With an uneasy feeling that she was attempting to make excuses for the way her body responded to Tacitus' touch, she pushed the thought aside. She couldn't afford to become distracted from her purpose. She struggled to recall his last remark. *He has no intention of letting me go.*

"And I have no say in this matter?" She trailed her hand over his shoulder and dragged her fingers along the proud line of his jaw. He was rough against her skin and vague recollections of having done this once before plagued the outer reaches of her mind.

"No." His voice was husky. "You'll stay with me until I decide otherwise."

She speared her fingers through his short hair and marveled at her lack of indignation at his arrogance. But then, what did it matter what he said? When she was ready to leave, she would. After all, she wasn't staying with him because he commanded it.

Or because I want to. Yet that thought lacked conviction and her fingers tightened involuntarily in his hair. Of course she didn't want to stay with him. She was simply using the circumstances to her best advantage.

"Is this the way of your world, Roman? To give your women no choice?" Not that she was really interested in his world. She had no intention of ever living in it so his customs were of no interest. It was only a ploy to show token resistance to his authority. She didn't want him to suspect her real motive for succumbing to the lust between them.

Except, unaccountably, she wanted to hear his answer.

With infinite care, he lifted his cloak from her, leaving her entirely naked beneath his intense gaze. Her nipples tightened and shivers raced over her skin as she saw his jaw clench and heard his sharp intake of breath. Never before had merely a look from a man caused her body to respond this way and instinctively she arched her back so her breasts thrust enticingly toward him.

"What choice do you need?" His full attention was focused on her breasts. "You're with me. You're mine."

She was wet with need, lust curled deep in her womb and yet his casual words of possession pounded through her blood. He said them as if they were the natural order. As though he was merely repeating something she should already be aware of.

Her senses urged her to ignore him. He could say what he wished and none of it touched her. All that mattered was that they fucked so Tacitus would lower his guard around her. And yet she couldn't remain silent.

"I'm with you, but I'll never be *yours*."

Finally he dragged his attention from her breasts and looked at her. There was a smile of masculine satisfaction on his face. Did he think her words meaningless?

"Nimue." The way he said her name in his exotic Roman accent caused quivers of desire deep in her pussy. He trailed his fingers up her body and cradled her jaw between his hands. His fingers branded her flesh, blatantly possessive, and instead of outrage flooding her at the thought, she didn't want him to stop. Her chest tightened, lungs contracted, making it almost impossible to draw breath. "Why must you question this? You want me as much as I want you." His lips grazed hers, a kiss as insubstantial as mist in the morn yet fire scorched low in her belly and curled with seductive promise around her clit.

She knew she should keep her thoughts to herself and not question his every word. That wasn't the way to gain his trust. She should agree with him so he imagined her malleable and not a threat.

"I know." Their lips brushed as she spoke and sharp desire spiked between her thighs, splintering all thought of stoking his male Roman pride. Did he intend to drive her insane before taking her? Her hand slid from his head and feverishly she fisted his linen and pulled, wanting him naked and on the bed with her. "Remove your tunic."

For a moment, he looked startled. Had a woman ever commanded such a thing from him before? But then, with an irresistible smile, he obeyed without further question. And once again she feasted on the magnificent sight of his broad shoulders, his muscular chest and taut abdomen.

He looked like a foreign bronzed god, and although the

notion should have repulsed, it served only to heighten the need thundering through her veins and incinerating her reason.

"Come here." Her voice was hoarse and she reached out to drag him from the ground. Pain lanced through her shoulder and she gasped, her arm dropping uselessly onto her lap. How had she forgotten about her injury? This insane lust fogged all her senses. A deadly condition for a warrior.

Before she had time to mask her unthinking reaction he was on the bed beside her, looming over her like a predator guarding its prey. But despite the lust that glowed in his eyes, she detected concern too.

"Be careful." He brushed her hair back from her face in an oddly tender gesture. "You don't want to reopen the wound."

Of course she didn't, but she didn't appreciate him telling her that as if she was ignorant. Yet even as the thought flared through her mind, uncertainty hovered. Why was he so concerned for her comfort?

"I have no intention of reopening my wound." Her voice was breathless and the lingering pain in her shoulder faded as desire thudded through her veins. He was so close that his uneven breath dusted across her face. She wanted to crush her aching breasts against his chest, slide her wet pussy along his rigid cock and relieve the exquisite pressure spiraling through her clit.

A stifled moan of frustration razed her throat. If she wasn't hampered by her injury she would do all that and more to him.

"You tempt me beyond reason." He wound his arm around her waist, his hand supporting her between her shoulder blades. His other arm slid under her knees and before she quite realized his intention she was flat on her back. She glared up at him, torn between indignation at his maneuver and a delicious sense of helplessness. *Since when have I ever enjoyed the sensation of helplessness?* Tacitus' grin at her submissive position was worthy of any of the trickster gods of her people. "Now you are fully within my power."

His words should infuriate her. But against all reason they didn't. Perhaps it was his smile that took the threat from his words. "If my arm wasn't useless," she was compelled to inform him. "You wouldn't find it so easy to pin me to the mattress."

For answer, he kneed her legs apart, bracing his weight on his hands as he loomed over her. "I would have no difficulty pinning you anywhere, no matter whether you were injured or not."

The exotic spices that scented his hair and body engulfed her. It was heady, evocative and weaved through her blood and clouded her mind. She wanted to claw his face for his arrogance, and she wanted to fuck him senseless to still the ravening need shredding her sanity.

She wound her hand around his throat, mimicking what he had done to her earlier that day. His pulse thudded beneath her fingers and still he grinned down at her, arrogantly mocking her display of strength.

"Believe that if you wish, Roman." She loosened her grip around his throat and dug her nails into the hard ridges of his shoulder. "One day we might put that assumption to the test."

What am I saying? Why couldn't she hold her tongue when she knew her strategy should be one of subservience? Most of all, why did she find their exchange of words so cursed arousing?

He nudged her thighs farther apart and lowered himself, until the aching tips of her breasts brushed against the dark hair that dusted his chest. It was agonizing, excruciating and she dragged her nails with murderous intent along the rigid contour of his breathtaking biceps.

"I have never," his voice was strained, as if he clung onto his control by sheer willpower alone, "met a woman who insists on answering back with such frequency."

She abandoned his arm and clasped his taut arse. Goddess, he felt good. The way he jerked against her as though he couldn't help himself proved he found her touch equally arousing.

"I wonder you don't gag me." It was a breathless taunt and she squeezed his hard flesh, raising her knees and wrapping her ankles around his thighs. Still he didn't take what she offered. He remained rigid above her, his hot gaze locked with hers.

"Don't tempt me."

She scraped her nails along his spine, relishing the way he shuddered, the way he so doggedly refused to relinquish his cursed Roman pride and follow her lead. If she had full use of both arms she wouldn't be flat on her back, where she could do little but squirm. She'd have him on his back, and by Goddess, she would already be riding him into orgasmic pleasure.

"I do tempt you." She dug her heels into his buttocks and attempted to raise her hips to encourage penetration but curse the man, he had her pinned securely to the mattress and her ability to control even this was negligible. "Fuck you, Tacitus, what are you doing?"

He bared his teeth, whether in a grin or grimace she could not decipher. His hot breath panted across her face and he lowered himself onto her. His erection slanted over her pussy, so close to where she wanted him and yet not close enough. She groaned, tried to squirm, but only succeeded in rubbing her swollen clit against his cock. It was a torturous pleasure and she squirmed again, the friction causing her juices to spill over his rigid length. He still didn't answer her unspoken demand, but instead continued to press against her, crushing her breasts against his chest. Pushing her securely into the mattress so she could no longer even move.

Yet even in the midst of her frustration, she was aware he hadn't come close to touching her injured shoulder.

"That's not the language I expect to hear from a noblewoman."

Her clit throbbed for release. Her nipples ached for his mouth. And all he could think about was her *language*? She hitched in a shallow breath, all she could manage, and glared into his lust-filled eyes.

"I'm not a *Roman* noblewoman, and I can say as I please."

"But you are noble-born."

Where was he going with this? For an instant, the circumstances of her birth haunted her, before her current circumstances once more overwhelmed her.

Goddess, he drove her mad. She could feel how hard he was, how hot and ready, and she could do nothing about it. It wasn't just because she was injured. Despite her earlier words, she knew that even without her wounded shoulder she would still be at his mercy. The knowledge slammed into her, and a flicker of fear ignited at her vulnerability.

She had never been so securely pinned beneath a man before. She had always maintained a degree of control. But Tacitus had wrenched all control from her. She couldn't even impale herself on his cock and watch his mocking smile transform into mindless need. Then, she would know what to do. He would be under *her* command and she could slake her lust while retaining her freedom to move as she pleased. She didn't want to talk about her heritage. She didn't want to talk to him at all. All she wanted, all she needed, was for him to take her, for her to come, so once again she could think clearly.

Her frustrated confusion made her reckless. "Why? Are you unable to *fuck* a peasant, Roman? Aren't you man enough for me after all?"

Breath hissed between his teeth and he rose from her. His tough, bronzed body radiated tension in every muscle and for a fleeting moment, he looked like a conquering warlord claiming his prize. The image burned into her brain but before she could suck air into her deprived lungs he slammed into her so hard, so fast, for a dizzying moment the world turned black.

"Is that man enough for you, Celt?" Leashed fury whipped through each word but she didn't have the breath to answer. His cock was inside her, stretching her, invading her, and Goddess help her, but she could feel him all the way up to the entrance of her womb.

She couldn't speak. She was afraid to breathe, in case she shattered. All she could do was stare up at him and remain utterly still for fear of rupture.

"Nimue?" His growl penetrated her fogged mind. *"Nimue?"* This time a thread of doubt entered his voice, and he eased off her, enough to relieve the pressure deep inside.

She gasped, clutched at his back and gingerly flexed her internal muscles. She rippled against his rigid length and desire coiled where a moment ago she'd been paralyzed with shock.

He was inside her, and it was nothing like she had fantasized.

It was so much *more*.

"Are you all right?" He braced his weight on his left arm and his right hand cradled the side of her face. His touch should mean nothing yet she found it oddly endearing. "Did I hurt you?"

She wasn't sure if he'd hurt her or not. *Shocked* was how she felt, but she would never tell him.

Nothing in her limited experience had prepared her for this. She should be furious he had taken her with so little regard. But instead, a hazy voice whispered in the back of her mind. Wasn't this what she had wanted? Hadn't she deliberately pushed him to the edge of his control? The knowledge unnerved her and she tried to glare at him in condemnation but knew she failed. Because she didn't condemn him. "You might have warned me you were about rut like a barbarian."

His fingers gently speared through her tangled hair. He remained motionless inside her, as if aware her body was still adjusting to his forceful penetration.

She still couldn't move in the way she was used to, but delicious tremors licked through her pussy and her nipples throbbed in a way she had never imagined possible.

"I've never been accused of rutting before." He eased out of her a little farther and involuntarily her legs tightened around his thighs. His cock filled her to a degree that hovered on the precipice of discomfort and yet it was a sensation she savored more with every passing beat of her heart.

There was no need to answer him. And yet she couldn't help herself. "You can't help your nature, Roman." Her voice was breathless and she couldn't tear her gaze from his. "It's not your fault if you lack finesse in such matters."

He gave a raw laugh, as if her words amused him despite himself. She eased her thighs farther apart, cradled him more comfortably with her legs. And tried not to utterly succumb to the enigmatic beauty of his eyes.

"If you held your tongue," his voice was uneven and she could feel the tension radiating from his body as he held himself so tightly in check, "you wouldn't drive a man to the brink of his control."

But she wanted him at the brink of his control. She wanted him to lose his control. Feminine power surged through her, and she tightened her internal muscles around his cock. He hissed in shock and reared back to gaze down at her through lust-glazed eyes.

"And where is the fun in that, Tacitus?" she gasped, scarcely coherent as her senses focused on the delirious sensation of his cock against her swollen clit.

"Nimue." He sounded as if he was in the throes of the harshest of barbaric tortures. "Gods, you're so tight and hot around me. *Be still.*" The last was an agonized order, and because she took orders from no Roman, she clenched her muscles again, possessive and demanding around his thick shaft.

He rammed into her, as hard and fast and brutal as before, but this time she was ready and this time she welcomed his invasion. She wrapped her arm around his back, clung onto him, even though she couldn't breathe; even though she couldn't think.

She could feel. Goddess, how she could feel the length of him inside her, stretching her sensitized flesh. Her wet sheath quivered around him as he began to thrust, faster, harder, and what sanity she retained splintered.

Hands flat on the mattress bracing his weight, he rose above her. Again he reminded her of a conquering barbarian and the thought fueled her desire. She matched his rhythm, increased the pace and gasped with mindless delirium as he once again took over, once again set the pace; once again hammered her into the mattress as if he intended to impale her for eternity.

She gripped his shoulder and relished the feel of his muscles flexing beneath her fingers. His gaze bored into her, and his intense focus stoked the feel of him pounding into her slick cleft. His balls slapped against her tender flesh, his harsh breath caused erratic shivers across her damp breasts. For a moment, a thread of panic surfaced. *This is too much.* But it was impossible to struggle against the rising wave of sensation that claimed her pussy. His eyes mesmerized her and his thighs were hard and unyielding where she gripped him with her legs. The scent of sex and sweat and foreign spices swirled in the air, intoxicating her senses as fiery tendrils of pure desire swirled around her clit.

Tension coiled, spiraling through her pussy, twisting low in her stomach. The lingering fragments of her restraint shredded, forgotten, as she tumbled over the edge. Her orgasm shuddered through her, rippling with abandonment through every particle of her convulsing body. Beyond the frenzied beat of her heart, the erratic pound of her blood, she heard Tacitus roar his release, and his hot seed pumped deep and flooded her quivering womb.

CHAPTER 12

The world slowly came back into focus. She stared up at Tacitus. He hadn't instantly collapsed on top of her, as she had expected. Instead, his gaze meshed with hers and their breath mingled, uneven and jagged. A sensuous counterpoint to the erratic thunder of her heart.

Her hand dropped to the mattress and her legs slid down his thighs. Her ankles hooked over the back of his knees and she couldn't help giving him an exhausted smile as she once more contracted her pussy around him.

His grin in response sent a peculiar shaft of pain through her chest. It lingered for a moment, oddly reassuring, before she forcibly smothered it. Not that she had needed to smother it. It had nothing to do with Tacitus or what they had just done. It was likely a strange reaction to the fact she had not eaten for more than a day.

"Do you never do as you're told?" He lazily traced one finger along the line of her face. Disbelief quivered at the realization that his touch set off tremors of renewed desire. Her few previous sexual encounters had always been enjoyable and she had invariably reached climax but she had never so utterly lost herself before. And while she'd had every intention of savoring the times she and Tacitus fucked it was, after all, only a means of securing his trust. She wasn't supposed to have experienced the most mind-blowing orgasm of her life. And she certainly shouldn't crave to have him again already.

She couldn't let him know his touch wielded such power. Allowing him access to her body was *her* strategy. She needed to remember that, and regain her focus. "Would you prefer I simply lay here like a log?"

"I don't believe I ever asked you to behave like a log." He was still inside her, his fingers were playing with her tangled hair, and he looked completely relaxed as he continued to grin down at her. As if she was the most enchanting thing he had ever encountered.

She didn't know what she'd expected in the immediate aftermath of their joining but she certainly hadn't expected such intimate jesting. Just because she found his bantering disarming was no excuse to encourage him.

"Do you expect me to ask permission before I make any move?" And now she was responding. But how could she not? There was something deliciously seductive about this Roman that edged through her defenses. Was it truly so wrong to enjoy his company?

Guilt whispered through her soul and she instantly stiffened. *I'm not betraying the heritage of my foremothers.* She was a prisoner and she would do whatever she needed to do in order to survive.

Yet the excuse sounded false to her ears.

His grin faded into a frown. "Does your shoulder hurt?" He sounded concerned. "I tried to avoid touching it."

It would be so much easier to convince herself she was doing this only for survival if Tacitus was not so oddly *thoughtful* at times.

He was a Roman. He was not supposed to possess a

thoughtful side to his nature. And yet so far his every action belied her long held beliefs about the barbarity of his race.

Except she knew from personal, bloodied experience of the cruelty of Romans. She'd always believed it inherent in their nature. The fact that Tacitus didn't appear to share his countrymen's contempt for one not loyal to his Empire was disconcerting.

She realized he was still waiting for her answer. "It does hurt," she conceded. "But not because of anything we just did."

Carefully he eased out of her and she clamped her lips together to prevent a sigh of protest from escaping. He rolled onto his side, her uninjured side, and propped himself up on his forearm, his other hand cradling her waist.

"Do you need some opium?"

Take the opium. The thought pulsed into her brain, insistent and demanding and completely unexpected.

"No." The word burst from her mouth as unease weaved through her mind. How could she have become so desperate for the drug after just one time? "But tell me where you keep it, in case I need it when you're not here."

Where had that come from? She didn't want to know. Why would she want to know?

Yet the insistence persisted. She needed to know.

His thumb caressed the curve of her waist. "I can't do that." He didn't sound regretful. "You might find a way to poison me in my sleep."

If she had the contents of her medicine bag, she could certainly find any number of ways to poison him. But it hadn't even occurred to her that she could use the opium.

"Then I shall suffer in silence."

"I can't imagine you doing anything in silence."

She laughed. She hadn't meant to. But she couldn't help herself. "Even a gag would fail to silence me."

"I confess, I doubt I'd ever use a gag." His gaze dropped to her lips. "I enjoyed hearing your gasps of impending climax too much."

His words shouldn't affect her so. But no other man had ever said such things to her. And never in her wildest dreams had she imagined hearing such evocative confessions from a Roman officer.

Everyone knew Romans were barbarous heathens who took what they wanted without a thought of the devastation they left behind. They were murderers, rapists and mutilators of all who opposed their filthy Empire.

But when Tacitus looked at her with mingled desire and amusement, it was hard to recall his heritage. Hard to recall why she could never risk him discovering her true calling.

Harder than she had imagined to view him purely as her enemy she needed to disarm. Just because he'd inexplicably chosen to pay for her healing, and treated her better than she had ever imagined a Roman capable of treating a woman, he would still crucify her if he discovered she was a Druid.

Into the silence that followed his remark her stomach gave a loud, intrusive gurgle. Mortified, she clamped her hand over her stomach and her face flamed. But it didn't help. Her stomach growled again, horribly demanding.

"Gods." Tacitus sounded on the verge of laughing again. "You must be starving, Nimue. I intended to feed you, not fuck you."

"Of course you did," she said between gritted teeth. He didn't take offense at her tone, merely flashed her a grin that did something entirely illicit to the pit of her stomach, before pushing himself from the bed and strolling to the casket.

Unwillingly, she focused on his tight, perfectly formed arse. She had come. She had been more than adequately satisfied. So why did she still fantasize about having him? Even now, when she was still recovering from his *primitive* rutting technique, she was more interested in exploring his cock than filling her stomach.

It was only because they had not taken the time to discover each other's bodies. Next time, they would. And then she would be rid of this unwelcome fever that raged through her blood and caused her to lose all sense of focus.

Then she could use him at nights to sate their mutual need, and forget about him during the days when she could regain her strength and strategize.

∽

TACITUS CARRIED the basket of fruit and bread back to Nimue and smothered another grin at the haughty expression on her face. She was obviously mortified by the way her stomach had rumbled and yet she lay exactly as he'd left her on the bed, utterly unconcerned by her nakedness.

His cock stirred, more than willing to fill her tight, luscious body once again. But next time he wouldn't be distracted from his purpose by her provocative taunts. Next time he would explore her body with intimate dedication.

Unfortunately, that time was not now. They would scarcely have time to eat before they needed to leave.

He sat on the edge of the bed and watched her wriggle upright, her breasts jiggling with every move she made. She didn't attempt to cover herself with his cloak. She obviously didn't mind in the least that he found it all but impossible not to stare at her naked breasts and ripe, rosy nipples.

Hunger gripped low in his gut, and it wasn't hunger for the food he offered her.

Abruptly he stood and marched back to his casket. If he didn't cover temptation he would likely succumb once again, and that was intolerable. Every moment that passed increased the possibility of interruption from another tribune.

"I don't recognize half of what's in this basket," Nimue said, sounding put upon. "Do you have nothing that is not imported from your precious Rome?"

He glanced over his shoulder and couldn't help himself. "Yes. I have you." His humor was short-lived when he trod on something sharp. Bending, he picked up one of Nimue's earrings. "Besides, it's not all imported. Just eat, unless you wish your stomach to continue to complain for the rest of the day."

When she didn't respond to his taunt, satisfaction curled through him. Now she accepted that she belonged to him, now that he truly possessed her, her sharp tongue had mellowed. Certainly, he didn't want her to agree with his every word—he doubted she would ever do such a thing. But finally she would realize acceptable boundaries.

He retrieved his key ring that had fallen to the ground along with his tunic, and began to unlock the casket. It was already unlocked. Frowning, he stared at it. Surely he hadn't forgotten to lock it last night, after he'd put the embroidered Celtic bag inside?

He wasn't entirely sure why he'd taken the bag after Marcellus had appropriated the contents. He didn't have any use for it. It certainly wasn't because of the insidious sliver of doubt that the bag belonged to Nimue.

There was no possible connection between Nimue and the bag. Because if the bag was hers then she had been traveling with Caratacus' queen. That would point to her being connected to the royal family and possibly having information on the Briton king's whereabouts. If she was suspected of being the healer who had tended to the princess' injury, Nimue would be interrogated. The fact she was his slave wouldn't save her from that.

He had vowed to protect her from his fellow countrymen. Just because Nimue had healer knowledge didn't make her the owner of that bag.

But still he had hidden it, to prevent any further investigation into who might have once possessed it.

Another glance over his shoulder confirmed Nimue was eating, even though she had a pained expression on her face. He turned back to the casket and lifted the lid. Under the top layer of linen the bag remained. It didn't look as if anything had been disturbed. Surely if Nimue had taken advantage of discovering an unlocked casket, she would have rummaged through it? And if that bag had belonged to her, wouldn't she have taken it?

Still frowning, he found what he was searching for and locked the casket before sliding the key ring back onto his finger and dropping her earring on the lid.

"Here." He laid the plain white tunic over her feet. "You can wear that until I find you something more suitable."

She barely gave it a glance. "I won't wear it. I'll wear my own gown."

He paused in the process of helping himself to some bread. "Your gown is ruined. There's nothing else available until we return to the garrison." There were many markets in the settlement that had sprung up around the garrison. He'd easily be able to find her something more suitable.

"I don't care." She appeared supremely unimpressed that he was offering her one of his own short tunics to wear. "I'd rather wear a tattered rag that is my own than something of Roman origin."

Irritation prickled through him. Why did she have to disagree with *every*thing?

"It's covered in blood and filth and needs repair. If you wish, you may keep it, but you're not wearing it until it's been cleaned."

Finally she looked at him, her resentment clear on her face. "Of course I wish to keep it. It's all the clothing I possess." She waved her arm at him. "What about my bracelets? Do you have some obnoxious Roman jewelry you wish to exchange them for?"

Anyone would think, by her attitude, that he'd just told her she would remain naked for the rest of the journey. Then, he could understand her anger. But he'd offered her a clean tunic.

One of his *own* clean tunics, a gesture that would draw unwelcome attention from his fellow officers who would be as likely to offer a slave their own tunic as they would offer their horse.

"Nimue." It was a warning to be silent. Once again she was pushing too far.

"Tacitus." She mimicked his tone and maintained eye contact. By the gods, did she speak to all men in this manner? Or was it just him?

"If you prefer, I'll have your gown burned. Then the question will no longer arise."

Her fingers clenched around the bread she was holding. He wanted to maintain his rigid sense of injustice at her ingratitude, but it was hard when she was naked and her tangled hair tumbled over her tempting breasts. And when her bound shoulder was a constant reminder of how she had been injured.

None of which improved his mood.

"So you wish me to dress as one of your Roman noblewomen." The derision in her voice was unmistakable. "It will take more than a *gown* to make me a Roman."

"I have no wish to transform you into a Roman noblewoman. I doubt Juno herself could manage such a miracle." He snatched his discarded tunic from the ground and pulled it on. "And why you imagine I have women's gowns in my casket I fail to comprehend. You'll wear my tunic until such time as I decree otherwise."

Gods. He sounded like his father. The thought caused a hard knot to form in his chest.

She glowered at him for a moment longer and then transferred her glare to the cursed tunic.

"Very well." Her voice was haughty. "I'll wear your tunic on the condition you don't burn my gown."

She was giving *him* ultimatums? He stared at her in stunned disbelief, not only at her audacity but at her sudden change of mind.

He could remind her she was in no position to issue demands.

But what did it matter? She had acquiesced to his command. It would be easier to simply allow her to believe she had gained a small victory.

"Agreed." Thank the gods no one would ever know of this conversation. He would be ridiculed throughout Rome for being unable to keep his own slave in check.

The thought clawed through his brain. She was only a slave. But she was still unaware. All he needed to do was keep her in ignorance for another day. It shouldn't be difficult. No legionary would dare approach her and his fellow officers wouldn't engage her attention without his permission.

She sniffed and picked at the linen between finger and thumb. "I need to consult with your healer."

He shot her a sharp glance. "Why didn't you tell me earlier?" But she had told him her shoulder hurt. And he hadn't thought to pursue it further because she hadn't complained further. "Let me look." He hoped the stitches were still intact.

She looked at his hand, as he hovered over the bandage, as if she had no idea what he thought he was doing.

"I'm not talking about my wound." She pushed his hand aside with one disdainful finger. "I need to flush out my womb."

"You need…to what?" Had he heard correctly? Surely not. *Flush out her womb?* The implication of what she might mean sent shudders through him.

She scowled as if she thought he was being deliberately obtuse.

"Cleanse my womb of your seed, Tacitus. I have no desire to bear your bastard." She made it sound as if that was the worst thing imaginable. In the outer reaches of his mind he wondered that he should be offended by her obvious disgust at such an outcome but it was a vague, insubstantial thought. Because his senses were reeling with incredulity that a woman was discussing such things with him in the first place.

A woman's fertility was none of his concern. Not until he

married. The lovers he'd taken in the past had never breathed a word about the possibility of conceiving his child, and he'd never inquired as to what they did to prevent such event from occurring.

In truth, he had never considered the matter at all. He'd taken it for granted that the women would take the necessary precautions. That was what women did. It was only a man's wife who was subject to his scrutiny.

And a man's slave. But he had never taken a slave before. Had never even been with a prostitute, and so the question of using a sheath to protect his health—and prevent conception—had never arisen.

His glance slid to her belly. Was it possible she had conceived his child? The thought chilled his blood sufficiently to diminish his erection. Despite his privileged upbringing, he'd been acutely aware of the difference in status between him and his many half-sisters. He'd never wish such prejudice to touch his own child.

Nimue's child.

"How likely is that…outcome?" He swallowed and mentally girded his loins. Perhaps she was already protected. Perhaps she was merely wishing to be absolutely certain.

She gave an impatient sigh and shrugged her uninjured shoulder.

"It is not *likely*." She sounded disgruntled. "I'm still in my moon quarter so conception should be impossible. I merely wish to be prepared for the future."

Her moon quarter? Unease crawled along his spine. This was not talk meant for a man's ears. How could she even broach this subject with him—and without a shred of embarrassment?

She was his slave. Who else could she speak of it to?

Slaves never mentioned such things to their masters. But then, Nimue was no ordinary slave and he had no wish to be her master in that sense of the word.

For the last nine months, he'd been the second-in-command

of the Legion; had strategized with the commander and led troops into battle. None of it compared to facing this woman and speaking of matters he had no business discussing with anyone.

But he had no choice.

"I'll make the necessary arrangements for the future." He knew he was scowling but it was the only way he managed to push the words along his throat. He'd speak to Marcellus. Face the inevitable mockery. But better that than having Nimue consult with his friend on such intimacies.

Even before the thought finished forming, he saw her forehead crease, saw her preparing to once again dispute his word. But before her evident displeasure at his decision found voice, he heard the tent flap being ripped open, heard his commander make a sordid jest.

"Cover yourself." He barked the order at her, grabbing the edge of his cloak as he did so and for once, she didn't argue. Instead, she wrapped his cloak around her, gripping the edges together at her throat so her body was entirely concealed.

Tacitus swung back and glared as his commander strolled into the tent. The commander offered him a knowing grin before transferring his leer to Nimue.

His grin slid from his face and an all too familiar look gleamed in the commander's eyes. Infuriated, Tacitus stepped in front of Nimue and folded his arms. With clear reluctance, the commander refocused his gaze on Tacitus.

"You're behind schedule." It was a reprimand. In front of Nimue. But as far as the commander was concerned, Nimue was only a slave. And one could say anything in front of a slave.

It did nothing to alleviate the simmering anger roiling through Tacitus' blood. Especially since the rebuke was deserved. He'd had no business taking Nimue when he was still on duty. And yet after she'd regained consciousness, he'd forgotten everything but the need to possess her.

"Sir." It could have been worse. Blandus could have accompanied his commander.

Instead of leaving, the commander strolled farther into the tent, his attention on the bed. Tacitus stepped forward, blocking his advance. "Is that all, sir?"

The older man regarded him. There was a calculating look on his face, an expression Tacitus had witnessed in the past but never before had it been directed at him, and never had it caused his gut to tighten with such rigid distaste.

"We'll talk later." The commander's voice was deceptively mild. He turned to leave then paused and glanced over his shoulder. "I understand, now, why Blandus was so pissed you reneged on your deal." He shot Tacitus a mocking smile. "Don't allow it to cause any professional ill-feeling. You understand?"

He understood perfectly. Blandus had complained to his uncle who, having now seen Nimue, appreciated the situation.

But that wasn't the reason why the savage urge to smash his fist into his commander's face thudded through his blood. His hands fisted by his sides, his muscles tensed in readiness for battle.

His cousin held no threat. But after seeing Nimue, the casual interest in his commander's eyes had been replaced by something far more dangerous.

It was no longer mild amusement that Tacitus had bought a slave girl. Just as Tacitus had known he would, his commander lusted after Nimue.

CHAPTER 13

Since Tacitus had no intention of allowing Nimue out of his sight during the journey, he once again defied convention and had her ride with him on his horse. But then again, she belonged to him. She was his personal responsibility. She could no sooner travel with the other slaves, who trudged in chains at the rear of the convoy, as she could ride with the injured legionaries in the medical wagons.

The unsettling notion that he was making too many excuses for his actions crossed his mind, but he banished it with the contempt it deserved. He wasn't making excuses. There was no other option.

No other officer made any comment, and if they considered the fact she was wearing his cloak a breach of protocol, they kept their thoughts to themselves.

Nimue sat in front of him, ramrod straight, as proud as a heathen queen. He wore his spare cloak, and had insisted she wrap his other one around her. She displayed far too much flesh wearing only his tunic. He'd been surprised she hadn't argued, but also relieved. He hadn't felt up to explaining his reasoning.

How could he tell her he didn't want his commander to see her naked thighs as she straddled the saddle?

Even now, on the open road, he could detect a tantalizing hint of the wild, abandoned sex that soiled the cloak she wore.

Involuntarily, his arm tightened around her waist. The tempting notion of fucking her once again blurred his vision and thickened his cock. So much for not thinking of her during the day. But how could he not when she was so close to him? When, despite her frigid posture, the curve of her delectable bottom nestled against his erection?

He exhaled and tried not to think of her smooth, rounded buttocks. Tried not to imagine her bent over a couch, thighs spread, naked and willing and ready for him.

Tried, and failed. Gods, it was going to be an agonizingly long journey before they camped for the night.

~

Nimue glared straight ahead as the Roman Legions charged through her land. And she was at the front of the onslaught, held securely in Tacitus' arm, as if he had every right to hold her so possessively.

As they had started this journey, she'd caught sight of the other prisoners. They were chained together like animals, and herded into obedience.

She'd been torn between relief and horror. Relief, that so many of the women and children who had been on the mountain had apparently escaped the Romans. And horror that not all of them had.

The queen and princess had not been with the other women and children. It would seem the Romans knew exactly who they had captured, and were intent on ensuring their royal prisoners arrived without further harm at their destination.

Her stomach had churned at her fleeting glimpse of the captives. A shaming relief streaked through her when she realized she didn't know any of them, but that vanished instantly. It didn't matter if they were from a different tribe than hers. They had all come together with one goal in mind. To rid Cymru and Britain of the invaders.

And now they were enslaved to the Roman Empire.

How had she escaped that fate? If another Roman had found her by the stream, would she be chained with the other captives now? A hard knot formed in the pit of her stomach at the thought. But the question echoed in her mind.

It was more than the fact Tacitus wanted her to warm his bed. He—any of the Romans—could take any of the enslaved they desired, and the Celts would have no choice in the matter.

She was the daughter of a high-ranking noble. Royal blood flowed in her foremothers' ancestry. She was a chosen one of the Moon Goddess herself, descended from powerful Druids in an unbroken line since the beginning of Creation.

Arianrhod—or perhaps even Arawn, the lord of the Otherworld—had ensured she remained free for a purpose. So she could complete her mission, return the queen to Caratacus and then they could continue the fight against the Romans.

～

They finally halted as dusk hovered overhead. She dismounted and ignored the tremors of lust that assailed her as Tacitus' strong hands spanned her waist in unwanted assistance.

She turned to face him and with seeming reluctance, he released her.

"Remain here. I will return shortly." But he didn't leave instantly, perhaps waiting for her to confirm obedience to his command.

He would wait forever. She tightened her one-handed grip on

his cloak, hating how his scent permeated the scarlet wool yet at the same time offered her a sense of false security.

"Your Legion is diminished." Was it a tactical error? Somehow she couldn't believe the Romans had accidentally lost a vast portion of their numbers. Yet it was quite obviously so.

Tacitus looked taken aback by her observation. It was obvious he hadn't imagined she would notice such things.

"Only marginally." For a moment she thought he was going to say more, to elaborate, but instead he brushed his fingers over her tangled hair. "Don't attempt to escape. I can't guarantee your safety outside this camp."

He turned and she couldn't drag her fascinated gaze from the way his cloak swung about his muscled legs, nor the arrogant way he marched through the legionaries. Only when he finally disappeared did she heave a silent sigh and sweep her glance around the glade.

She was desperate to relieve herself. And she had no intention of waiting for Tacitus to produce a loathsome bucket. Stealthily she made her way to the tree line. She would be only a few moments.

No one accosted her. No one gave her more than a fleeting glance. If she had intended to escape, who would stop her?

The thought hammered through her brain. *Would* anyone try? How far could she get before Tacitus returned and began a search?

As she slid into the edge of the forest, the thought persisted. She was under no illusion that all these Romans and their mercenaries knew Tacitus considered her his personal property. And yet clearly he had not given orders that she was to be prevented from wandering as she pleased.

Peering through the barrier of bushes at the activity as a camp was constructed, that knowledge glowed, bright with promise. She couldn't escape tonight. Not only was she ill-prepared but she still had to find the queen and princess.

But she'd discovered something valuable. Something she intended to use. Tacitus trusted her to obey his command. When the time was right, she would use that trust to secure the freedom of the Briton queen and her daughter.

Feeling considerably more cheerful with an empty bladder and new possibilities of escape, she stepped back into the glade. A shadow loomed from the darkness of the trees and her heart slammed against her ribs in sudden alarm. *Has someone been watching me?*

"Don't you know how dangerous it is for a Celt to wander alone out here?" The voice was mocking, accented and she couldn't place it at all.

"Who are you?" Her voice was haughty. She would never show how his sudden appearance had so badly startled her.

He moved from the shadows and she glared at him. He was no Roman but one of their auxiliaries. How dare he creep up on her?

"I'm the one who saved the worthless skin of the Roman you intended to gut."

Jagged thoughts pounded through her brain. She had never intended to gut Tacitus, but she remembered advancing toward him, dagger poised.

"You shot me." She didn't feel particularly angry at him. She was, after all, his enemy and in his shoes would likely have done the same to save one of her own.

"I did." Although the sun was sinking onto the western horizon, the twilight illuminated the glade and she could clearly see the dislike ingrained in the auxiliary's features. "Next time I'll ride away."

What did he mean? That he regretted shooting her? Why would he regret something like that?

"Bearach." The voice was sharp, authoritative. "What in the gods' names are you doing?"

Another auxiliary. Nimue drew the cloak around her more securely and stiffened her spine further. If Tacitus came upon her now he would never believe she hadn't been trying to escape. He'd jump to the conclusion these two barbarians had prevented her, and then she could forget about her tribune extending even a modicum of trust toward her again.

"I'm doing nothing, Gervas," Bearach said. "Isn't that right, Celt? I haven't touched a hair on your head."

"Enough." Gervas towered over her, but his attention was focused on the other man. "It's not the girl's fault. Get out of here before her master discovers to whom she speaks."

Her master? Nimue shot Gervas a glare of intense dislike, but he missed it since he was entirely focused on Bearach.

Bearach gave a bitter laugh. "He must value you highly, Celt. Not many Roman officers go so far as to buy a foreign slave when her charms can be had for free. You must be a mind-blowing fuck."

"Go." Gervas didn't raise his voice, but it was enough for Bearach to turn and stalk back to camp.

Nimue glowered after his retreating back, his words pummeling inside her skull. She didn't believe him. Not for a moment. Tacitus *had not bought her*.

"You must forgive his uncouth tongue," Gervas said, indicating with a sweep of his arm that he expected her to precede him back to camp. She remained rooted to the spot, and could do nothing to prevent the waves of mortified heat from pounding through her body and flooding her cheeks. *Am I a slave?*

Gervas shot her a glance. "He meant nothing by it. He's merely…irked by his punishment."

She tilted her head and gave Gervas a proud look. "So he lied about my status?"

Gervas narrowed his eyes and lowered his arm. For a moment he stared at her, assessing her, and she maintained eye contact. Finally he exhaled a slow breath and took a step back.

"You didn't know." It wasn't a question. But his words answered so much. Too much. Her stomach cramped and only by sheer force of will did she remain utterly still and not curl up with humiliated disbelief. She *was* a slave.

"I was not paraded on the block." The words choked her. She'd been so smugly certain she had escaped that fate. So sure she was Tacitus' *special prisoner*. But what was a *special prisoner* except a sex slave?

Nausea roiled. Somehow, while she had been unconscious, she'd been put up for sale. And Tacitus had bought her.

As if she was nothing more than a horse, or a goat, or a piece of fine jewelry he admired.

"No." There was a thread of sympathy in Gervas' voice. She wanted to cut his throat for his sympathy. *I don't need a filthy auxiliary's sympathy.* "You were never with the other slaves. The tribune bought you after he brought you back from the mountain."

CHAPTER 14

Nimue couldn't look at the auxiliary. She couldn't bear to risk seeing the sympathy in his voice reflected in his eyes. Instead she glared straight ahead, to where the camp was constructed, and attempted to smother the pain coiling through her breast.

Just because she was Tacitus' slave didn't change anything. She would still earn his trust. Still make plans to find the queen and princess and ensure their escape. The fact she was his slave made no difference in how she felt about the relationship she had with Tacitus.

He was a Roman. She was a Druid. And yet no matter how logically she tried to look at the situation the knowledge that she was his slave changed everything.

He had intended to enslave her from the moment he'd come across her on the mountain. And when she'd been shot, he'd taken instant advantage. How naïve of her to believe, for even one moment, that he could have intended anything else.

What else could there have possibly been? She would never have gone with him willingly. But her wounded pride recoiled from the truth.

She hadn't for one instant seriously considered the possibility Tacitus had bought her. Nothing in her life had prepared her for such an ignoble revelation. Druids were tortured and murdered by the Romans. They weren't kept as slaves.

"I see." Her voice showed none of her turmoil. Her spine was so rigid she feared it might shatter. Tacitus might have reduced her to the status of a slave in his world, but she was not of his world. She would never be of his world. And in her own, she was not only freeborn. She was a noble and the blood of the gods flowed in her veins.

"The tribune saved you from a worse fate." There was a hint of distaste in the auxiliary's voice. "If he hadn't bought you from the quaestorium you would be with the other captives. And they are all destined to be bought by the slave traders back at the garrison."

A shiver trickled along her spine. She knew of the brutality of slave traders and the possibility of being under their control chilled her soul.

"I imagine that fate waits for me, also." Her voice was as icy as her blood. Arianrhod hadn't prevented Nimue's enslavement but the Goddess had given her enough freedom to complete her mission. It was enough. Her wounded pride was nothing but an indulgence.

"No." This time when Gervas indicated she should head back to the camp she forced her feet to move. "He'd never recoup the price he paid if he sold you to traders. Continue as you have, and I'm certain the tribune will remain entertained by you for some time yet."

She stopped dead and slung him a freezing glare. "I'm not a whore who entertains men for *their* benefit." But she was a slave, and Tacitus had bought her for sex. If that didn't make her a whore, what did?

Gervas gave her a calculating look, as if he saw far more than he should. "I'm from Gaul. Unlike the Romans, I'm not blinded to innate strength by gender alone. Your beauty has captivated the tribune. That and your apparent fragility are your biggest weapons if you want to survive."

Once again, she moved toward the camp. Her weapons of choice were her dagger and her bow. She relied on speed, on surprise, because in hand-to-hand combat she knew she stood little chance against a male warrior.

Never before had her looks or delicate bone structure been considered assets when it came to battle strategies.

"I wonder why you tell me such things."

"I'm a warrior. And I recognize a fellow warrior when I see one."

They neared Tacitus' horse. She glanced at the Gaul who walked by her side, close enough for confidential conversation yet not close enough to raise undue comment from any passing legionary.

"You would have shot me too, wouldn't you?"

A brief smile touched his lips. "Had we been alone, yes. In the presence of a Roman tribune?" For a fleeting moment he caught her gaze. "No. Their women aren't warriors. When confronted by one who looks as you do, they cannot even conceive such a thing."

Gervas inclined his head, a mark of respect, of farewell, and as she resumed her place by Tacitus' horse, she watched him until he disappeared from view.

To survive, Gervas expected her to disarm her Roman master with her face and her body and a sweet-talking tongue, until he believed her incapable of making any decision without his prior approval.

She gritted her teeth. What was so different between the Gaul's expectation of her strategies and the ones she had already formulated?

Nothing.

Except she'd never thought of Tacitus as her master. Never considered herself his slave. And while she had deliberately made the decision to fuck him in order to lower his suspicions, until now she'd never imagined that might equate to whoredom.

Her fingers clenched around his cloak and as if an invisible thread guided her, her gaze shifted and caught on the figure of Tacitus as he marched through the camp toward her.

She despised the tremor of lust that caused her pussy to quiver and nipples to harden. No matter how she tried to convince herself she had taken him purely for strategic gain, her body disdained the lie.

She'd taken him because she'd wanted to. Desire had fogged her brain. Would he have trusted her enough to leave her alone just now, if they had not rutted like wild creatures?

As he approached, her heart hammered against her ribs in a tangled wave of fury and despair. Her strategy was working. It should make no difference to her feelings whether Tacitus considered her a free woman or his slave. Except now that she knew the truth, her plans of seduction no longer held any appeal. As a free woman, she had the choice. As a slave, she had none. Yet this should make no difference to how she felt because she had been a slave from the moment she had woken in the Roman camp.

But I didn't know then. And now that she did, the knowledge that she had willingly had sex in the hope it would help Tacitus trust her brought her no pleasure, only an aching sense of disgust.

"Come." He held out his arm, a silent command to follow him, but ruined the effect with a warm smile that twisted her rage and fed her self-revulsion. He showed no surprise that she was standing exactly where he had left her. Why should he? She was his slave. It was her duty to obey without question or demur.

Without a word, she stepped toward him. She would play her part. She would play it so perfectly that when she finally left him, he would be staggered by her duplicity, horrified by his own gullibility.

"I've arranged for a bath for you in my quarters. You'll have as much time as you need to dress your hair." He shot her a sideways glance, his eyes glinting with apparent mirth at how she'd been unable to tame her hair to her satisfaction earlier that day.

She didn't respond; merely ground her teeth so she wouldn't be tempted to tell him what she thought of him. She'd never respond to his taunts again. She would be the perfect, *silent* slave, obedient to his every wish. And his guard would tumble and she would take her revenge.

For a moment, he continued to look at her and she continued to stare doggedly ahead, refusing to succumb to the insistent voice in her head that urged her to turn. *I won't look at him.* She would give him no reason to doubt her.

Her fingers ached, they gripped his cloak so tightly. Better to focus on that, than the scorching words that incinerated her brain.

"Are you unwell, Nimue?" His voice was low and a thread of false concern weaved through his words. "Did the journey tire you overmuch?"

Did he think her incapable of enduring a half-day's march? When she had been on *horseback*? A scathing retort scorched her tongue, and then she recalled Gervas' words.

When Tacitus looked at her, he didn't see a woman who was trained as a warrior. He saw a woman of noble birth. A woman he believed more familiar with a loom than a bow.

"No." She forced the word between her teeth, and couldn't bring herself to call him *master*. She would likely choke on her own vomit if she attempted such base humility.

"Does your shoulder pain you?" He sounded so genuinely

concerned it was hard to remember he had enslaved her without her knowledge. Without even having the decency to inform her of her status afterward, before he'd taken her with such forceful disregard.

She pried open her lips to respond with another surly *no* when once again Gervas' words echoed in her brain.

Romans believed women were weak, not only in body but also in spirit and mind. She'd heard rumors in the past, and hadn't always believed them. But now she knew for certain.

It went against everything she believed in, but if it helped weave a web of complacency around Tacitus then she would bury her pride a little more.

"Yes." It wasn't a lie. Her shoulder did pain her. But not enough to comment upon. Not enough to expect sympathy or special treatment. But she was no longer in her clan. She was fighting for survival in the enemy camp, and she had to use tactics she had never before in her life contemplated.

He cursed under his breath and for a moment she thought he was about to wind his arm around her. But then he pulled back, as if recalling the lowly status he had thrust upon her. It was unheard of for a master of any race to embrace his slave in public.

No matter what they might do in private.

She entered his tent. Lamps illuminated the interior, casting a magical golden glow but it did nothing to ease the injustice curdling her stomach. When he approached her she forced herself to remain absolutely still, instead of lashing out and gouging the flesh from his arrogant, aristocratic face.

"Let me see." Without waiting for her response—as if her response would make any difference—he gently eased his cloak back from her shoulders. She smothered the urge to cling onto the cloak and instead allowed him to drop the offending article to the ground.

Of course he wanted to examine her wound. He wanted to ensure his investment wasn't putrefying.

How much had he paid for her? How much pleasure would she take in forcing those cursed coins down his throat, until he choked on them?

∼

Tacitus eyed the thunderous glare on Nimue's face and waited for her outburst. It was sure to erupt. She'd been almost incandescent with stifled fury from the moment he'd returned to her.

But she didn't say a word. Had he read her mood wrong? Was she so silent only because her wound gave her so much pain?

Since it was unlikely she would hold her tongue if something had annoyed her, he could only assume the ride had exhausted her more than she was admitting. Not that he was surprised by her fortitude. Nimue had scarcely complained about her injury at all.

His tunic was far too big for her. The material had slipped over her right shoulder, exposing her creamy skin and tempting swell of her breast. Through the linen, her nipples were clearly defined, erect and proud and the lust that had thudded between his thighs all day broke through his rigid control.

For a moment he was tempted to cup her breasts and drag his thumbs over those luscious nipples. But if he started he wouldn't be able to stop. And he had no intention of repeating the hasty coupling they'd enjoyed earlier that day. He battened down his smoldering desire before untying her leather belt. It was her own and several leather pouches hung from it. He'd examined their contents the previous day for possible weapons, but they had mostly contained personal items.

He dropped her belt on top of his cloak and still she didn't say a word. But the look on her face said volumes.

For a moment he hesitated. He hadn't known her long but he

knew her well enough. And when Nimue looked at him with such venom she never remained silent.

The bandage was clean. Relief surged through him. At least the wound was not weeping poison. She stood absolutely still and if he was inadvertently hurting her, she didn't let it show.

With infinite care, he began to unbind her dressing. It would be easier if the tunic wasn't in the way, but if she was naked he'd be tempted to admire her body. He didn't want her to think all he was interested in was fucking her. No matter how much he desired her, he also wanted her to know of his concern for her physical well-being. He might not have shot the arrow that had injured her but he was responsible. He should have been able to protect her, and he had failed.

He frowned at the wound that marred her perfect skin. Marcellus' stitches were neat, but Nimue would still be scarred for life. But at least she would still have her life.

"It looks to be healing well." He scrutinized her face, as she peered at her shoulder, and wondered if her unnatural silence was because she'd been afraid of what she might see beneath the dressing.

Yet it didn't make sense. She'd shown no feminine fear earlier that day when Marcellus had examined her. Perhaps, with her knowledge of healing, she was used to seeing such battle wounds? But even so, it was different when the wound was inflicted on herself.

"Yes. It appears Roman knowledge of such matters is impressive."

He waited for the barbed comment that was sure to follow her remark, but it didn't arrive. Nimue merely pressed her lips together as if complimenting Roman medicine pained her more than any arrow.

Why then had she deigned to say it in the first place? He certainly didn't expect any gratitude from her on that matter.

Unwelcome suspicion ate through his brain. "Did something happen while I was gone?"

She gave him a look designed to paralyze. "Like what?"

The suspicion solidified but he fought against it. If Nimue had discovered she was a slave she wouldn't be giving him the silent treatment. She would be clawing out his eyes.

There had to be another reason why her mood had degenerated so swiftly. "Did anyone speak to you? Insult you?" No one insulted his woman. But if anyone had, they would soon learn the error of their presumption.

"No one insulted me while you were gone." She flicked her gaze over him, from his head to his boots and then up again. Her beautiful green eyes darkened, and an answering tug of need gripped low in his gut. "Most of your legionaries look through me, as if I don't even exist."

The tightness in his chest relaxed. Was that all? She was only irked at being ignored by his men. She was undoubtedly used to being constantly admired.

He had no problem with other men admiring her. Once they returned to the garrison and Nimue became his concubine he would ensure she wanted for nothing. Gowns, jewels—anything she desired. Men would lust after her, but they would keep their hands and thoughts to themselves if they valued their lives.

Even his commander hadn't commented on Nimue when they'd spoken a few moments ago. It was as if the blatant desire Tacitus had witnessed on the older man's face when he'd seen Nimue in bed had never occurred.

Surprising, but a relief. It would not have been pleasant to outright deny the commander's request, had he wanted a night with his Celt.

"I assure you, they know you exist." His fingers trailed over her left shoulder, along her biceps and gently clasped her hand. She didn't wince from the pain she must be experiencing from her wound, although she dropped her gaze to focus on his jaw.

She was in optimum health to recover so swiftly from her injury. He knew she was of noble birth and the strong, supple condition of her body suggested she had never faced the rigors of debilitating disease or starvation. And again, he wondered what she had been doing wandering alone in the aftermath of battle.

Faint unease echoed in his mind but he instantly banished the thought. Nimue had not been the healer traveling with Caratacus' queen. Because if she had…

No. He refused to consider it. Her proximity to where the barbarian queen and her daughter had been discovered was pure coincidence. Another healer had been accompanying them, and had escaped capture.

"But they would not attack me?"

All thoughts of Nimue's possible connection to the queen vanished. Gods, it had never occurred to him that she'd been afraid of attack from his own men. Hadn't he told her she was safe so long as she remained within the camp?

Obviously, his words hadn't been sufficiently clear.

"No. None of them would dare to approach you, let alone touch you." Gently he raised her arm and brushed his lips across her knuckles. "They all know you're mine. To dishonor you would be a direct attack on my name."

He could give her no higher assurance of her safety. His name, his lineage, ensured her protection was absolute. Yet the swift look she stabbed him with, before once again focusing on his jaw, suggested she imagined he had just leveled a coarse insult her way.

"You don't intend to pass me around your compatriots for sport?" The question, loaded with vulnerability, punched through him, and yet she didn't cast him an anxious glance and neither did her voice tremble.

She sounded haughty, proud—as if she had issued a demand instead of displaying the depth of her deeply buried fear.

It didn't matter how she denied it. Someone had frightened her. He intended to discover who that *someone* was.

"I don't intend that any other man will have you, Nimue." Fleetingly he recalled that within three months he was due to return to Rome. But he wasn't looking that far ahead. For now, Nimue was his and no other man had rights over her. "Do you understand? No matter his rank or heritage. The only bed you will share is mine."

CHAPTER 15

Nimue withdrew her hand and flexed her fingers, as if they ached. Once again she was looking at him, and he couldn't decipher the expression on her face.

He recognized the lust in her eyes, though, and his cock thickened with anticipation.

Not yet. He had no intention of taking her when she needed to eat, to rest—to bathe. No intention of losing control the way he had earlier. No matter how she tempted him otherwise. He was, after all, a Roman. And a Roman should never be at the mercy of his lust.

Without breaking eye contact, she began to tug his tunic from her body. It was an inelegant process with her damaged shoulder but he couldn't tear his fascinated gaze away.

He knew he should stop her. This wasn't what he'd intended. But the words lodged in his throat as she finally managed to pull the linen over her head and toss it onto the ground.

The lamplight bathed her body in a golden glow; her tangled, windswept hair framed her face and gave her a strangely ethereal appearance. She stood before him, proud and uninhibited, her breasts full and ripe and ready for his touch.

"Is that a promise, Roman?" Her gaze never left his. He could scarcely fathom what she was asking him, but right now he would promise her anything.

"Yes."

She trailed her finger over her lips in a deliberately slow, sensuous manner designed to inflame. His glance dropped to focus on her pouting lips, even as her finger drifted over the proud angle of her chin and along the column of her throat.

"Can I trust the word of a Roman tribune?" Her voice was low, smoky. Bewitched, his gaze followed the languid progress of her finger.

"You can." If any other man touched her, Tacitus would castrate him. If any man insulted her, Tacitus would rip his tongue from his filthy mouth. "I give you my word as a patrician and on the names of my forefathers, Lucius Marius."

Her left hand splayed across her belly while her right continued its provocative exploration over the pale globe of her breasts. She circled her erect nipple and then clasped the rosy bud between her finger and thumb.

His breath rasped between clenched teeth. He'd watched women strip and pleasure themselves before, but only in company when they were the evening's entertainment. Never had any of his lovers stood before him in such a manner. Never had any of them taken the initiative to put on such an erotic, personal show.

Never before had the desire to simply stand and watch or take control of the situation warred so violently between every frenzied thud of his heart.

She held her breast, her nipple peeking provocatively between her thumb and finger. He battled the overwhelming urge to grasp his cock and gain temporary relief. He'd never been tempted to do such a thing in company before. He had no intention of starting now.

But gods, he was so hard. Every particle of his being was

focused on his groin, pounding through his erection, making it all but impossible to concentrate on anything else.

On anything but Nimue. But Nimue was intertwined with the lust thundering along his veins, fogging his senses. Nimue was the reason he was struggling for control, a control that was sliding from his grasp with every erratic thud of his heart.

She abandoned her breast and her hand molded the curve of her waist and flare of her hips. Her body was not that of a wild barbarian. It was slender, supple, delicate and enchanting and despite his best intentions an agonized groan escaped his throat.

Fuck his good intentions. He would claim her first, and then see to her other needs.

"Wait." Her breathy command halted him, before he even realized he'd moved toward her. "Watch."

He was beyond watching. If he didn't have her soon he would disgrace himself for all time. And then his jagged thought processes stalled, nailed him to the spot, and he was unable to move a muscle as his gaze riveted on her.

Nimue parted her thighs and two fingers delved into the pale golden curls that cradled her sex. She caressed her swollen pussy lips, back and forth, and he glimpsed the hood of her clitoris, ripe with seductive promise.

"Nimue." It was a command to stop, yet sounded like an entreaty to continue. He couldn't drag his fascinated gaze from her fingers.

"Yes." There was a wisp of triumph in her whisper, but he scarcely heard above the pounding in his temples, the throbbing need in his groin. With agonizing disregard for his sanity, she slowly slid one finger inside her pussy, and his cock jerked with tortured frustration.

"I need to have you. Now." His words were jagged, rasped against his raw throat. The head of his cock was wet, his balls were tight and hard and he was so close to coming lightning streaked through his groin, an excruciating ecstasy.

"Will you fuck me hard and fast?" Her breathless whisper inflamed his mind, and before his hypnotized gaze she slid a second finger into her lush body. "Will you fuck me until I scream your name out loud, Roman?"

"Yes." It was a primal growl. "I'll fuck you until you can't think straight, until you beg for mercy."

She dragged her fingers from her glistering sheath and flattened her hand against his chest. Instantly he gripped her wrist and pulled her toward him. Their gazes meshed, her eyes so dark they appeared black, and with the last remnants of his tattered control he slowly sucked her finger deep into his mouth.

Her eyes widened in shock but he scarcely comprehended as her musky scent flooded his senses and drenched what sliver of sanity he retained.

His.

"No." Nimue leaned into him, rising onto her toes. "Tonight I'm going to fuck *you*. Until you scream *my* name. Until you beg *me* for mercy."

She shoved him backward and he wound his arm around her waist and pulled her with him as they tumbled onto his makeshift bed. Never before had words so inflamed, but everything Nimue said scorched his blood. "Mercy is the last thing I'll ever beg from you."

As an answer, she wrenched up his tunic, but her eyes never left his. Her glorious hair cascaded over her shoulders, caressing her breasts, and she looked wild and wanton and utterly irresistible.

She straddled him and looked down at him as if she was Aphrodite herself, the Greek goddess of love. The treacherous thought was faint, insubstantial, as Nimue angled her wet pussy against the head of his cock.

"Are you ready for me, Roman?" Her whisper was sultry and she rocked her hips, rubbing her clit over his swollen glans. She looked infinitely fuckable and his body throbbed to take her, but inexplicably a shard of disquiet flickered through his mind. Why had she called him Roman, and not Tacitus? But it was too fleeting, too inconsequential to question her when she looked at him with such blatant lust.

"Yes." Through the pounding in his brain, he knew she should be the one flat on her back. She was injured, and it should be him bracing his weight on the bed. Yet he couldn't move, couldn't summon the strength as Nimue slid down his erection, taking him deep into her slick core.

A strangled groan thudded in his ears. Was that him? He gripped her delectable arse cheeks, her smooth skin silken and taut against the palms of his hands. Her tight cleft grasped his length, and he dragged his gaze from her bewitching eyes and looked to where their bodies joined.

Gods, he'd never seen a more arousing sight. Nimue's thighs were spread wide, and a tantalizing glimpse of pale curls shielded her swollen folds that stretched to accommodate his girth.

She wrapped one finger and thumb around the root of his erection, and her touch wasn't light or fragile but brutal and his hips bucked involuntarily as he collapsed back onto the bed.

He could no longer see his cock buried inside her pussy, but the image burned into his brain.

"Nimue." Her name pounded in his mind, tangled on his tongue. Her pink lips parted but she didn't speak. Instead she increased the rhythm, the glide of her silken slit along his cock glorious. She had to slow down. But he couldn't find the words or the will to stop her, and he abandoned her bottom to cradle her breasts.

She arched her back and he tightened his grip, relishing the feel of her firm flesh. She filled his palms, her full breasts warm against his fingers. The sensation of her heated sheath clasping him, her slender fingers working him, combined into a maelstrom of primitive need. He grazed his thumbs over her erect nipples and wanted to pull her down so he could suck those rosy peaks into his mouth. But the view was too intoxicating.

She looked every inch a heathen Greek goddess, exotic and uninhibited and when she looked down at him and slid the tip of her tongue over her lips his control shattered. He surged upward and her balance rocked, pushing her forward. Only his hands around her breasts supported her and his harsh breath rasped into the sex-drenched air surrounding them. He buried himself in her tight pussy, felt her contract around his cock. Raw lust consumed him and he squeezed her ripe nipples as he came in a wave of unbridled release.

His tortured groan echoed in his ears as the aftereffects of brutal pleasure thundered through his blood. Chest heaving, breath labored, he focused on Nimue as she loomed over him, her hand now flat against his shoulder, bracing her weight.

"Did I please you?" Her whisper drifted through his mind like a summer breeze and his hands slid from her breasts to clasp her shapely waist. He was well pleased. And she knew it. The only discord was he still wore his tunic, but that was easily remedied.

"I trust," his voice reflected the warm sense of contentment that flooded through his blood, "that you'll never please another man in such a manner, Nimue." The memory of her sensuous strip and erotic foreplay caused sparks to reignite low in his groin. How many men had she entertained like that in the past? He would kill any man she so entertained in the future.

Through the linen of his tunic her nails dug into his shoulder as she pushed herself off him. His hands trailed from her waist to her hips and caressed the firm contours of her thighs. Whatever had displeased or upset her earlier had now been driven from her mind.

Satisfaction snaked through him and as she turned to face him, on her knees on the floor beside the bed, he shoved himself upright. Once again lust had consumed him before he'd fed her.

It was becoming a habit. But not one he could seriously condemn.

They would eat, she would bathe, and then the night would be theirs.

CHAPTER 16

"If that is your wish." Her voice pierced his languid thoughts and he frowned at her. She was looking at him, but it was nothing like the way she'd looked at him the last time they'd fucked. There was no soft smile on her face, no unfocused glaze in her eyes. Tension radiated from her as if it took a great deal of willpower for her not to leap on him and scratch out his eyes.

Suspicion stirred. He took her hand and tugged her toward him, but she was surprisingly resistant. "Come back to the bed." He'd been so ensnared by her sensuous seduction that he'd failed to notice Nimue hadn't come. "Let me please you as you've pleased me."

She wrenched her hand from his loose grasp. "There's no need." The look of venom she glared his way belied her words and he stared at her, bemused by her contradictory mood.

"Does your shoulder pain you?" He knew he should have stopped her. He should have been the one bracing his weight but lust had blinded his reason. And now Nimue was suffering for his indulgence.

She bared her teeth but it was nothing like the smiles she had bestowed his way earlier. Was she truly snarling at him?

"My blood is not poisoned," she said, although poison dripped from every word. "Therefore what does it matter if my wound pains me or not?"

Irritation spiked through him. He might have been remiss during their recent coupling but it wasn't as if he'd deliberately set out to deny her pleasure from the act. "It matters to me." His voice was sharp and he swung his legs off the bed, imprisoning her between his thighs.

"Pray, do not think of it." She pushed the words between gritted teeth and then shuffled backward until she was free of his embrace. "Do you wish to eat now?"

Did he want to *eat*? She glared at him as if she wanted to gut him and instead of telling him what was on her mind, she offered him *food*? He stared at her in disbelief. Nimue was naked, on her knees before him and the evidence of his lust soiled her thighs. He had never taken an unwilling woman, but for one gut-churning moment, he imagined she looked as if that was exactly what he'd done.

But she'd wanted him as much as he wanted her. Her arousal had scented the air, her body eager and willing. Despite her status in the eyes of Rome when they were together like this she was free. And she had a choice to deny him. A choice he knew she wouldn't hesitate to claim if she wanted to.

He knew full well that some of his peers used women purely for their own pleasure. Whether the woman was a wife, lover or slave made no difference. A slave could expect nothing more. And to his knowledge, no gently bred Roman noblewoman would complain if her husband or lover had failed to satisfy her.

But Nimue was no Roman noblewoman. She wouldn't pretend satisfaction merely to stoke a man's pride.

So why was she holding her tongue when he knew she wanted to accuse him of denying her climax?

He leaned toward her. She didn't flinch as a slave might have done nor lower her gaze as he might expect from a Roman woman. "I wish you to tell me what the matter is."

A blush swept over her aristocratic cheekbones, but it wasn't from modesty. It was mortification. "Why? Do you also own my thoughts?"

Realization punched through his chest. *She knew.* Who the fuck had told her? Rage thundered through his brain. It didn't matter who had told her. The damage had been done. Now he had to defuse it.

"I have no desire to own your thoughts."

"Only my body." The derision in her voice slammed into him as if she had physically attacked him.

"That's not true." But if anyone saw her now, naked and on her knees before her master, what else would they think?

Except he wanted more than simply her willing body. He wanted her irreverent responses, no matter how shocking he sometimes found them.

It was too late for regret. He would have to explain his plans for her now, and then she would see he had no wish for her to be a slave. That it was only temporary. That, in reality, he offered her an honorable status as his concubine.

Her lip curled. "So you bought me for my conversational skills."

∼

Nimue watched Tacitus grit his teeth and she dug her fingernails into the palms of her hands. *What in the name of the Great Goddess am I doing?* Every word out of her mouth deliberately provoked him and she couldn't seem to stop herself.

She hadn't meant to say anything after he'd finished rutting with her. She'd held onto her control only through the formidable strength of her Druidic willpower, but it had all but shattered her to rise from his body before embracing her own glorious orgasm.

But frustration thundered through her blood and clouded her good reason. She had intended to be the perfect, malleable slave so he'd find no reason to doubt her. Yet the look on Tacitus' face suggested that any advance in gaining his trust had now vanished.

All because she couldn't hold her rebellious tongue.

"I did what I had to do in order to protect you." He sounded irked. She was torn between wanting to goad him further and belatedly behaving as an obedient slave should.

Except she had never been a slave, and the thought of submitting her will to a master caused her stomach to churn and bile to rise. That the master in question was Tacitus, whom she had foolishly believed to possess honor despite his Roman heritage, made everything unimaginably worse.

If she didn't bury her pride she could bury all hope of saving the Briton queen and princess, and Nimue's own honor would be forever tarnished.

She might not be able to fake subservience for her own sake, but she would do it for the sake of those she'd been charged to protect.

"I understand." She fixed her gaze on the ground between them so he couldn't see the fury in her eyes. "Do you wish me to bring you the food now?" *And I hope you choke on it.*

He hissed out a violent curse in Latin, one she had never heard before but its meaning was plain. Clearly, food was not on his immediate agenda.

"I don't expect your gratitude, Nimue," Tacitus said and she only just stopped herself from clenching her fists in reaction. She had to view this as she would any other battle maneuver and not allow her personal feelings to dictate her next strategic move. "It was never my intention to enslave you. Once we reach the garrison I intend to secure your manumission."

He made it sound as if he was bestowing a great favor. She ignored the dull throb in her injured shoulder, ignored the eerie whisper that craved the cursed opium, and focused on finding the right words to respond.

Curse your barbarous Roman guts would gain her nothing but fleeting satisfaction.

"And then I may leave?" She risked glancing up at him, and then couldn't tear her gaze away. Why did he not look like a hideous monster? Why did he have to glare at her with that indefinable air of injury, as if she was the one in the wrong?

Why could she not simply hate and despise him, the way she should?

"Then you will be my concubine."

"Your *concubine*?" What did he mean? In her world a concubine was little more than a sex slave. But Tacitus said the word as if there was no shame attached.

"You will have status as my concubine. You'll be free but still under my protection and therefore no other man will dare accost you."

"I'll be free?" Being the concubine of a Roman sounded different from being the concubine of a high-ranking Celt chieftain. "I can leave if I wish?"

Tacitus' jaw tightened. "You misunderstand. I'm offering you my continued protection as my concubine. As a free woman as opposed to being a slave."

He was speaking in riddles. "As your concubine I'll be free? Why would I need your protection if I can leave at any time?"

Tacitus curled his hands over her shoulders, taking care to avoid her injury. She refused to acknowledge the treacherous tremors that attacked her wherever he touched her. Then he frowned, pulled a cover from his bed and draped it around her as if he had noticed her chilled flesh.

Curse the man. He likely had noticed. Why did he have to be so considerate of her comfort? It made it so hard for her to remember that everything between them was nothing more than a strategy for her survival. But if he was offering her freedom that meant he trusted her. It meant he didn't truly consider her his slave. She knew it shouldn't make any difference to how she felt, and yet it did.

"No, Nimue." He continued to frown at her, his large hands grasping the edges of the blanket across her breasts. "As my concubine you'll belong to me until the contract is dissolved. Until that time you can't leave without my permission."

The foolish hope that he might think more of her than a spoil of war sputtered out of existence. Disbelief flooded her veins, but it was more than disbelief and anger. She was hurt that the best he considered her worthy of was the status of a whore in all but name.

Tacitus wasn't offering her freedom at all.

She straightened, secretly shocked that somehow she'd leaned closer to him during their exchange.

"I don't see the difference between what you've made me now and what you offer me in the future."

He actually recoiled, as though she had physically attacked him. When all she'd done was unravel his lying Roman words and displayed the truth for them both to see.

"You don't see the difference?" He sounded as if she was being deliberately difficult. "You'll have everything you desire as my concubine. You'll be safe and want for nothing. It's an honorable status, Nimue. Not so different from a contracted marriage."

A Roman contracted marriage. Furious that she needed help to rise from the ground she braced her weight against his leg with her good arm and shoved herself upright. Clutching her makeshift robe around her she glared into his eyes.

Don't think of his eyes. But it was impossible to look away.

"A Roman wife is little better than a slave." Her voice was haughty but it took everything she had to keep the foolish tremble locked inside. She wouldn't let him see how easily he could wound her. She despised the fact he could upset her. "I see no advantage in becoming your concubine when my freedom remains subject to your will."

"You're refusing my offer?" Tacitus sounded staggered, as if such a response had never occurred to him. "You don't wish to become my concubine?"

Why did he care? If he wanted to make her his concubine, what choice did she have?

She tilted her chin at him. It was a futile gesture of pride when, for the moment at least, he wielded power over everything she held sacred. But she couldn't bow her head, couldn't beg for his mercy. It would crucify her from the inside out. Yet it was more than that. She knew, deep down, that this Roman would never fall for such a false display of humility. Not from her. She'd lost that advantage, if it ever could have been an advantage, from the moment they'd met in the mountains.

"No, I don't wish to become your concubine." It would be tantamount to agreeing she wished to be his slave. "I don't wish to *belong* to you at all."

The silence after her words pressed against her ears and thudded inside her skull. Tacitus just looked at her as though he'd never seen her before. As if the fact she'd thrown his offer back in his face was somehow blasphemous.

Then he stood and it took everything she possessed not to take a hasty step backward. He towered over her, a mighty Roman warrior. Her bitterest enemy. And yet she didn't crave for her dagger so she could carve out his blackened heart. She craved, despicably, for him to hold her in his arms.

He stepped around her, as if by touching her he would become contaminated. He strode to the flap of the tent where he paused and glanced over his shoulder.

"What you want is irrelevant. You belong to me." His words should have infuriated her, but there was no trace of autocratic pride infusing his voice. Instead his tone was oddly flat, as though his statement gave him no pleasure. "Bathe and eat. Don't attempt to escape. I will return later."

He disappeared through the flap in the tent. She followed, pushed open the flap with her shoulder and watched him march into a gloom that was kept at bay by the torches that burned around the Roman camp.

Her fingers clenched around the material and she took a deep breath. The urge to take more opium seeped through her mind, a compelling imperative that Tacitus' presence had managed to subdue. But now that she no longer constantly fought her body's responses to the Roman, the alarming need for the drug increased.

She would search the tent in his absence. Surely she would find his hiding place.

As she began to lower the flap, a flurry of darkness swept across the cloudy sky. She froze and narrowed her eyes, peering into the night, but the nocturnal creature had vanished into the surrounding woodland.

And then the unmistakable, haunting sound of an owl shivered through the darkness. Nimue gasped, strained her eyes but could see nothing through the shadows, but it didn't matter.

Her beloved Arianrhod was with her, in the form of her sacred owl. It didn't matter how dire her situation appeared. She would prevail. The Goddess had sent her a sign.

With a smile, Nimue closed the tent flap, and the ravaging need to find the opium faded.

CHAPTER 17

The following afternoon, as they approached the settlement that had sprung up around the garrison, Tacitus still couldn't comprehend how Nimue had so contemptuously dismissed his offer. It was unheard of. Foreign women simply didn't refuse when a Roman patrician extended such privilege.

How could she possibly imagine there was any similarity between slavery and concubinage? Every time he thought of it—and he thought of it more frequently than he cared to admit—her total disregard for the honor he'd intended caused fresh disbelief to pound through his head.

He hadn't expected her to fall at his feet with gratitude. But he hadn't expected her to react as though he had deeply offended her, either.

It didn't help that she sat before him on the padded saddle, her back straight, as proud as a heathen queen, without the slightest regard for how she had insulted his honor. But where else could she be but here with him?

She was his slave. His responsibility. And now he faced the stark truth that unless he could change her mind, Nimue would continue to remain his slave for as long as he remained in this primitive province.

Thank the gods he hadn't procured her manumission before extending his offer. In that case she would be free, no longer under his protection and therefore vulnerable to any of his compatriots who lusted for her.

Did she have no idea of the danger she'd be in? Even if she left the Legion as soon as they reached the settlement, that was no guarantee of her safety. She would be an unprotected woman alone. Did she imagine she could stop a man from raping her if that was his intention? Could she really not understand that he had bought her because it was the only option open to him at the time?

In the back of his mind, the recurring voice reminded him. Nimue would be alone once he left for Rome. Who would protect her then?

But it was a faint voice of reason. Because his cursed pride could not get over the knowledge that Nimue, a native of a conquered land, had refused him.

~

TACITUS LED NIMUE, still dressed in his tunic and wearing his soiled cloak, to his quarters in the garrison. As befit his status, his quarters comprised of several rooms for his own private use, as well as servants who tended to his everyday domestic needs. Had Nimue agreed to become his concubine her elevated status would ensure all treated her with due respect. As it was, she would be viewed as nothing more than a pleasure slave.

The knowledge burned his gut. He'd never taken a pleasure slave. Had never even been tempted. But yesterday Nimue had acted the part to perfection. She had played it so well, he hadn't the slightest idea of what she was doing until it was too late.

She had serviced him. As any good sex slave should serve her master. And he had enjoyed every fucking moment. Even now, hours later, his cock jerked at the memory of her touch despite how his pride had been injured.

Her lack of climax had been deliberate. A calculated move to show him that despite appearances she was not, and would never be, under his command.

He opened the door and stood aside as Nimue entered. Despite how she'd sneered at his offer, she never behaved as a slave should. Smothering a grim smile, he followed her and watched her face as she glanced around the room that served as his office. She tried to hide her awe, but for one unguarded moment her eyes widened and a look of disbelief flickered over her face. He couldn't help but wonder how much greater her awe would be if he showed her his villa in Rome.

Perhaps when his term in Britannia ended, he would take her back to Rome with him. She was, after all, nothing but a slave and a slave was subject to her master's whims. At least then he would know she was still safe from harm. The thought only served to blacken his mood further.

He turned to his servants who were making a great effort not to stare at the exotic creature he'd brought with him. "Nimue will be staying here. She is to be accorded all due respect." How far more powerful this introduction would be if he could have called her his concubine. Yet nothing on earth would induce him to call her his slave.

With an imperial gesture, he indicated Nimue should follow him into his bedchamber. It was far smaller than his luxuriously appointed apartments in Rome but at least, thank the gods, it possessed a proper bed. He'd slept on the floor last night, leaving Nimue alone on the makeshift bed. His injured pride and bruised ego had been cold comfort. Every time she had turned over, every time she had sighed as if she was deliberately trying to keep him awake, his blood had burned with need.

Tonight he had no intention of sleeping on the floor. And

neither would Nimue. Tonight he would show her that he would not be manipulated when it came to sex. He would make her come and prove, without need for words, that she embraced his touch because she wanted him and not because *it was her duty to*.

She turned and looked at him.

"Am I to remain here?" She didn't sound defensive. She sounded regal. Although he wasn't sure what she meant by her question. Where else would she go?

"You're still recovering from your wound." Not that she looked in need of convalescence. Her recovery was nothing short of astounding. "You'll have ample opportunity to recuperate here."

An odd expression flickered over her face, as though she had all but forgotten about her injury. Then she swallowed, a strangely vulnerable gesture that inexplicably pierced his chest.

"Yes. I do need to rest." Then she pressed her lips together as if somehow the confession diminished her. Again he marveled at her fortitude. She insulted him with barely a blink yet she never complained of her physical discomforts. "But what of fresh air and exercise?"

He saw her point but also knew that given half a chance she'd attempt to escape. And although she wouldn't get far, the thought of her being dragged back to him like a common slave turned his stomach.

"When I return later we'll walk together."

Gods, he needed to arrange suitable clothing for her, otherwise she'd never be able to set foot outside his quarters. Even now, he could imagine the gossip his actions would cause. Who ever heard of a master walking with his slave for no other reason than she needed exercise? But scandal clouded his birth and gossip was something he'd got used to long ago.

Let them talk. Just because he appeared enamored of a foreign woman, a slave no less, would not impact his career.

Nimue pulled off his cloak and tossed it across the end of his bed. His tunic hung on her, too large and too long and yet somehow she managed to make the plain linen unbelievably sexy.

"What shall I do in the meantime?" Her voice was perfectly reasonable and yet he received the distinct impression that it irked her greatly to ask. And as he stared at her, the full weight of her question sank into him.

What in the gods' names was she going to do all day? Such a mundane thought hadn't crossed his mind. It appeared a great many things hadn't occurred to him when he'd made the decision to rescue her from her fate.

He didn't have the first idea what to tell her. His servants ensured his quarters were clean, his clothes were laundered and his stomach satisfied. Blandus' comment echoed in his mind. *She can be as idle as she pleases during the day. She'll certainly be kept busy enough at night.*

Tacitus resisted the urge to groan. Never before had he possessed servants—or slaves—surplus to requirements. He was certain that of his peers who had concubines not one of them had had to explain to the woman in question what her duties entailed. Nimue wasn't a gently bred Roman woman who would be content to do whatever it was ladies did during the day. And the one time he'd broached the subject with her she'd looked at him as if he was mad to suggest she might be proficient with the loom.

Still Nimue looked at him, waiting for his answer. He was supposed to be meeting with his commander. With an impatient gesture that he could only hope covered his mounting irritation, he swung away from her. "Do whatever you please." Would he come to regret these hasty words? Somehow he thought he would. "So long as you don't leave my quarters."

∽

After Tacitus left her, Nimue explored his quarters but finally returned to his bedchamber since that appeared to be the only room where none of his servants would follow her. Just before she closed the door, she was presented with a small pile of clean clothes. They were coarse, the type of garments a peasant would wear, and Nimue had bitten back her instinctive reaction when the woman had given them to her.

She stood in the middle of the room and glowered down at herself. She would rather wear her torn and blood-stained gown than this...Roman sackcloth. But since she was trying her best not to annoy Tacitus she knew she'd simply have to bear it.

As she fastened her belt around the rough material, she frowned. She couldn't understand why her refusal to agree with his demand to become his concubine had so affected him. One would think he required her permission. But how could that be so when the status of a concubine was nothing more than that of a slave?

She couldn't fathom the difference, and yet Tacitus' behavior suggested that, in his eyes, there was a whole *Empire* of difference.

With a sigh, she forced the image of Tacitus from her mind. She wasn't supposed to think of him when he wasn't with her. Whether he wanted her to be his slave or his concubine was irrelevant, because she had no intention of remaining with him for any length of time.

The journey from the battle site to this fortification had brought her a lot closer to the magical enclave where Caratacus had shielded his warriors and she knew it was a sign that she could no longer delay in her mission.

She should pray for Arianrhod's guidance, but even as the thought formed, unease fluttered through her breast. Her beloved Moon Goddess had been silent and remote since Nimue had been captured, no matter how desperately she'd tried to reach Arianrhod.

Was her Goddess displeased that Nimue had been captured by the enemy? Or was it because she had not yet managed to secure the escape of the Briton queen?

For a moment indecision warred through her heart. Since the night of her initiation, Arianrhod's presence had never been far. Although the Goddess didn't always answer Nimue's prayers, never before had she felt so oddly bereft. It was almost as though Arianrhod had turned her back on her.

No. That possibility was too terrible to even imagine.

Nimue took a deep breath and tried to calm her racing heart. There had to be a way to show Arianrhod that she was committed to her task. That now they were in the fortification she would no longer delay in her mission.

To save the queen and princess. And return the shard of bluestone.

Heat washed through her. She'd almost forgotten about the bluestone. Hastily she searched for the pouch hanging on her belt. She would hold the bluestone and once again beg for Arianrhod's advice. This time, surely, the Great Goddess would heed her call.

Where is it? She couldn't feel the shape of the bluestone through the leather pouches and disbelief punched through her. Frantically she pulled the belt from her waist and dropped it onto the bed. She knew, merely from looking at each pouch, what it contained. And the pouch she had put the bluestone in *wasn't there*.

But it had to be. How could it not? Ignoring the evidence of her eyes, she pulled desperately at the fastenings of the first pouch and tipped the contents onto the bed.

Her comb, and lengths of colored leather to tie her hair. Just as she had expected.

Her stomach churned as she tugged open each pouch. The bluestone wasn't hiding in any of them. Of course it wasn't. She knew she'd put it in its own pouch. She even knew the exact position on her belt where she had tied it.

It didn't matter how long she stared at her belt or her myriad possessions that were now scattered across the bed.

She had lost the bluestone.

Her legs gave way and she slumped onto the floor. How had she not known the bluestone was missing? Why hadn't she checked before?

Was this the reason Arianrhod refused to hear her pleas?

Her chest constricted as panic clawed through her breast, causing her heart to hammer erratically against her ribs. When was the last time she'd seen the bluestone? Now she thought about it, she hadn't touched it since before her capture. Did that mean she'd lost it before Tacitus had found her at the stream?

Or had he taken it from her afterward when he had taken her dagger and bow?

But that made no sense. The bluestone was no weapon. She gritted her teeth and pushed herself to her feet. Perhaps the leather ties had become worn and the pouch had dropped from her belt. Perhaps it had fallen onto the ground outside Tacitus' quarters. Perhaps, after all, this was merely Arianrhod's way of ensuring Nimue once more focused on her task.

She clung onto that possibility with grim determination as she left the bedchamber and made her way toward the door. The bluestone would be outside. She knew it. And once it was again in her possession, the Moon Goddess would forgive her for temporarily losing it.

As soon as she opened the door, the legionary on guard turned toward her. His face was a hard mask of enemy implacability. But she couldn't let a little thing like that stop her.

Dusk had fallen but the outside torches gave plenty of illumination. She stepped outside. He immediately blocked her way with one muscled arm.

"I'm looking for something." She offered him a guileless smile and hoped he fell for it and couldn't see the fear beneath. "I think I dropped it out here."

His arm didn't waver. Neither did his expression. "I have orders not to allow you to pass."

The fear inched higher in her breast and threatened to paralyze her throat. "I do not wish to pass." She hoped he couldn't hear the desperation in her voice. "I simply wish to look around."

He towered over her, a great hulk of a man and instinctively she took a step back.

"I have no wish to force you back inside," he said. "But I will if I have to."

She took another step back, her gaze scanning the ground. But no familiar leather pouch greeted her. Had she really believed it would be this easy? She gripped her unraveling courage together and tried once more. "I must—"

He didn't even wait to let her finish. He simply shut the door in her face.

For a moment, she stared at the door until the reality of her situation slammed through her mind.

She had lost the bluestone. And although she'd taken it without permission and had intended to use it for her own ends, an insidious sense of something far greater than her own plans hovered on the edge of her consciousness.

Return what you have taken. The imperious command echoed through her mind, but why did it? And why did it sound so eerily familiar?

Slowly she turned around, to see Tacitus' servants staring at her as though she was something unspeakably foul. Her heart jerked in her chest as she remembered all her treasured possessions, scattered across Tacitus' bed, and she hurried back to his room.

Relief streaked through her. Nothing had been taken. She sat on the edge of the bed and with shaking fingers returned the contents to their respective pouches, until she came to her mother's exquisitely engraved torque.

A shaft of bittersweet pain engulfed her heart as she traced her finger over the gleaming silver. The torque had been passed from mother to eldest daughter for generations, and the bestowal had always been cause for great celebration.

Except there had been no celebration when her mother had given her the priceless heirloom. Only terror, disbelief and the rank stench of betrayal.

Her fingers tightened around the silver as she tried to push the memories to the back of her mind. It would do no good dwelling on them now. Not when she had to somehow find the bluestone. And work on gaining Tacitus' trust—at least enough for him to allow her free access throughout this cursed Roman fortification. How could she discover the whereabouts of the queen if she was forbidden to leave Tacitus' quarters?

Voices in the adjoining room penetrated her thoughts. It was a deep, masculine voice but it wasn't Tacitus and before she could investigate for herself what was happening the door flew open.

A large Roman in flowing white robes with a purple stripe smiled at her from the doorway. He was the same Roman who had burst into Tacitus' tent the other day. The one Tacitus had attempted to prevent from seeing her, as she had sat on his bed covered only by his cloak.

She gave him her haughtiest look and rose to her feet, her heart thudding with trepidation against her ribs. There could be few reasons why this Roman was here, and she doubted any of them had to do with negotiating her freedom.

The lust in his eyes was evident. And this time Tacitus was not here.

Her fingers clenched around her torque, but as a weapon it was useless. If only she still had her dagger. To be so defenseless and vulnerable was intolerable. She had never been without a personal weapon at her hip since she had been a child and the extent of her vulnerability tasted foul on her tongue.

She didn't need to glance beyond the Roman to know that Tacitus' servants stood, useless, in the next room. They wouldn't come to her aid. All she could rely on was her wits and speed, and she was sorely compromised because of her injured shoulder.

"Greetings," the Roman said, stepping into the room. He continued to smile at her as if he imagined that might lower her guard. Did he think her a fool? And before the question had even finished forming, she acknowledged the truth.

Yes, he did. He looked at her and didn't see a captured enemy warrior. He saw a woman he wanted in his bed. The Gaul, curse him, had been right. It was not a dagger she needed in order to slay this Roman. It was his perception of her that would prove his downfall.

When she didn't respond he took another step toward her. "Don't be afraid," he said and it was only then she realized he was speaking her language, and not Latin. Did he think her ignorant of his barbaric tongue? The notion stung her pride but she kept silent. Let him think her an uneducated peasant. And on the heels of that thought came another.

If he thought her a peasant, he would never imagine for a moment what she truly was. Hadn't she, back in the mountains when Tacitus had first come upon her, known that concealing her identity was her best hope for survival?

But then she had been dressed as a noble. Now she was dressed as a slave. For all this Roman knew, she might have stolen the bracelets from her dead countrywomen.

"What is your name?" He injected a false friendly note in his voice. Nimue imagined impaling an arrow through his lying mouth. "Come now, I won't hurt you."

Despite her precarious situation, his arrogant assumption that she was paralyzed with terror irked her. She tilted her jaw at him and only just remembered not to give him a withering glare for good measure. "My name is Nimue."

His smile faltered and for a fleeting moment confusion wreathed his features. Belatedly Nimue understood why. Great Goddess, would she never learn to hold her tongue? She might look like a peasant but she certainly didn't speak like one.

"Nimue." She wasn't sure whether he spoke to her, or himself. "A beautiful name for a beautiful girl."

And now he attempted flattery? By calling her a *girl*?

He gave a low laugh and took yet another step into the room. But he didn't close the door behind him. "There's no need to look so apprehensive," he said, and he was so close that if only she still possessed her dagger she could have plunged it through his corrupt heart before he drew another breath. "I mean only to make your acquaintance, nothing more."

She flicked a scornful glance over him. His dark chestnut hair was short, as all Romans kept their hair, with only the faintest sprinkling of silver to belie his advancing years. His entire bearing exuded aristocratic authority and the assumption that his slightest command would be obeyed without question.

"Then there is nothing more to discuss." He had her trapped between his body and the bed. Self-disgust flooded her veins. Why had she allowed herself to be maneuvered into such a vulnerable tactical position?

"I can see why the tribune likes you." The Roman appeared to be amused by her response, which hadn't been her intention at all. "Although by Jupiter I cannot fathom why he dresses you like the meanest creature of the gutters."

The Roman's criticism of Tacitus oddly annoyed her. She might be offended by the garments he'd left her, but that was between her and Tacitus. "My own gown was ruined." She didn't even try for humility anymore. It appeared such a feat was beyond her capabilities. "At least these are clean." True enough. Even if the rough material did scratch her skin.

There was no mistaking the amusement that gleamed in his eyes this time. "You should be dressed in the finest of silks and softest of linen." His lip quirked as if the image pleased him. "I see I shall have to instruct the tribune in such matters."

"There's no need." She didn't know why the Roman's unsubtle censure of Tacitus bothered her so, but the thought of him lecturing Tacitus because of her plagued her senses. And because this Roman's casual assumption that she couldn't understand Latin scraped her nerves she decided to reply in his own cursed language. "I am, after all, merely a slave and dressed in garments fit only for a slave." As she shot the words at him she fixed her torque around her throat. She didn't know why he managed to so raise her ire, or why she told him she was nothing more than a slave while she flashed priceless jewelry in his face. She knew he was Tacitus' superior. If he wished he could have her flogged or worse for her behavior. Yet somehow she knew he wouldn't.

He didn't want to disfigure her body. He wanted to possess it.

The silence after her last thrust stretched between them until finally Nimue risked a fleeting glance. He was staring at her, entranced. It was clear the fact she could not only speak his language but could speak it fluently staggered him.

A dozen barbed comments danced on the tip of Nimue's tongue. Yet they remained locked within as her gaze meshed with the Roman's. And a terrifying thought gripped her heart.

Had she gone too far? Had this powerful Roman guessed she was no ordinary Celt noblewoman? *Does he know I'm a Druid?*

CHAPTER 18

The moment Tacitus entered his quarters he knew Nimue was in danger. It wasn't simply the way his servants, who should have been busy at their tasks, scattered at his arrival. It was a gut reaction that hit him with the force of a physical blow.

He marched through the room and then stopped dead at the sight of his commander, in his bedchamber, looming over Nimue.

White rage seared through him and without thinking of the consequences, he stamped into the room. His commander had trapped Nimue by the bed and it was obvious what would have happened if Tacitus hadn't returned.

"Sir." He ground out the word, clenching his fists. To lay hands on his commander could end his career, no matter how good friends he was with Tacitus' father. But gods, if the bastard didn't step back from Nimue instantly, Tacitus would bring down the full force of the law on his commander's head.

Slowly his commander turned to him, and for a fleeting moment Tacitus could have sworn the older man threw him a look of fury. What the fuck did he have to be furious about? That Tacitus had interrupted his sport?

"Tribune." Once again the commander's face showed no trace of emotion. "Your latest acquisition is enchanting." Without another glance at Nimue he turned and strode into the other room. Tacitus threw Nimue a black scowl but she didn't look pleased with herself that she'd managed to snare the interest of his commanding officer. Instead she rubbed her fingers gingerly over her wounded shoulder and guilt flooded through him.

He'd been so consumed by her refusal to accept his offer and the knowledge she'd used sex to prove a point that he'd forgotten about her injury. He should have left the opium with one of his servants so Nimue had access to pain relief. And then something else punched into his brain.

What in Hades was she wearing? Did it give her perverse pleasure to disobey every word he uttered, even when he was attempting to ease her situation?

There wasn't time to take issue with it now. His commander was in the other room and didn't look happy at being kept waiting.

"Wait here." His voice was gruff and she looked at him, but he couldn't decipher the expression on her face. Or perhaps he simply didn't want to. Because she looked at him as if everything about him sickened her.

Abruptly he turned and marched after his commander. It was obvious what the older man wanted. And Tacitus had no intention of agreeing.

Hands clasped behind his back, his commander turned to face him. "How much did you pay for her?"

That wasn't the question Tacitus had expected. He considered refusing to answer but there was little point. His commander could discover the price easily enough if he so wished. And so he named the amount.

The commander didn't move a muscle, even though the price

was hefty for an injured captive. The silence became oppressive but still the other man didn't speak or break eye contact. Was he waiting for Tacitus to extend hospitality in the form of using Nimue for the night?

Then his commander was in for a long wait. Tacitus was not his father, who saw nothing wrong in offering the sexual service of his slaves to favored friends.

"I'll pay you double for her."

Tacitus clenched his jaw, rage threatening to demolish his civilized veneer. "She's not for sale."

Something dark and dangerous flashed in his commander's eyes. "Name your price, Tacitus."

"There is no price. Sir." The honorific sounded almost insulting, affixed to the end of his remark in such a manner but Tacitus didn't care. It wasn't him defying convention here. It was his commander. Tacitus decided to make the situation absolutely clear. "She belongs to me. I've pledged to keep her safe from harm." Let the other man make what he liked of that. The intention was plain.

Tacitus would not stand by and allow Nimue—*his property*—to be used by any other.

His commander narrowed his eyes, his piercing gaze burning into Tacitus' mind. "I have no intention of harming her, tribune. If you're too enamored with her to part with her yet, then give me your word on this. When you tire of her, I claim first right of purchase. Do you agree?"

The image of his commander fucking Nimue turned his guts. He would never agree to such a thing. Because he had no intention of selling Nimue.

But what if, when the time came for him to return to Rome, his commander refused to grant Nimue manumission? If she was free she could return to her people, wherever they were. But if she remained a slave how could he continue to protect her unless he took her home—and acquired her freedom there from an unbiased magistrate?

Gods, how would Nimue survive as a freedwoman in Rome, unless she *did* agree to become his concubine?

"Should I decide to sell Nimue," Tacitus said, and the words corroded his soul; as if he was speaking of a prize mare his commander had taken a fancy to, "I give you my word you will be the first I approach."

His commander didn't respond. After a fraught silence he finally jerked his head in acceptance and left. Tacitus expelled a frustrated breath, kicked the door shut and returned to his troublesome slave.

She hadn't moved from where he'd left her, but she was no longer rubbing her wounded shoulder. The look she gave him, however, hadn't altered in the slightest.

He resisted the urge to massage his pounding temples. Nothing had gone smoothly from the moment he'd found Nimue by the mountain stream. But at least this conversation with his commander, as much as it had irritated him, had clarified one thing. His commander now knew Tacitus would not stand by and allow any man to abuse Nimue, and he needed to make her understand.

"There's no need to fear. You'll never belong to the commander. And while you're under my protection, his honor will never allow him to touch you."

That should ease her mind. It had certainly eased his although nothing would induce him to admit such a thing aloud.

"I don't fear him." As always she spoke to him in Latin, but for the first time he acknowledged the quality of her Latin. Her accent would always mar her as a foreigner but her grasp of his language was akin to that of a patrician.

The haughty glance she gave him to accompany her words were at sharp odds with the garments she'd chosen to wear. He couldn't fathom where she'd got them. Even his servants dressed better than this.

"Why aren't you wearing the gown I arranged for you?" He knew she was proud but she didn't have to look like a beggar to prove her objection to her situation. He was fully aware of how she felt.

So why in the name of all the gods had she refused his offer? If she hadn't been so stubborn he could have acquired her manumission already, before his commander had taken it upon himself to meet with Nimue and decided he wanted her for himself.

"I *am* wearing the gown you arranged for me."

Air hissed between his clenched teeth. Without another word he swung on his heel and marched from the room. His orders had been specific, but obviously not specific enough. It was clear that when it came to Nimue nothing was ever going to be straightforward.

And again the infuriated thought pounded through his head.

If Nimue was his official concubine, his servants would never have dared to offer her such coarse clothing.

~

Nimue followed Tacitus to the door and watched him storm toward the kitchen and servants' area. That he was displeased with her gown was clear. Why that somehow eased her wounded soul she couldn't imagine. Because it didn't change her status.

Neither did the fact he had just assured her she was safe from his superior officer. Her pride demanded that Tacitus' word meant nothing to her. In Rome's eyes, she might be nothing but a slave but in her heart she was free. And no matter how brutally the enemy might use her she would survive and complete her mission.

But the truth was sorely different. Because in reality the thought of being used by countless barbarous Romans to satisfy their carnal lusts terrified her. And she despised her terror. Was she not a warrior? Had she not participated in many ambushes and skirmishes with the enemy since they'd invaded her beloved Cymru?

Yet it didn't change the fundamental truth. Despite how she'd refused to be cowed by the older Roman, she had been very aware of the possibility that she could end up in his bed. Not because Tacitus would allow it. But because Tacitus could not prevent it.

The realization that Tacitus could, indeed, prevent such a fate shouldn't be cause for such deep relief or—Goddess forgive her—gratitude.

What would she gain by continuing to delude herself? She had never given herself to Tacitus simply as a strategic measure. Could she have experienced such glorious orgasms with his superior officer? The image of attempting to seduce *him* made her feel ill.

The questions swirled through her mind, tangled and edged with unformed alarm. She desperately needed to commune with Arianrhod. Not to ask her about her mission, but because her wise Goddess would soothe her battered soul and calm her turbulent thoughts. Without considering the consequences, she went to the front door and pulled it open. This time the legionary didn't attempt to prevent her escape. She looked up and a deep, thick darkness shrouded the skies.

Nimue frowned, but no glimmer of the silver moon could be seen. Of course it wasn't unusual for clouds to obscure the Moon Goddess on her nighttime passage across the skies but still a shiver spidered along Nimue's spine.

Something was wrong. She could feel it in the spiritual essence of her being; the special place where the Great Goddess had entered and filled her young acolyte with adoration on that long-ago night of initiation. She closed her eyes, willed her thoughts to still, and opened her heart to her Goddess. *Please forgive me.* Please return. She hadn't meant to lose the bluestone.

"Nimue." Tacitus voice punched through her senses and she swung around. He was glaring at her from the center of the room. "What do you think you're doing?"

Would he understand if she told him the truth? He was only a heathen Roman, but even Romans acknowledged the power of foreign deities and Tacitus was not an ordinary Roman.

"I was attempting to commune with my Goddess," she said with as much dignity as she could. "I feel barren without her love to comfort me."

"Do you need to stand before an open door in order to do this?"

No, she didn't. But neither did she generally call upon her Goddess while inside a dwelling. "I usually worship her at night." Although she generally worshipped her Goddess whenever she had a quiet moment, she felt something more was needed so he appreciated just how important Arianrhod was to her. "In a sacred glade." Because Tacitus had not told her to, she turned and closed the door, since that was clearly his intention despite how he didn't move toward her.

"You'll have to find alternative arrangements. There are no glades, sacred or otherwise, within the garrison."

"I won't use your heathen temple."

He flashed a smile that appeared genuine, and she was once again enchanted. And a treacherous thought weaved through her mind.

Why couldn't he be a brave Celt warrior that she could, at least, dream of having a future with?

"I'd never expect you to use our temple. I fear such sacrilege would bring plague and pestilence upon us all."

Before she'd met Tacitus she had never imagined a Roman possessed a sense of humor. Certainly not when it came to his barbaric gods.

"You're right to fear such retribution." Although, in the back of her mind, the unnatural blackness of the night ate into her, she couldn't help smiling back at him. "My gods can be mighty in their wrath."

He came toward her and held out his hand. Without thinking she took it. His strong fingers folded around hers, and even that small touch caused delightful tremors to lick across her skin.

"Perhaps I should offer sacrifice to your gods in appeasement." His smoky voice curled through her senses.

He wore the Roman tunic and cloak of her enemy, yet all she could see when she looked at him was the man who invaded her thoughts when he shouldn't; the man whose touch she craved no matter how hard she tried to deny the truth.

"Surely your Roman gods would strike you down for honoring mine."

"The gods of Rome are surprisingly tolerant of such indiscretions."

She didn't want to be intrigued, and yet she was. "My gods would never countenance such a thing."

He tugged her forward and she went without resistance. Why pretend something they both knew to be false? Her refusal to climax the last time Tacitus had taken her had done nothing but cause her frustration. It hadn't changed her status. Hadn't changed the way she felt about him.

She might as well enjoy the time they had together because when she left with the queen and princess, they would never see each other again.

"Then whose gods are the more enlightened, Nimue?" He was laughing at her, mocking her beliefs, and yet fury didn't rush through her veins or the desire to cut out his blasphemous tongue flood her senses.

Fascination weaved through her instead. "That's easy to say, Tacitus." They entered his bedchamber and he kicked the door shut behind them, and the lamps cast a mystical glow across the room. "But in reality your gods would strike you down if you worshipped another."

He grasped her braid and then slowly slid his fist along the length of her hair, still damp from when she had washed it earlier. "Yet still I survive."

They no longer held hands. Tacitus pulled her braid over her shoulder and began to leisurely loosen her hair. It shouldn't feel so seductive or arousing, and yet she was both seduced and aroused by his gentle touch. She struggled to recall what they had been talking about. Because what he was suggesting was truly —outrageous.

"You do not worship the gods of Rome?" That couldn't be so.

"I do worship them." He speared his fingers through her hair and arranged her damp curls over her shoulders. "And I also worship the gods of my maternal heritage."

She'd had no idea Romans considered their maternal heritage worth preserving. Not if it went against their despicable Emperor's decree. "Your mother is not of Rome?"

His fingers stilled in her hair and an odd expression crossed his face. As if her question had caused him pain.

"She is of Rome. But she holds onto her old ways. I made the decision while still a child to embrace her gods to honor her."

Goddess, she didn't want any more reason to find Tacitus irresistible but his confession undid her. She'd always been taught Romans thought little of women. That their wives and, by extension, their mothers were not given respect and honor.

"In that regard at least," she said, as he began to tug the rough fastenings at her breast, "your mother will be proud of you."

He laughed. "I assure you, my mother is excessively proud of my achievements, Nimue. Yet I intend to exceed her expectations, whatever the cost." His voice hardened, as if reiterating a pledge he had made long ago.

More intrigued than she had any right to be, Nimue stared into his hypnotic eyes.

She wanted to ask him more of his mother. As Tacitus gently eased the rough gown over her injured shoulder, she realized that she wanted to know everything about his family, about his way of life in Rome.

The questions burned her tongue, closed her throat. Tacitus wasn't her lover. Not in the same way a warrior of Cymru would be. If he had been, she could ask whatever she wished. But how could she ask Tacitus such personal questions? It gave rise to a level of intimacy she wasn't comfortable in embracing. No matter how dearly she wished to embrace it.

To do so would reek of betrayal to her slain countrymen.

CHAPTER 19

Nimue's gown slid to the floor, but Tacitus didn't take his gaze from her face. But his eyes darkened and it became harder than ever to recall why she couldn't simply indulge her desire to speak to him as she wished. Ask him whatever she pleased. Learn of his strange Roman ways that did not condemn its citizens for embracing foreign gods.

She reached for the brooch that held his cloak in place, but he captured her wrists in his hand, preventing her. "Lie on the bed."

"Are you giving me orders, Roman?" There was no malice in her voice. She might hate her status and blame Tacitus for it, but she wasn't stupid. The confrontation with his commandeering officer this night had clarified more than one question for her.

Tacitus hadn't lied when he'd said, "*I did what I did in order to protect you.*" She didn't have to like it to appreciate its truth.

"Yes." He stepped back from her, removed his cloak and flung it across his casket. Dark flutters of lust kicked low in her pussy as she complied. His gaze raked over her, scorched her naked flesh. Instinctively she crossed her ankles, feeling suddenly vulnerable although she wasn't sure why. Tacitus had seen her naked before.

"Does this please you?' The words tumbled from her mouth before she could prevent them, but although she knew she was defying her Goddess by enjoying this encounter, she couldn't help herself. The raw need that flared in Tacitus' eyes at her provocative remark was worth any soul-searching she would inevitably need to conduct later.

"Spread your thighs so I might see you properly."

She had never done such a thing before. Her lovers before Tacitus—to her shame she had taken only two before this Roman—had never demanded she display herself so utterly. She would never admit to such extraordinary inexperience.

Slowly she uncrossed her ankles and just as slowly parted her legs. Tacitus gazed at her, transfixed, and the knowledge that he found her so alluring intoxicated her senses.

"What would you have me do now?" She scarcely recognized the sultry note in her voice. Never before had such a question passed her lips while with a lover. But Tacitus was different, in every way, and not just by virtue of his foreign status.

His burning gaze licked over her body. How could just a look cause desire to curl through her core and make her nipples ache for his touch? She wanted his hands on her skin, his mouth on her breasts. But he made no move toward her, just continued to visually feast on her nakedness.

She shifted restlessly. Her exposed pussy lips, spread for his satisfaction, throbbed with need. Could he see her swollen clit? The slick arousal that betrayed her hunger?

Her ravenous gaze roved over his short military hair. It was nothing like that of any Celt warriors she had known. Until she'd met Tacitus, the thought of spearing her fingers through such short hair had never occurred to her. But now she longed to rake her nails over his head and feel the soft spikes of his hair graze her palm.

His entire focus centered between her thighs. Quivers claimed her wet sheath and she rolled her hips, unable to stop herself. His aristocratic jaw tensed and she curled her fingers into a fist to stop herself from reaching for him.

It's only sex. She tried to convince herself but if that was all this was why did she care about his relationship with his mother? Why was she so deeply moved by the strength of his honor when confronted by his commanding officer?

Her regard was wrong. All wrong, and yet deep in her soul it felt so inexplicably right. Tacitus was a Roman, the enemy of her people. But that, in itself, didn't make him inherently an evil man.

"Touch yourself." His voice was hoarse and for one eternal moment their gazes clashed. "Show me what pleases you."

You please me. The words remained locked in her mind. She could never speak them aloud, for they were more than a confession of carnal pleasure. Her lust was supposed to have subsided once she'd had him. Yet his face and his body and the way he could make her writhe with mindless delight haunted her waking thoughts and invaded her lust-fueled dreams.

She cradled her breasts, ignoring the twinge of discomfort from her shoulder. It meant nothing when Tacitus' attention was riveted on her fingers, as she tweaked her aching nipples.

Primal power surged through her blood and desire swirled low in her pussy. The Dance of the Moon Goddess, performed on the night when Arianrhod's full magnificence glowed in the sky, was a sacred ritual. Only the Moon Goddess' priestesses and acolytes were permitted to attend. Yet last night, consumed with fury, she had danced for Tacitus, the first man she had ever bestowed such honor upon.

Tonight she would dance for him again. She didn't have to be on her feet to worship her body the way her Goddess commanded. The thought of pleasuring herself while Tacitus watched tightened the need building between her thighs. He had watched her before, but then she had been consumed with fury and the desire to show him she could rise above the lust that thundered between them.

But she couldn't rise above it. Had no desire to rise above it. Because it was more than mere lust even if she could never accept it.

She trailed her fingertips over her ribs, the dip of her waist and curve of her hips. In her mind she imagined the hypnotic thud of the drums and seductive notes of the flutes that the older Druids played while the dancers worshipped the power of the Moon Goddess. She imagined she was alone in the sacred grove, bathed in the silvery nighttime light and Tacitus, her Roman warrior, watched from the shadows of the trees.

Her fingers slid between her parted thighs and caressed the folds of her sex. She saw Tacitus grit his jaw and knew he kept his distance only by rigid willpower. She would break his proud Roman will and have him on his knees, begging for her favor.

"This pleases me." She could scarcely push the words along her throat but it was worth the effort when Tacitus dragged his gaze from her exposed pussy and looked at her as if he was already clinging to the precipice. She stroked the soft inner lip of her sex then teased her swollen clit and sighed as pleasure spiraled through her wet channel.

"Nimue." He knelt on the end of the bed between her open legs, his hands bracketing her ankles. "Push your finger inside."

Again he gave her orders, the kind of order no man had the right to give a Druid or even an acolyte. But his command was dark, exciting, and without taking her gaze from his bewitched expression she slowly slid her finger into her slick crease.

"Like this?" Her whisper was a ragged caress that stoked her sensitized flesh.

His breath escaped in a tortured hiss. The sound inflamed more than her imagined Druidic music.

"Does that please you also?" He appeared mesmerized by her finger buried deep in her pussy. How was it possible that his utter concentration could enhance her own pleasure so immeasurably?

She withdrew and trailed her finger, coated with her juices, over her stomach and between the valley of her breasts. Tacitus followed her progress, enthralled, and although she was the one flat on her back, although she was the one enslaved by Roman law, Tacitus was no less imprisoned by the shared bonds of their desire.

"Yes." Her finger hovered against her lips and her musky scent drifted like gossamer in the heated air. Without breaking eye contact she slowly, seductively, sucked her finger into her mouth.

His grip on her ankles tightened and she slid her finger from her mouth until only the tip remained between her pouting lips. She had never before teased a man this way. It had never before occurred to her. But every move she made appeared to inflame Tacitus, and his reactions entranced.

"How do you taste?" He crouched over her spread thighs, his gaze intent.

With deliberate provocation the tip of her tongue trailed over the seam of her lips. "I taste of freedom."

He licked his lips and lowered his head toward her exposed flesh. She saw him inhale and it shouldn't have been so erotic, and yet sharp arrows of need speared low in her pussy. The tip of his tongue flicked over her sensitive clit and with a strangled groan, she clutched the bed linen as Tacitus continued to torture her.

"How do I taste?" Goddess only knew how she managed to squeeze the words out when her heart hammered in her breast and blood pounded against her temples. She felt Tacitus smile against her vulnerable clit, felt his breath fan her damp folds, and the sensation was like nothing she had imagined in her wildest fantasies.

"You taste like ambrosia from the gods."

She didn't know what ambrosia was, but his inference was plain. Illicit delight swirled low in her belly, enhancing the desire that thundered through her veins. His tongue circled her swollen bud, building the pleasure to unbearable heights. She buried her fingers in his hair, except his hair was not long enough to grip. The very foreignness of the touch of his hair against her palms caused renewed waves of desire to pound through her, and she pressed his head harder between her thighs.

Gasping, she raised her head to look down at him. The sight of her Roman on his knees eating her pussy was as arousing as the feel of his tongue, the graze of his teeth; the rough scrape of his day-old beard.

She collapsed back onto the bed. He thrust his tongue into her as his thumb caressed her throbbing clit and she wanted to scream at him to take her, take her *now*, but she could scarcely breathe and speech was beyond her.

He slid his other hand beneath her bottom and gripped her arse, angling her upward, shifting his penetration. Then he pushed two fingers inside her and sucked on her sensitized nub, and she forgot how to breathe at all.

∼

Tacitus sucked hard on her clit and felt her pussy clamp around his probing fingers. His cock jerked as her musky scent enveloped his senses. She was wet and hot and her juices trickled over his knuckles as he massaged her tight slit. Every frenzied thud of his heart urged him to fuck her, but he ground back the imperative. She would come first. His pride demanded it. She would never use him the way she had used him before.

Her strangled whimpers and the feel of her fingers digging into his head were a sweet torture and his resolve stretched tight. *I won't succumb.* He edged back, just enough so he could look at her aroused clit. Swollen and pink, peeking from its hood, he'd never seen anything so tempting. He stuck out his tongue and prodded her bud and her hips jerked and thighs clamped around his head.

He licked her clit, slowly, and her moan vibrated through her body. "You like that?" His voice was hoarse. He didn't expect an answer but she gave him one just the same. Her hand clutched the back of his head and her message was plain.

He circled his fingers deep inside her pussy, gripping her arse to keep her still. Her slick sheath undulated and he savored her taste as the tip of his tongue trailed along her slit. She bucked helplessly beneath him as her climax shuddered through her, clenching around his probing fingers, vibrating against his mouth.

Her choked gasps were all he could hear above the pound of his heart. She came over his hand, and he rammed his tongue against her aroused peak, forcing every last tremor from her shaking body. Only when her rigid muscles relaxed did he finally raise his head to look at her.

She lay before him, eyes closed, mouth open, her hair spread across his pillows. Her breasts rose and fell with every erratic breath, her erect nipples ripe and inviting. Quivers claimed her body at satisfyingly frequent intervals and the scent of her come was a musky drug in the sex-drenched air.

She looked thoroughly fucked. There was no hint of pretense in her look or doubt in his mind. He had mastered her, in the only way he had ever desired to master her. Never again would she attempt to delude him in such matters. With a pained breath, he pushed himself up and ripped off his tunic.

His cock throbbed; his balls ached with need. Nimue's eyes were half-open, watching him as he straddled her. His thighs pushed against her breasts and he loomed over her until the head of his erection brushed her jaw. Her eyes widened as she appeared to finally realize what he had in mind.

"Take me." It was a hoarse command and he grasped his cock and angled it against her parted lips. Her uneven breath panted across his wet slit, a blend of hot and chilled air and for an agonized moment, he thought she would refuse.

Then she opened her mouth and he pushed into her, past her

lips, over her tongue. She felt like heated silk and he watched, transfixed, as her lips sealed around him.

He braced his weight on his knees and wound a length of her hair around his fist. She sucked hard, her cheeks hollowing with effort. He pushed in farther, releasing his grip on his cock, relishing the tight cocoon of her wet mouth.

She flattened her hands against his rigid thighs, her fingernails digging into his muscles. For a moment he closed his eyes, gritted his teeth. Her compressed tongue rippled beneath his shaft, sending streaks of pleasure straight to his rock-hard balls.

He tightened his grip on her hair, caught and held her gaze. He pulled out a couple of inches and the scrape of her teeth against his cock threatened to shatter his self-control.

One hand fisting her hair, the other flattened on his bed beside her head he fought the urge to thrust down her throat and spill his seed deep inside her. It was hard to think, hard to speak, but somehow he forced the words out. "Finally I've discovered a way to silence your tongue."

She choked and her eyes watered as she attempted to laugh and clearly found it impossible. He shoved farther inside her, connected to the back of her throat and gave her a feral grin. He had never seen anything more arousing than the way Nimue looked with her green eyes focused on him and her mouth full of his cock.

A primitive groan burned through him and he rocked into her, back and forth. The feel of her mouth surrounding him was like nothing he had experienced before. His thighs tensed, arse clenched and he buried himself into the tight clasp of her throat.

She convulsed, gagged and dug her nails into him. He bared his teeth at her, forced himself to stop and it was the hardest thing he had done in his life. Bizarrely, her taunt when they'd first met thundered through his mind. "Too much of a man for you, am I?"

In response, she gripped his arse and tried to jerk him

forward. He remained rigid above her although every sense demanded he relinquish control and pour himself into her. But despite the way she clutched his body and worshipped his cock, her eyes were glazed and she was no longer breathing.

Curse her stubborn Celtic pride. She would never admit she needed air. His muscles protested as he eased out of her delectable wet heat, the slide of her tongue against his flesh mocking his restraint. Her lips pouted around the head of his shaft, pink and swollen. *For him.* Somehow he found his voice. "I accept your surrender on this matter."

Her erratic breath feathered across his erection as she cupped his heavy balls and squeezed. He almost forgot about fearing she might choke and battled the desperate need to plunge back inside her tempting mouth.

She gasped up at him, her breasts heaving as she sucked air into her lungs. "I didn't surrender, Roman. You made a tactical withdrawal."

To Hades with his tactics. He knew if she wasn't injured he would have continued. She never complained of pain but how would he know if he hurt her if she couldn't even make a sound?

When she had fully recovered, he would take her this way. He would take her in every way.

She reached up, licked the swollen head of his cock and any future plans he had in mind vanished. He jerked, gritted his teeth and then cushioned his shaft between the valley of her breasts. "My withdrawal is temporary."

He pulled her hand from his sac and she appeared bewitched when he had her cradle her breast against him. He cupped her other breast, his thumb grazing her rosy peak, and together they created a seductive embrace around his hot erection. Her breasts enveloped him, a scented haven of soft skin and he gripped the root of his cock and rocked between her luscious flesh.

There was a look of wonderment on her face as she watched him ride her, as though no man had ever done this to her before.

The thought enflamed and his thrusts became urgent, his breathing ragged. Her tight valley became slippery from sweat and she tentatively stroked a finger along the length of his engorged shaft.

He couldn't tear his gaze away from his cock pumping between her breasts. From the way she pinched her ripe nipple between her finger and thumb. *I have to slow down.* But gods, she looked so glorious beneath him offering her breasts and throat for his pleasure.

And then she spoke. "Come for me," she whispered. "My barbaric Roman warrior."

Her words flayed the last of his control. A primal groan seared him in a primitive wave of lust and need. The force of his climax caused his thigh muscles to lock, his vision to blur. All he could see was Nimue's flushed face. And then raw possessiveness engulfed him as his hot seed pumped over her breasts and throat, branding her *his*.

CHAPTER 20

Nimue watched as Tacitus languidly cleaned her with his discarded tunic before tossing the soiled linen aside. Then he propped himself up on one elbow and looked down at her. "How is your shoulder, Nimue?"

Experimentally she rolled her shoulder. It ached, and after the night's exertions was a little sore, but certainly it was nothing to warrant mentioning. Then she saw the frown on Tacitus' face, and realized he'd noticed her inadvertent wince. And something occurred to her.

Tacitus wouldn't scorn her if she admitted the injury still caused her discomfort. Unlike her own people, he wouldn't think her weak or complaining unnecessarily. And while, at her core, she valued the strength of mind and body that her people expected from their Druids, she couldn't deny the flare of comfort that Tacitus' obvious concern gave her.

"It's a little uncomfortable." She felt blood heat her cheeks at her confession. But Tacitus didn't look at her as though she had just displayed self-indulgent weakness. He looked concerned as though he imagined she blamed him for her discomfort. "But nothing to concern yourself with," she added hastily, as guilt ate through her at the way she had succumbed to this Roman's perception of her. But it had been so long since someone had asked her how she was. So long since her well-being had been genuinely enquired after. Since the Romans had invaded, as long as a warrior could stand, then they were expected to fight, no matter how many injuries they had sustained. And she agreed. If her shoulder had been injured while she was with her people, then she would have found another way to attack the enemy until she was able to once again use her bow.

But she was not with her people. She was with Tacitus. And Tacitus, even though he was a hated Roman, didn't crave to see her suffer.

"I still have the opium Marcellus gave me." Tacitus shifted on the bed and then gently brushed back an errant curl that had fallen across her cheek. "Shall I get it for you?"

Shame burned through her at how she had misled Tacitus. She wasn't a fragile woman of Rome. She was a Druid of Cymru. And yet despite it all she could not deny how Tacitus' concern warmed her battered heart.

"It's not that bad," she began, and then the rest of her words locked in her throat as a shaft of blinding sunlight dazzled her mind's eye. She froze, and from the light saw a shadow approaching. A majestic figure and terror whipped through her, although she could not grasp why. And then the figure held out its hand and all she could see was a shard of magical bluestone; the bluestone that she had lost.

An eerie trickle of familiarity caused the hairs to rise on the back of her neck. She couldn't think why this scene was familiar, and yet it clawed through her soul as if the fact she had forgotten was somehow shocking.

A vision.

But a vision of what? Of whom?

Gwydion. The name brushed through her mind like the scuttle of spider legs. But why would that great god come to her, a mere acolyte? And why did she have this overwhelming urge to accept the opium from Tacitus when her injury didn't warrant it even when she acknowledged it still pained her?

The uneasy notion that Gwydion was sending her a message haunted her mind. But she knew she was mistaken. He was not a god who wasted his time with a Druid who was not one of his Chosen.

"Nimue." Tacitus' voice was sharp and she looked at him, her thoughts still racing through her mind. Before she could stop herself, she wrapped her hand around his wrist.

"I've lost my bluestone, Tacitus." The words were out before she could prevent them, but strangely she didn't regret them. Perhaps, as remote as the possibility could be, Tacitus might somehow find the sacred shard.

He stared at her as if she had lost her mind. "Your bluestone?"

She took a deep breath. Understanding illuminated her mind as the strange vision of Gwydion suddenly became clear. Why else had Arianrhod sent her brother god to her at this precise moment, with the bluestone in his hand if not to show Nimue that Tacitus could help?

"It's very precious to me." Her voice cracked and she hastily cleared her throat. "Is it possible one of your men might have found it?" *After I was shot?*

An odd expression crossed his face. At any other time, she might have thought it was guilt, but what did Tacitus have to be guilty about her bluestone?

"I took a sharp stone from one of your pouches. It looked very much like part of a broken weapon to me." His frown was formidable but instead of outrage that he had taken her bluestone, relief washed through her and she laughed.

It was safe. She hadn't lost it. Surely now Arianrhod would come to her?

Tacitus cursed under his breath and pushed himself from the

bed. "I trust you won't slit my throat with it if I return your precious bluestone."

"It's a sacred shard, Tacitus. It's never occurred to me to use it as a weapon before now."

"I find that hard to believe." His tone was skeptical but the smoldering glance he threw her way caused her pussy to quiver. She watched him march to his casket, unlock it and then search inside. But her attention slipped and instead she admired the poetic play of his muscles, his firm sculpted flesh and irresistible backside that she had the extraordinary desire to bite.

She licked her lips and tried to order her thoughts. But they would not be ordered. Any more than the insidious need to take the opium could be scrubbed from her mind. Yet, for some reason she couldn't fathom, the opium and the vision were somehow linked.

As Tacitus stood and turned back to her, holding two leather pouches in his hand, the answer struck her. On special days dedicated to the gods, the greatest of Druids would prepare sacred concoctions known only to the Elders. During the ritualistic celebrations they would ascend into trance and mingle with the deities and then return with great wisdom to impart.

Awe unfurled in her breast as she watched Tacitus sit on the bed and open the largest pouch. She had only just started to learn the power of such magical potions when the Romans had invaded. She knew it was dangerous to attempt such a connection without proper training and support. But suppose Gwydion had just delivered a second sign from her beloved Goddess? A sign that she should take this Roman opium so that she could commune with Arianrhod in an elevated sphere?

"Here." Tacitus tipped the bluestone onto her palm and she closed her fingers over it, relishing how the jagged edges bit into her flesh. Why hadn't she searched his casket more thoroughly the other day?

Tacitus untied the smallest pouch. "There isn't much," he said, frowning at the hidden contents. "Marcellus is uncommonly miserly when it comes to his precious medications."

Nimue hesitated for a moment and then threaded her fingers through his. "Could I save it until my need is greater?" She wasn't lying. But if Tacitus assumed her need involved pain from her injury instead of communing in the higher realms with her Goddess that was scarcely her fault. She needed to persuade him to let her have the opium. Somehow, the thought of taking it from his locked casket, after he left her the following day, didn't feel right anymore.

He weighed the pouch in the palm of his hand and gave her a smile that tugged at her heart. She didn't bother trying to deny it. There was no need. She liked this Roman, despite all the reasons why she shouldn't. But that fact wouldn't blind her to the truth or what she needed to accomplish.

"Can I trust you not to poison me in my sleep?"

She smiled back. She couldn't help herself and again she had to forcibly remember that he was her enemy. "Yes. Why do you so readily assume I wish to kill you? I have no desire to be handed over to your commanding officer for committing such a crime."

"I'm relieved to hear it." He placed the pouch on her thigh. "It would be an ignoble end, even for me."

"Even for you?" His enigmatic comment intrigued her more than the contents of the pouch and she stared at him, trying and failing not to become ensnared by his eyes or his smile or— everything about him. "A mighty warrior from Rome?" Contempt edged her words but it was faint, insubstantial. Because her contempt was for Rome, not for this warrior even though she knew, logically, the two were intrinsically entwined.

"Is that how you see me, Nimue?" Far from appearing insulted by her barbed words he looked anything but. "A mighty warrior from Rome?"

Goddess, he was laughing at her again. Did all Romans possess this sense of irreverence, or was it peculiar to Tacitus?

Or was it simply something corrupt within her blood that found him so irresistible?

That possibility stung, but not as much as it should. She ignored it, as she had ignored so many things since she'd been captured. There would be time enough later, after she'd completed her mission, to repent of such oversights.

"What else can you be?" And then, although she knew she shouldn't continue this conversation because of its inherent dangers, she couldn't stop herself. "What do you see when you look at me, Tacitus?"

A lazy smile tilted his lips as he proceeded to scrutinize her from her tangled hair to her bare toes. She told herself it was not the scrutiny of a master to his slave and convinced herself with little difficulty. How easily she could delude herself when it came to Tacitus.

"I see a beautiful woman who looks in sore need of nourishment."

What else had she expected? That he would look beyond his Roman prejudices and see her for who she truly was?

She didn't want him to see her as she truly was. If he ever did, it would be her death sentence. Yet her emotions warred within her breast, and she couldn't fathom what it was she really wanted.

For Tacitus to acknowledge her warrior strength? When she had just admitted that her injury still pained her? No wonder he thought she was a weak woman, akin to the milk-blooded Roman females.

Yet that was exactly what she wanted him to believe. The Gaul had told her it was her only weapon, and the longer she remained under Roman rule the more she accepted its truth. No matter how it jarred her senses.

Except she didn't want Tacitus to believe that of her. She

didn't want to lie to him, even by omission. Yet if she didn't stop such treacherous thoughts from polluting her mind then how could she hope to summon the conditions necessary in order to launch her rescue?

"I am hungry." It was the truth but it sounded like a confession of weakness. She glared at the pouch on her thigh so Tacitus couldn't see the confusion in her eyes. "Tacitus, am I permitted to leave your quarters during the day?"

When he didn't answer straightaway she looked up at him, and caught a bemused expression on his face. As if he couldn't understand her sudden shift in conversation.

She should have been more subtle. Stoked his ego, bolstered his pride and then made her request when he was thoroughly convinced she was as harmless and incapable as he clearly suspected she might be.

But she couldn't do it. It was one thing to gain his trust so she achieved freedom of movement. But it was, she had discovered, quite another to forcibly subdue her nature in order to deliberately misdirect him.

"Why do you want to leave my quarters?"

So I can discover where you're keeping the Briton queen and princess. It was the overriding truth, but it wasn't the only reason. And while she couldn't tell Tacitus her primary motivation, she could share her other reasons without betraying her loyalty.

"I'm not used to—" She hesitated, suddenly unsure whether she wanted to share this particular confession. But Tacitus remained silent, remained focused on her, and in the end what did it matter what she confessed if it achieved her aim? "Being confined inside for such extended lengths of time."

"I fear my quarters don't extend to a private courtyard for your use." For some reason that appeared to irk him, as if the lack of a courtyard—whatever that might be—reflected badly on him. "I didn't forget my promise to take you for a walk this evening, Nimue. But I was unavoidably detained."

She should be offended at the way he assumed she needed to be taken for a walk. But his obvious irritation at the fact he had broken his word charmed her. Not least because he had actually *recalled* making such a promise.

"I wasn't suggesting you'd broken your word." How odd she could say such a thing to him and mean it. "But I'm used to being active all day. I fear I may lose my mind if all I see all day are these walls and ceiling pressing down on me."

The words were out before she could prevent them and she stared at him, appalled at how easily she had let him see her vulnerability. Yet it was true. No matter how magnificent Tacitus' quarters were—and she had to admit, the intricately patterned stonework floors and astonishing proportions of the rooms were like nothing she had ever imagined before—they still confined her.

His frown intensified. "Active?" he repeated, sounding mystified. It was obvious he couldn't imagine what she might mean. "Surely you had servants and slaves of your own, Nimue, to undertake menial tasks outside?"

Of course she had—before the invasion. But everything had changed with the coming of the Romans.

She opened her mouth to explain, and then realized to do so would be a grave mistake. Because how could she tell him that she had spent most days engaged in memorizing the sacred Druidic knowledge of the ages?

As an acolyte just over halfway through her training she had also been expected to help their people whenever necessary. Her skills as a healer and special affinity with the Moon Goddess had quickly spread among the women who had sought her advice and wisdom on the complexities of their feminine cycles and fertility.

She couldn't tell Tacitus the whole truth. But she could share…a little.

"I would comfort my people in need," she said with quiet

dignity. "And commune with my Goddess. All I ask is that I'm permitted to leave your quarters during the day."

"And am I to believe you wouldn't attempt to run away at the first opportunity?"

She had no intention of running away like a common thief. When the time was right, she would execute her carefully planned escape. But first she had to find the queen.

"You have my word I won't run away at the first opportunity." It wasn't a lie, so why did it feel like one? Tacitus should phrase his questions more carefully. But thank her Goddess that he did not. "Where would I go, Tacitus?"

He cradled her face in his hand and his gaze touched her soul. "You could go nowhere, Nimue." There was an odd note of regret in his voice. "By Roman law you would be brought back to me in chains, and gods know that's not what I want. I'll arrange for my seamstress to accompany you on a daily walk, on condition you don't leave the garrison and that you're back before I return from duty. Do you agree?"

She bristled at the thought of one of his insufferable servants accompanying her, but at least she had negotiated a measure of freedom. She would find a way to discover the information she required without raising the suspicion of her spy.

"I do," she said, and when Tacitus leaned toward her and kissed the tip of her nose it was hard to remember why there were so many things she had to keep secret from him.

CHAPTER 21

By the third day the seamstress, a Roman woman well into middle age and not conversant with the Celtic tongue, had mellowed sufficiently to allow Nimue to explore the markets by herself, so long as she remained within visual contact. It was a vast improvement on the first morn when the woman had shown her disapproval with her folded arms, pursed lips and dagger-like glares.

Clearly she believed the upstart slave would be troublesome and autocratic, and so Nimue had conversed with her in Latin, adjusted her stride to the woman's slower pace and consulted her on the purchase of lengths of fine wool.

Nimue wasn't sure why she was compelled to barter two of her bracelets for the wool. Tacitus' servants had presented her with more than sufficient clothing—even if the two gowns were far too Roman for her liking—and yet the need had been insistent and so she had succumbed.

When they had returned to Tacitus' quarters on that first day, Nimue had further charmed the seamstress by requesting her wisdom on the best methods of converting the wool into serviceable over-gowns. Not that Nimue was incapable of such tasks herself yet, once again, she had felt compelled to ask for assistance. And this morn, as she wandered unchaperoned among the market stalls, she understood why.

It had been to gain the other woman's trust.

Surely her Goddess worked in the most wondrous of ways. For such a tactic would never have occurred to Nimue by herself, of that she was certain.

Now when she conversed with stallholders, she could direct the conversation how she wished. She had a good idea of the structure of the interior of the fortification, and knew where the officers' and legionaries' quarters were, where the healer practiced his arts and the location of the heathen sacrificial altars. She had yet to discover where captives were held.

What she had discovered, though, was that the fortification was not closed to those who lived in the surrounding settlement. There was a freedom of movement she found astonishing and while only part of the fortification was open to the general populace that was more than she'd anticipated. She was certain that, somehow, it would aid in her plans for rescuing the queen.

"My lady. I hope you're recovering well from your injury."

Nimue swung round and stared at the Roman officer who had spoken her language and stood smiling down at her. Did she know him? Why did he address her as if they were acquainted? Or perhaps he was merely enquiring after her health because he was a friend of Tacitus.

She inclined her head in acknowledgment. And then, obscurely, the Gaul's words came back to her. Her only weapon and means of defense was to use the Romans' perception of her against them. She might be well on the way to full health but there was no need to let this Roman know.

"As well as can be expected." It occurred to her she should wince in pain, or perhaps hold her injured arm. The image turned her stomach and besides she wasn't sure she could carry off such a masquerade.

"Rest assured," the Roman said, taking another step toward her, a look of concern on his face, "I personally ensured that the one responsible was duly punished for his crime."

The auxiliary who had approached her as they'd set up camp. She hadn't understood why he'd been punished for shooting her but it appeared this Roman was the one responsible.

And he expected her to be grateful for it.

"In a battle it's expected that the enemy will shoot each other." She tried to keep her voice even so this Roman wouldn't guess how his remark had irritated her but by the way he raised his eyebrows she wasn't sure she'd succeeded. Perhaps her best course of action was to keep her mouth shut altogether.

"The battle was over, my lady. And no warrior worthy of the name would shoot an innocent woman in cold blood."

How blind these Romans were. She bit her tongue and embraced the sharp pain that cleared her mind. There was no point defending her position. It would achieve nothing but the possibility of angering this officer. Instead she should use her feminine wiles, the way the Gaul had indicated. The way she had failed to use them on Tacitus, because Tacitus, despite their short acquaintance, knew her too well to fall for them.

Besides, she didn't wish to pretend to be someone she wasn't with Tacitus. The one time she had tried, by refusing to embrace the orgasm that had threatened to consume her, what had she gained? Nothing but rabid frustration and an unpleasant coldness that had lingered between them until his commanding officer had shaken the shades from her eyes.

She affected a soft sigh, as if the memory of being shot was too traumatic to recall. "I'm eternally grateful that Tacitus didn't leave me to be rounded up with the rest of the captives."

The Roman's eyes widened at her use of Tacitus' name and again she stamped down the flare of anger. Why was it so odd that she used his name? First the healer, and now this officer reacted as if it was something extraordinary. Was she supposed to refer to him by his rank?

Another thought occurred to her. One that should have occurred to her immediately. It was more likely that, as his slave, she should call him her master. It was how slaves referred to their owners in her society so why would it be different for Romans?

The difference was that this time she was the slave. And even to keep up this flimsy masquerade she wasn't certain she could force *that* word between her lips.

"My lady," the Roman said, and in her peripheral vision she saw the seamstress edge closer, clearly unsure whether to intercede or not, "such a fate for you never crossed my mind. My first imperative was to ensure your wellbeing."

She trawled through her memories, but after the arrow had struck she could recall nothing clearly until waking in Tacitus' tent. Had this officer seen her unconscious by the mountain stream? The knowledge that she'd been so vulnerable and unaware sent a trickle of unease along her spine. "You were there?"

He smiled, and a detached section of her mind acknowledged that he possessed an autocratic beauty of his own. But almost instantly, the impact of his words wiped out any other consideration.

He had been there when Tacitus had claimed her freedom. Did he know anything about the queen and princess?

"I persuaded my esteemed cousin to save you from the indignity of being herded with the others. You are clearly no peasant, my lady, and deserve a better fate than that."

None of her people deserved such a fate at the hands of the Romans, but it was equally clear this Roman had no idea he'd just insulted her by his words. And then his other comment fell into place in her mind.

He and Tacitus were cousins? And he had persuaded Tacitus to save her?

Somehow that didn't feel right. Did this barbarian think to flatter her with such talk?

She was just about to take issue with his comment when something made her glance at the stall to her left that sold small carved timber goods. At eye level, fixed to the wooden pole that supported the awning above the table, an exquisite rendition of an owl observed her with unblinking intensity.

Nimue only just stopped herself from sinking to her knees before the image of her beloved Goddess. The owl was a reminder that she was in the heart of the enemy's camp, that she had to watch her tongue. With this Roman at least, she should play the weak female he clearly imagined she was.

With reluctance, she dragged her gaze from the owl and mentally stiffened her spine. Her pride might weep at what she was about to do, but she would recover. She needed vital information.

"Thank you. I'm most grateful for your benevolence." How the words burned her throat. But the self-satisfied smirk on the Roman's face was more than enough to convince her that she'd sounded genuine. "I don't think I could survive in the pit with the other captives."

Goddess forgive her. Nimue felt her face glow with shame at her words, but she was following Arianrhod's instructions. Yet even knowing that didn't help to ease the acidic scorch of betrayal that seared her. She sounded as though she didn't care about the suffering of her people, as long as she remained free and unchained.

"Do not distress yourself." The Roman's smirk faded as though he imagined she might dissolve into hysterics. "You'll never be put with the other slaves, as long as there's breath left in my body."

Had she a dagger to hand, the breath would leave his body a lot sooner than he imagined. She fought to subdue the enticing thought, in case it showed on her face. "You're very kind." She widened her eyes in the hope it would stop her from baring her teeth in frustration. The Roman stared at her, seemingly entranced, and she forcibly reminded herself of the reason for this deception. "I cannot sleep at night for fear of being thrown into the pit, chained like a wild beast."

"No man would dare chain you." He sounded shocked by the notion, as if the chaining of slaves was unheard of. "And there's no pit, my lady. We're not savages."

She might have been playing to this Roman's prejudices against her sex, but she was sure they kept their prisoners in a primitive pit, without protection against the elements. Perhaps her people had got that wrong.

"You keep the slaves inside?" She injected a note of awe into her voice. Surely he would strike her for her mockery but the Roman appeared completely oblivious to where she was heading. From the corner of her eye she saw the seamstress, a look of agitation on her face, clearly debating the wisdom of approaching while her charge conversed with another officer. It would seem Tacitus hadn't specifically given instructions that she wasn't to speak to another Roman, but that was likely because he never imagined she would.

And she wouldn't have. But this Roman had approached *her*.

"Of course," the Roman said, as though it was imperative she believe him. "We would never subject women and children to unnecessary hardship. They are housed beyond the Veterinarium." He indicated with a jerk of his head the direction that he meant. Nimue stared at him in disbelief at how easily he'd given her the information she sought. Did he even realize the importance of what he'd told her?

"The Veterinarium?" She sounded out the Latin word, although she knew full well what it meant and how to pronounce it.

"For the horses," he said, as if explaining to a small child. "It's next to the Valetudinarium where our physician attends to the sick and injured."

"You have greatly eased my mind." She lowered her gaze to his chest so he wouldn't see that she was anything but subservient or grateful in reality. "Now if you'll excuse me, I must return to Tacitus' quarters."

"It's been a pleasure, my lady. I'm sure we'll meet again very soon."

She offered him a perfunctory smile and watched him stride away. Then she looked in the direction the Roman had pointed out to her.

Seeing the owl just now had been more than a reminder to curb her words. It had been Arianrhod's way of telling Nimue that the Roman could help her. And he had. Surreptitiously she glanced around, but apart from the seamstress, no one took any notice of her.

She could discover where the queen was being held and let her know that Nimue was working on an escape plan. Heart thudding against her ribs she walked purposefully toward the Veterinarium. If she looked as though she had every right to be in this part of the fortification then she was less likely to be stopped. At least, she hoped.

She saw the building she was looking for by the legionary standing guard outside. She took a deep breath, tilted her head in a regal manner and strolled toward the door. The legionary looked her up and down, and clearly liked what he saw if the appreciative grin on his face was anything to go by. Would he be so lax if she had her bow and dagger?

"I am under the tribune's protection." She spoke in Latin and while the words made her feel more like a slave than ever, the effect on the legionary was dramatic. He straightened and took a step back from her, as though to get too close would condemn him to punishment.

Perhaps it would.

"I wish to speak to the prisoners." Nothing would induce her to call them slaves.

The legionary frowned. "Why?"

Why did he think? She forced a smile to her lips and hoped he didn't come from Gaul. Otherwise he'd never fall for her deception. "Because they are my friends."

He glanced around, then clearly came to the decision that she couldn't possibly pose a threat. "Very well." He turned and unlocked the door. "But only for a few moments."

Nimue took a deep breath and stepped inside. She was taking a risk but there was little else she could do. If one of the women or children recognized her and decided to betray her, all would be lost. But she trusted her Goddess and if the reaction of the legionary was anything to go by, then Arianrhod was by her side.

The conditions were not nearly as bad as she'd feared. They were clean, if sparse, and from a cursory glance it didn't look as if her people had been brutally whipped or been left in chains.

As a couple of the women approached her, she realized something else. The Briton queen and princess weren't there and panic shot through her. It hadn't occurred to her that they wouldn't be here and yet it should have. After all, they hadn't traveled here on foot with the rest of the captives, had they?

"My name is Nimue." She spoke softly, in the language of Cymru, certain that the legionary was trying to eavesdrop. "Where is the Briton queen?"

The women eyed her with suspicion and one of them curled her lip. "How did you escape our fate?" Her words implied that she had a very good idea how Nimue had escaped, and despised her for it.

Her stomach knotted in distress to know that, in truth, the woman was right. Nimue was nothing but a Roman tribune's whore.

But she didn't feel like one. She would never feel like one, not when it came to Tacitus.

There was no time to mourn what could never be. She ignored the woman's hostile glare and pulled the gown over her shoulder so her wound was visible. "I was shot and captured."

The women stared at her injury and their hostility faded a little. The one who had spoken before finally met her gaze again. "The Briton queen has never been with us. She and her daughter are in the building next to this one."

Relief surged through her. She'd feared the Romans had taken the queen somewhere else. She thanked the women and just as she was about to leave, a small child caught her attention. She was clinging to one of the women's legs, and her huge eyes stared up at Nimue in silent entreaty.

Guilt speared through Nimue's breast. How could she leave this child—all the children—the Romans had captured? How could she leave behind the women? But how could she hope to save so many? They were bedraggled and would be caught the moment they set foot outside their prison.

But there had to be something she could do. Her first priority was to the Briton queen but she would not—could not—forsake her countrywomen. She would ask for Arianrhod's guidance. Surely—

Her thoughts were severed by the sound of the legionary's voice addressing a superior officer. *Please don't let it be the commander.* Trepidation licked through her and with a feeling of dread she glanced over her shoulder.

And saw Tacitus glaring at her.

CHAPTER 22

Tacitus stared at Nimue as disbelief thudded in his chest. It had never occurred to him that she would seek out the other slaves.

But he should have. Nimue had made it plain that she resented her enslaved status. He reeled in his sense of betrayal, because logically he knew she hadn't betrayed him. After all, he hadn't specifically ordered her not to visit the slaves.

No. And the reason he hadn't was because he hadn't believed such an order necessary.

She looked at him and the fact she appeared as if she had every right to be there stoked his ire. "Come here." His voice was low, even, and although Nimue did not bat an eyelash, the legionary by his side suppressed a shudder.

Let him shudder. Let him imagine Tacitus was about to unleash fearful punishment upon his errant slave. The notion turned his guts and he spared the other man a lethal glare before once again focusing on Nimue.

She came toward him and once she stood before him, the legionary hastily locked the door.

Tacitus had the mad urge to grip her arm and drag her back to his quarters, as though he was an ignorant slave master who had no control over his property. Instead he marched several paces then stopped, waiting for Nimue to catch up with him.

She stood by his side, as silent as a good slave should be. The thought of Nimue doing anything that a good slave should was laughable.

Except laughing was the last thing he felt like doing.

"What do you think you were doing?" He glared down at her but she refused to cower. Did he really want her to?

"You didn't say I couldn't visit my countrywomen." Pride infused every word and he battled the urge to shake her. Didn't she understand that by going behind his back she eroded his authority? Didn't she realize that it was only his authority—his heritage, rank and honor—that protected her from the fate that awaited her countrywomen?

"How many times have you visited them?" Every day he'd imagined she went to the market, taking the air and exercise she so desperately craved. But had she, instead, spent that time with the other slaves? And why the fuck hadn't his seamstress told him?

"Today was the first time."

The anger simmering beneath the surface of his patrician façade cooled a little at her response. He knew he should doubt her word. Knew she could say anything, do anything, to alleviate his concerns but somehow he knew she spoke the truth.

He knew it, because Nimue wouldn't bother to lie to him in such a matter. She clearly found nothing wrong in what she'd done. He took a deep breath, exhaled slowly.

All she had done was visit the other slaves. If she'd asked him, would he have allowed her to? Why was he so irate by her actions?

But he knew why. It was because he'd imagined her doing one thing during the time he wasn't with her, and she had been doing something quite different. Something no other woman he had met would dream of doing without first asking his permission.

Yet again he faced the fact that Nimue was nothing like any other woman he had met. And as much as he'd managed to delude himself as to how she might behave in his absence, the proof of his misplaced trust had just played out before his eyes.

He didn't have time to take her back to his quarters. Didn't have time to try to analyze what it was about Nimue that so corroded his reason. She was only a woman and her actions shouldn't plague his mind the way they did.

It was good advice. He knew he'd be unable to follow it. "Return to my quarters immediately. We'll discuss this matter when I return this evening." His voice was harsh but he experienced no sense of satisfaction when she stiffened at his tone. She made no response but merely turned and walked to where his seamstress waited. Unease shifted through him. He had the feeling he should've been more specific in his order but what could she do once she was confined in his quarters?

The thought should have reassured him. Instead, inexplicably, it only increased his sense of unformed dread.

～

NIMUE RETURNED TO TACITUS' quarters in silence. The seamstress's frosty attitude confirmed that any small advance she had made in gaining the woman's trust over the last few days had irrevocably shattered.

Not that she cared about the seamstress's trust. It was the look on Tacitus' face as he'd ordered her back to his quarters that haunted her mind. Why had he chosen that very moment to pass the prisoners' building? Why hadn't Arianrhod distracted his attention?

She didn't want Tacitus to distrust her. It was a foolish thought because no matter how much they enjoyed each other's company they were enemies. They would always be enemies. But she craved his admiration in the short time they had left together.

Once she escaped the fortification, Tacitus would despise her. But at least she wouldn't be here to witness it.

Once inside Tacitus' quarters, the seamstress folded her arms and glared at Nimue. Her message couldn't be plainer. Not that it mattered. Nimue had no wish to engage her in conversation or sewing. She needed to answer Arianrhod's command and take the opium.

Although she hadn't encountered this Roman opium before, it had to possess the same magic as the sacred preparations the Elders used in order to enter the realm of the gods. Why else would Arianrhod have kept encouraging her to take the opium?

That she would be alone when she ascended into the higher realms while under the influence of the gods' magic elixir terrified her, but she didn't have a choice. If Arianrhod didn't think her capable of undertaking such a sacred rite, then surely the Great Goddess would not have summoned her.

Nimue couldn't imagine what Arianrhod wanted to command of her, that she couldn't convey during Nimue's normal daily worship. Neither could she imagine why Arianrhod hadn't answered her when Nimue silently begged for guidance. But it was not her place to question. Only to obey.

She picked up a lamp and went into the bedchamber. With trembling fingers she tipped the tiny amount of sticky opium into a small bowl. Tacitus wouldn't be back until that eve. She had plenty of time before she had to face him again.

She sat cross-legged on the floor by the wall opposite the door. From this position she was concealed by the bed should anyone casually open the door and glance into the room. Not that that was any great advantage, since if one of Tacitus' servants took it into their head to look for her, and couldn't see her, they would certainly investigate further and discover she was communing with her Goddess.

She'd face that problem should it occur.

Frowning, she prodded the opium mass with her forefinger. It was wrong to ascend into trance without appropriate rituals and incenses. But since it was also wrong for an acolyte to attempt such a thing on her own in any case, Nimue decided the lack of appropriate preparation was likely the least of her concerns.

She took a deep breath to still her erratic heartbeat and placed the bowl over the oil-filled lamp. It fitted snugly, as if the two pieces belonged together, and through the intricately carved openwork on the sides of the lamp she watched the flame flicker around its wick.

A sweetly pungent aroma drifted in the air and she wrinkled her nose with distaste. But since she would get nowhere by holding her breath she forcibly relaxed her muscles and inhaled deep into her lungs.

The Roman room vanished in a whirlwind and before Nimue had time to even gasp, she was plunged into an eerily familiar setting. A sacred oak glade surrounded her, and the silver moon descended in the starry sky. Fascinated Nimue gazed upward, and then looked back at the glade. And remembered.

This was the night of her initiation into womanhood.

Joy radiated through her and she embraced the feminine power that pulsed in tangible waves through the glade, strengthening not only the Druids but all the tribes of Cymru; reaffirming their position in the hierarchy of creation.

Nimue opened her arms, felt the magical potency of her foremothers surge through her blood. This night was hers. This night she had been chosen, and she would dedicate the rest of her life to the blessed Arianrhod.

And then her mother had taken her into her arms and whispered a secret so great, so terrible, that every dream Nimue had ever cherished trembled on a precipice of betrayal and despair.

Desperately she pushed her mother's arms away, struggled to be free. Yet even as the agonized look on her mother's face faded into the shadows of the forest, Nimue knew she would never be free of the burden that now crushed her heart.

From an incalculable distance came the haunting call of a single owl. Nimue turned, wildly searching for her beloved Goddess, but the glade was now deserted and even as she strained her eyes to see through the encroaching shadows, the night grew darker still.

Dread gripped her and she looked up to the sky. The moon was obscured by storm clouds, black and angry looking, and even Arianrhod's starry wheel was entirely concealed from view.

"Arianrhod, hear my prayer." The words fell from her lips but they were soundless, trapped inside her mind, and terror uncoiled deep in her breast and slid with malicious intent through her veins.

Why did her Goddess not come to her? Hadn't Arianrhod herself called her to this place?

A shadow splintered from the forest that surrounded the glade. For one glorious moment Nimue thought her Goddess had heard her plea. That she had taken pity on her petrified acolyte and would offer her comfort. But as the shadow approached a new fear gripped her, one that dug talons of terror into the core of her being.

It was not Arianrhod who came for her. It was Gwydion, the Magician God, but what caused her to fall to her knees and press her forehead into the grass was the frightening certainty that this wasn't the first time Gwydion had come to her in this sacred glade.

"Nimue, acolyte of my sister goddess Arianrhod, you have finally answered her call." His voice was rich, melodic and again the petrifying certainty that he had greeted her in a similar fashion before gnawed through her senses. "Are you ready to prove worthy of the loyalty your goddess bestows upon you, despite the grave sin that pollutes your blood?"

"Yes, my lord." Nimue kept her face plastered to the ground, too afraid to look at the great god who towered over her, illuminated by his own fearsome, glorious radiance. "I will do anything for my beloved Moon Goddess."

She felt herself rise from the ground, although it was not of her own doing. Her body felt weightless, disconnected, and she feared the slightest breeze might send her through the Veil into the Otherworld. Desperately she wrapped her arms around her waist in a vain attempt to reconnect with reality, but instead all she could do was gaze into Gwydion's fathomless eyes and fear for her sanity.

"Then fulfill your destiny and complete the vision of the High Druid Aeron."

It was her dearest wish to fulfill the vision of that martyred Druid. She clung onto that knowledge but couldn't prevent the unease that washed through her mind, diluting her purpose.

Before she'd met Tacitus, she'd wanted to destroy every Roman who dared set foot in her homeland. But now she was torn. And if Gwydion suspected how her loyalties conflicted, he would strike her dead in an instant.

"My lord." Her whisper barely squeezed through her constricted throat as the great god began to fade into the darkness of the forest. Nimue remained paralyzed, her body and mind severed, and fresh terror seeped through her blood.

Had the Magician God guessed her tangled thoughts? Was this her punishment, to remain forever in the Shadowlands between worlds?

A rush of wind and the soft brush of feathers across her face snapped her from her rising panic. Body and senses realigned; once again she felt solid earth beneath her feet and the dark outline of the sacred owl filled her vision and eased her heart.

Save them all. The powerful, feminine whisper weaved through her mind, and she clung onto the words even though she didn't fully understand their meaning.

The owl soared upward and Nimue followed its path across

the cloudy night. And then her reverential gaze froze. Light and dark combined, an unmistakable tableau created from the swirling clouds by the Moon Goddess' sacred wings.

The form of a newborn babe.

Nimue gasped, fell backward, and hit her head on something hard. Tacitus' bed swam into focus and she blinked slowly, trying to sort her pounding thoughts as she leaned against the wall and fought against the waves of nausea that threatened to consume her.

In a blinding flash of clarity, she understood. Arianrhod was telling her that not everything would be destroyed. That a new life would be created from the ending of the old. That it was her duty to save not only the Briton queen and her daughter, but all those taken captive by the Romans. To lead them back to the magical enclave where they could make plans for their future, before she continued onward with the queen to the land of the Brigantes.

That was why she'd been compelled to make the over-gowns. So that the prisoners wouldn't look like slaves when they made their bid for freedom. So they had a good chance of blending into the local populace.

Something sharp dug into the palm of her hand and with odd reluctance she uncurled her fingers. She knew what she would find. And she was right. It was the shard of bluestone she'd taken before the battle. The shard Tacitus had so recently returned to her.

The Moon Goddess' command could not be clearer. Time was running out and Nimue had to make her stand.

CHAPTER 23

As Tacitus entered his quarters, he mentally stiffened his spine. There was no doubt in his mind that Nimue would be waiting for him, claws unleashed, ready to defend her actions earlier this day. He supposed he should be relieved that she hadn't stood up to him when he'd accosted her in the slaves' quarters. But Nimue was not a fool. She knew certain boundaries couldn't be crossed in public. But when it came to just the two of them, she appeared to acknowledge no boundaries at all.

And curse the woman, but it was that very trait that so intrigued him.

He looked forward to her unorthodox conversation, the way she laughed at him, how she made no secret of what she truly thought even if she ran the risk of offending.

They had met only days ago and yet he could scarcely recall how he'd spent his free time before she came into his life. And with every day that passed the less certain he was that, when his tour of Britannia was over, he would be able to let her go.

The commander would never grant her manumission. Therefore he had no choice but to take Nimue to Rome with him. But it was a poor excuse for the truth. Because the truth had nothing to do with his commander at all.

Nimue drove him to the edge of distraction when they were together, and when they were apart she was never far from his mind. But today, instead of recalling the way she looked and gasped and the evocative scent of sex as she climaxed around him as he usually did, he'd been tormented by what she might be plotting next.

The thought of her in Rome staggered his mind. She would never fit into the role his society expected. Yet the thought of leaving her behind became more intolerable by the hour.

She wasn't waiting for him, as she usually did, in the small living area beyond his office. He wasn't sure whether to take that as a good sign or not. As he turned to make his way to his bedchamber, his seamstress appeared.

"Forgive me, sir." She looked as harassed as she sounded. Gods. What had Nimue got up to now? "The Cambrian took me by surprise when she went to the slaves' quarters. I didn't know whether or not she had your permission to do so."

He smothered a relieved sigh. At least Nimue had done nothing further to upset his servant. "Do not think on it. Nimue didn't disobey me. All is well." And now he was defending her. Yet he spoke only the truth. She hadn't disobeyed him.

But she certainly must know that she had gone against his wishes.

The woman didn't look reassured. "That's a relief to me, sir, but I feel obliged to tell you that before she visited the slaves she conversed most intimately with the tribune—your esteemed cousin—in the marketplace."

Blandus. Now he understood the sly glances his cousin had shot his way when they'd passed each other outside the commander's quarters just now. He'd imagined it was because his cousin had discovered that Nimue had taken it upon herself to visit the slaves' quarters without his permission. Not that he could imagine how his cousin had drawn such a conclusion. But the truth appeared even less appealing. Had Blandus attempted to coerce Nimue into a clandestine liaison? The very thought of it boiled his blood. How dare he?

"I see." He strode toward his bedchamber and with every stride his irritation increased. It was one thing for Nimue to flirt and speak her mind with *him*. It was another thing entirely if she had done the same with his cursed cousin.

He pushed open the door, but she wasn't reclining on the bed. Had he truly expected her to be? She wasn't a Roman noblewoman and not once had she ever tried to mimic one. For some reason that thought irritated him further, although he didn't know why. It wasn't as if he wanted her to pretend to be something she wasn't.

But if she wasn't here, where in the name of Hades was she? Had she managed to evade his servants and the legionary posted outside his quarters and escape?

It was an outrageous thought. Of course she hadn't. Such a feat was impossible. But the image of her standing in the slaves' quarters when she had no right to be there, thudded through his mind.

He had the sudden certainty that if Nimue wanted to elude her watchers, she could.

"Nimue." His voice was sharp, and relief stabbed through him when he caught a movement beyond his bed. He marched across the room and a faint, sweet odor drifted in the air that he could not immediately identify.

Then he saw her, sitting on the floor, her back against the wall, and shock punched through him. She looked up at him, her pupils strangely dilated, and in that same moment he registered the oil lamp in front of her and the burned residue staining the bottom of a small bowl.

He crouched beside her. "Nimue?" Relief that she hadn't escaped mutated into alarm. Gods, what had possessed her to use the opium in such a manner? He should never have entrusted her with it. He'd assumed that, if she needed the pain relief, she would have diluted it with wine or water. Surely, with her healing knowledge, she knew that? Nobody but Oracles inhaled the fucking stuff. It was too dangerous.

"Tacitus." Her voice was husky, as if she found it hard to speak. "I didn't mean for you to find me like this. But I find… I cannot move."

He glared at her to cover the flash of fear that whipped through him. Oracles and soothsayers were accustomed to taking the poppy to commune with the gods and to impart words of wisdom to their worshippers. But they had years of training, years of studying the ways of the gods and they understood how to protect themselves against evil shades that might try to enter their bodies while they were incapacitated.

Suppose Nimue had unknowingly entered that dangerous realm between the living and the dead? Suppose a malignant spirit had taken advantage of her innocence?

"What in the name of Zeus were you doing?" Without thinking, the name of the great god of his beloved mother's people fell from his lips as he scooped Nimue into his arms. Her head lolled against his shoulder and the fact she didn't protest at his action caused the worry to worm further into his chest.

He glowered around the room looking for the cloak he'd provided for her. Unlike the Roman gowns she wore it was a Cambrian garment, necessary for the chill weather, but he couldn't see it anywhere.

Nimue stirred in his arms. She unclenched her fist and he saw a glimpse of the bluestone lying across her palm. "Arianrhod called me."

He forgot about looking for her cloak and stared at her in disbelief. "What?"

Her eyelashes fluttered in an attempt to keep her eyes open. "I tried to find my Goddess. But she was…distant."

A shudder crawled along his spine at her whispered confession. To his knowledge only those most intimate with the gods were allowed passage into the higher realms through sacred rituals and spiritual enhancing preparations. That was how it worked in Rome and he saw no reason why it should be different for the Celts.

Except the spiritual leaders of the Celts were Druids. And Druids were the sworn enemy of Rome, the scourge of the Emperor and were to be eliminated from every last dark corner of the Empire.

The few that had remained here after the Eagle had conquered their people had been driven from Cambria a year ago when a great devastation had ravaged the land.

His gaze fixed on the silver torque around Nimue's throat. The other day he'd been taken by the elegant engravings on her bracelets and had found them oddly familiar. He recognized the same engravings, of the passage of the moon and detailed images of an owl, decorating the torque but that wasn't why he had found them familiar.

It was because the engravings on her silver jewelry were the same as the exquisite embroidery of the medicine bag that had been discovered with the Briton queen.

He could try to deny the truth, the way he'd denied it from the moment the suspicion had first arisen. But there was no longer any doubt in his mind.

Nimue was the healer who'd been traveling with Caratacus' queen. But it wasn't that knowledge that caused his gut to knot. It was the horrifying possibility that Nimue might be more than simply a Celtic noblewoman with an admirable skill for healing.

He wouldn't believe it. Nimue was not connected in any way with the hated Druids who, during the initial invasion of this western peninsula, had incited fear and uprising among the natives of Cambria.

"Tacitus, put me down."

"I'm taking you to Marcellus." He stamped through the doorway but no servants were to hand. Just because Nimue used the poppy in the same way the Oracles did, didn't mean anything. Perhaps she'd merely mimicked a ritual she'd witnessed an ancient Druid perform. "Where in Hades is your cloak?"

"If you put me down, I'll get my cloak." Nimue no longer slurred her words or slumped against him, but neither did she struggle to escape. *Of course she isn't a Druid.* Those heathen creatures were wizened with age and the burden of their barbaric rituals and brutal sacrifices.

He stopped glowering around the room and looked at her, secretly shocked. He'd expected her to protest about going to see Marcellus. To assure him that there was no need. Unease spiked and all thoughts of Druids faded into the depths of his mind. Did she also fear for her health? Somehow that possibility magnified his own concern a thousandfold.

Carefully he lowered her to the floor, holding onto her arms until he was reassured she wasn't in danger of collapsing. She shot him a glance he couldn't quite fathom—an odd combination of exasperation and amusement. He wasn't sure whether to be charmed or insulted.

"Do you often put your life in danger in order to commune with your goddess?" Perhaps, after all, the Celts did such things differently from his own people. It made more sense than the other possibility. He watched her go back into the bedchamber, push the bluestone into one of her leather pouches and retrieve her cloak, which had slid onto the floor behind his casket. He followed her and swung the heavy material around her shoulders. The cold fear that had gripped him just moments before faded. Nimue's eyes were focused; her balance restored and as far as he could tell no malignant spirit fought a battle for her body.

She was still going to see Marcellus, though. And he hadn't yet discarded the idea of taking her to the temple located within the garrison and offer sacrifice for her safety, just to be on the safe side.

"My life wasn't in danger." There was a haughty note in her voice and his relief increased. With every word she uttered she sounded more like her usual self. How long would it take her to recall the way he'd ordered her back to his quarters earlier? He was sure she had no intention of letting that pass uncontested. "You weren't supposed to discover me meditating. I wasn't expecting you back for the midday meal."

His relief vanished. He'd last seen Nimue shortly before the midday meal, but that had been hours ago. Was she truly unaware that it was early evening? "How long did you commune with your goddess, Nimue?"

She gave an impatient sigh as if his questions wearied her. "Not long. And the experience has left me famished."

He pulled open the door and led her outside. She paused, a frown on her face, and glanced up at the sky as if the position of the sun puzzled her. He knew Oracles could spend countless hours in trance and then behave as if mere moments had elapsed. The look on Nimue's face suggested that she had no idea how long she'd been insensible and couldn't fathom why the sun had moved so far to the western horizon.

If she had inhaled the poppy before, she would know of its time-altering perceptions. If she was a Druid she wouldn't look bemused by the fact many hours had passed since they had last spoken.

As they made their way toward the Valetudinarium he almost convinced himself. But one fact hammered in the back of his mind, an insistent refrain. Abruptly he stopped and pulled Nimue toward him, uncaring of who might see or later comment. "What possessed you to smoke the opium as if you were a priestess?"

Her eyes widened and for one eternal, tortured moment he saw guilt flare in her beautiful green depths. His chest constricted and heart slammed against his ribs in denial, and only years of rigorous training prevented him from reeling back in shock.

I'm mistaken. There was no guilt in her eyes, only confusion. And she was right to be confused because how could he think to accuse her of being a priestess? To even suspect she was in any way connected to the Druid cult that had once polluted this corner of the Empire could result in her death.

"I don't know." She sounded unsure, as if for the first time she was actually considering the matter. "My Goddess commanded it." Still she did not sound entirely convinced and he gritted his teeth before he could ask any other probing question.

Since when did the gods—or heathen goddesses in this case—demand such things from their ordinary followers? It was the kind of command they issued to the devoted, to those who dedicated their lives to serving the gods' obscure wishes.

To those who would know how to conduct themselves in the presence of immortals; those who were trained in the ways to channel demands from the deities to the common man.

Nimue was no Druid. But others might see her differently. He couldn't take the chance that her ill-advised use of the poppy could be misconstrued. The less people who knew of it the safer she would be. And while he trusted Marcellus with his life, he would trust no one but himself with Nimue's.

"Say nothing of this to Marcellus." He kept his voice low, his gaze locked with Nimue's and hoped that, for once, she would obey him without question. "Not everyone is willing to overlook the worship of foreign gods."

He wasn't including Marcellus, but let her believe so if it would ensure she held her tongue. Then he saw her frown, recognized the question in her eyes, and belatedly recalled what he'd told her the other day.

Rome embraced the gods of other cultures, so long as their own deities remained supreme. Would she remind him?

"I understand." There was a hushed tone in her voice that convinced him she truly did understand. That did not ease his mind. "I don't know what possessed me, Tacitus. Arianrhod has never commanded me to do anything like that before."

Heedless of protocol he wrapped his arm around her shoulders and resumed walking. She spoke of her goddess not as if she were an unreachable deity to be worshipped from afar, but as though they were on intimate terms.

He tried to shove the word from his mind but it lingered all the same.

Priestess.

Was it possible to be a Celtic priestess yet not be a cursed Druid as well? The question hovered on the tip of his tongue but he swallowed the words.

He didn't want to know.

CHAPTER 24

As Tacitus led her into the healer's dwelling, a surprisingly large structure, Nimue's heart hammered against her breast and her stomach churned with nerves at what a foolish, irresponsible risk she' taken.

But when she'd returned to her body, she'd thought only moments had passed while she had trembled before Gwydion and seen the mystical message in the cloudy sky. She had never intended for Tacitus to find the evidence of what she'd done, much less discover her in such a disoriented state.

She'd seen the question in his eyes. Yet he hadn't accused her outright. Did that mean she'd deflected his suspicion? Or was it merely her own guilt at her reckless behavior she had seen reflected back at her?

Perhaps the thought that she was an acolyte, a Druid in training, had truly not crossed his mind. If it had surely he wouldn't have wound his arm around her shoulders. His loyalty to Rome would demand he take her to his commander where she would be interrogated and tortured until they decided to crucify her.

The pit of her stomach knotted, causing familiar waves of

dread to burn through her veins. She wanted to believe that Tacitus didn't suspect her but she couldn't fully believe it. Because if so, why had he warned her against telling Marcellus the truth of what she'd been doing?

As they entered the building a faint scent of astringent lingered in the air. Distracted from her troubling thoughts she gazed at the scrubbed floor and then looked up along the passageway. It appeared that many rooms inhabited this dwelling. How different it was from the sacred glades or simple huts where her people tended the sick.

They were shown into a small room that looked to be Marcellus' private office. How dearly these Romans loved their offices, but unlike Tacitus' one back at his quarters there were no detailed maps of the area on the wall. Instead there were astonishingly accurate portrayals of the human body.

Fascinated, Nimue stared, once again forgetting her current precarious predicament. She knew Romans had a better grasp of healing than her people gave them credit for, but it appeared their knowledge in matters of the internal body was also more advanced than she'd imagined.

If only she and Marcellus could talk as one healer to another. Less than a moon ago, she would have scorned the thought that a Roman might teach her anything when it came to the healing arts but now she was not so close-minded.

The thought might be sacrilege to her people but the thirst for knowledge was ingrained into the fabric of her being. Yet even as she harbored the fragile hope, she knew it was futile.

She wouldn't be here long enough to learn anything of significance, even if she was permitted to barter her knowledge in exchange.

"Medicine intrigues you." Tacitus' hand slid along the length of her arm before resting possessively over her hip. She turned to him and didn't even try to hide how fascinating she found the contents of this room.

"I love learning new ways to heal." The knowledge of the Druids was vast and went back countless generations. How ancient was the knowledge of the Romans? "My grandmother was a revered healer. I knew I wanted to follow her path when I was but three summers old."

His lip quirked, clearly amused that she had been so strong-minded at such a tender age. "How fortunate you were permitted to follow your heart's desire."

Although he smiled, there was something in his tone that intrigued her.

She threaded her fingers through his as they cradled her hip. "Did you not always wish to be a great Roman warrior, Tacitus?" She'd taken it for granted that he was following his choice of career. But then, what did she truly know of a Roman's choice of career?

"My career was preordained before I was even conceived." He gave a short laugh but he didn't sound especially amused anymore. "My mother wishes me to secure an excellent military record and then progress to the highest echelons of the Senate."

It was the second time he'd referred to his mother in such a manner that clearly showed how deeply he respected her. While she admired him for it, she couldn't help wondering about his father. "And what does your father wish for you?"

He gave her an oddly haunted look, although she couldn't imagine why her question appeared to wound him. "That is my father's wish." There was a hollow note to his voice that pierced her heart. "My mother's dearest desire is that I please him."

Nimue couldn't tear her gaze from him. It was wrong that his evident familial conflict touched her so, but it did. And the fleeting glimpse of vulnerability that had flickered in his eyes at the mention of his mother's dearest desire tormented her. Why was he so torn between his parents' ambitions for his future when both his mother and father appeared to be in accord?

"But what do you want to do with your life, Tacitus?"

He stared at her and she had the strangest certainty that no one had ever asked him that question before. She held her breath, prayed to her Goddess that Marcellus wouldn't appear yet, and willed Tacitus to tell her his deepest, darkest secret.

"I intend to go into law," he said at last and she frowned, bemused. That didn't sound so terribly rebellious or shocking to her. "And for that, naturally, I need an excellent military record and influential support from members of the Senate." There was no mistaking the edge of contempt in his words. It was obvious the fact he was required to follow his father's designated career path, in order to secure his own, rankled.

She tried to see it from his view, but couldn't. As a matter of course, Druids learned all aspects of their culture that had evolved since the time of Creation, including the intricacies of their laws. An acolyte specialized according to their special gifts and the will of their heart, but it didn't stop them from becoming an esteemed scholar in more than one discipline.

And then something occurred to her. "Your father doesn't wish you to practice your laws? Is it not an honorable career in Rome?"

"No, it's an honorable career path. But whereas my father wishes me to use my time in the courts as a stepping stone in my political advancement, I intend it to be far more than that."

"More?" Enthralled, Nimue leaned toward him, delighting in the evocative scent of leather and forests and horse that emanated from him. "What do—"

Her question lodged in her throat as the door swung open and Marcellus entered. She swallowed her disappointment, along with the haunting certainty that the moment had been lost forever.

Tacitus would never confide in her like that again. Because she could no longer delay making plans for the queen's escape.

"And how is my favorite patient?" Marcellus shot Tacitus a

grin, clearly daring him to respond, but Tacitus remained silent, although his fingers tightened against her hip.

"I'm recovering well." Should she mention that she had taken the opium? It was, after all, the reason Tacitus had insisted they come to see the healer.

"Nimue had a bad reaction to the opium." Tacitus glanced at her and she understood what he was saying. Marcellus could know she had taken the opium, but not her method.

Marcellus' grin faded into a frown. "Were you nauseous? Disoriented?"

"Yes," Tacitus said before she could respond. "I merely want you to ensure that she is suffering from no lingering aftereffects."

Any other time she would have taken offense at the way he answered for her. But since she was not entirely certain how much to confide in Marcellus, she decided to hold her tongue. The look Tacitus shot her conveyed that he was both surprised and relieved at her forbearance.

Marcellus continued to ask questions as he examined her shoulder and the back of her head where she'd hit it on the rock. Surely he would question why she'd taken the opium now when there was no need? But he didn't.

Finally he pronounced her well enough and she gave a silent sigh of relief. There was something she wanted to ask of him. It was the reason she hadn't argued when Tacitus had suggested they visit Marcellus. And although there was no need—after all, she would be leaving soon and what did another night or two truly matter—she wanted to make the most of the time she had left with Tacitus.

"There's something else."

The two men turned and looked at her and she gave Tacitus a reassuring smile, since the alarm that flashed in his eyes was oddly endearing.

"It's unconnected to my injuries. But it's a matter that I've wanted to speak with you about for some time." Since she'd met

Tacitus, and although it was only six days it somehow seemed she had known her Roman for so much longer than that.

"You didn't mention any other problem." Tacitus sounded irked by the fact and she gave him a comforting pat on the arm before turning back to Marcellus. Who had a look of combined disbelief and barely concealed amusement warring for dominance on his face.

"I would dearly like," she said, "the means to prevent conception and cleanse my womb of—"

"Nimue!" Tacitus sounded as if he was being strangled. "I've taken care of this."

She glanced at him and then couldn't look away. The expression on his face suggested she had just grievously insulted his honor when all she'd been trying to do was make things easier for them.

Once again she reached out and curled her fingers around his biceps. Goddess, she enjoyed touching him. How dreadfully she would miss this contact. "I know. But I don't like the feel of that..." What had he called it? "Condom. And it's an odious task to perform when we should be thinking of nothing but each other."

This time it was Marcellus who choked. Tacitus simply stared at her in what looked like rising horror. She slid her hand along his arm and threaded her fingers through his. What had she said that was so terrible? Tacitus was her lover and Marcellus was a healer. It wasn't as if she had shared such intimacies with his servants or strangers, was it?

"Alas," Marcellus sounded like a fist blocked his throat. "I'm not conversant in such feminine matters."

Aghast at such lack of basic knowledge, Nimue stared at him. "But understanding the cycle of the moon and her power over her children is one of the fundamental teachings for healers." Certainly, the moon governed women in a more noticeable manner but men were just as bound by her rule. She was, after all, the One who presided over fertility—and provided the means for counterbalance.

"Gods." Tacitus gripped her arm and swung her around. "Marcellus is a physician in the Legions, Nimue. He has no need for such understandings."

"If you have no objection, Tacitus," Marcellus said, "I would be interested to hear what Nimue has to say. I'm always open to new ideas."

Nimue nearly spluttered at the thought of such knowledge being new but instantly realized what the healer had just revealed. A willingness to learn. Was it possible she would be able to trade knowledge with him after all?

"Very well." Tacitus' voice was stiff. It was obvious the concession gave him great pain. "But I insist on absolute confidentiality in this matter."

"You have it." Marcellus turned to Nimue and there was no mistaking the anticipation in his eyes. "Would you care to visit the herb gardens?"

~

THE HERB GARDEN, situated in a paved area in the center of the four-sided Valetudinarium, was impressive. With Tacitus hovering beside her, a dark scowl on his face, she traded tidbits with Marcellus in exchange for acquiring the herbs she needed.

As well as a couple she didn't. But the impulse to take the plants that induced sleep was overwhelming, and since they were also useful in pain relief Marcellus didn't query when she added them to her pile.

She wasn't entirely sure why she needed them. She had no intention of using them on Tacitus in order to facilitate her escape. To do so would somehow be an insult to her honor, although she didn't investigate that emotion too closely.

Shouldn't she be prepared to use every weapon possible to gain the advantage?

When they finally left Marcellus, the sun had dipped low in the sky. A sudden burst of loud, raucous laughter ripped through the cocoon of tranquility that had settled around her and she swung about. A group of legionaries lounged against the wall of the prisoners building, jostling each other and trading coarse jests.

Horror crawled along her spine as she watched one of the Romans saunter up to the door and enter. Instinctively her hand went to her shoulder, searching for an arrow, but her bow was no longer her constant companion.

"Nimue." Tacitus' voice was low. "Come away."

Rage boiled in the pit of her stomach. "It's wrong, Tacitus." Her voice was as low as his, although the legionaries appeared oblivious to their presence.

"I know."

His simple agreement, without any attempt at justifying the situation, pierced through her outrage. She looked up at him, in the dying rays of the sun, and saw a hard gleam in his eyes as he glared at the legionaries.

This was what he had saved her from. With a flash of insight she knew that, if it was within his power, he would have done the same for all the captives. Given them the freedom she now enjoyed, even if that freedom came at the price of being called... his slave.

She bit her lip and frowned back at the legionaries. While she had willingly shared Tacitus' bed, her people had been subject to unrelenting rape and abuse. And while she would have been a liability with an injured shoulder, her wound was sufficiently healed for her to now take up the mantle of responsibility.

A hollow sensation filled her chest at the knowledge that she didn't have the luxury of even another day with Tacitus. Was that why Arianrhod had called her into the higher realms? To remind

Nimue of her responsibilities? Tacitus had served his purpose. It was time to serve hers. She needed to strategize and execute her plans, and quickly, before further harm befell the captives.

"I must help them, Tacitus." The words fell from her lips before she could prevent them, but as horror at her unguarded tongue flooded through her, it was instantly calmed by the strange certainty that she had done the right thing.

Tacitus wouldn't condemn her for speaking from her heart.

His heavy sigh weaved through her blood and sank into the hidden depths of her soul. Instinctively she clasped his hand, as though on some level it was him who needed comfort. "There's nothing you can do. This is an inevitable repercussion of war."

She pressed closer and fought against the absurd sting of tears that prickled the back of her eyes. There was something she could do to save her people but she couldn't tell Tacitus of the plan beginning to form in her mind.

She could only share with him her half-formed preparations. "I could give them clean clothes. Blankets. It's not much but it might help ease conditions."

As Tacitus turned to give her a brooding look, something cracked deep inside her breast. She wanted to give the prisoners the clothes she and the seamstress had made during the last few days. Yes, it would ease conditions—and when they escaped they wouldn't look as if they'd been held captive.

Yet lying to Tacitus, even though she had no choice if she wanted to help her people survive, hurt more than she had ever imagined possible.

"Is that why you went there today? To see what conditions they were living in?" There was a guarded note in his voice as though that possibility had only just occurred to him.

"Yes." She wondered that he could hear her response, her voice was so choked with tears she could never allow to fall.

"That could be arranged." There was the slightest hint of suspicion in his voice as if he doubted her true motives, but at least he'd agreed. She should be elated at this added concession but all she felt was the acrid scorch of betrayal. "I'll inform the legionary on guard duty tomorrow to expect you." His grip around her hand tightened. "Don't try anything dangerous, Nimue."

CHAPTER 25

*I*n the back of her mind, Nimue knew this night was the last night they would have together. She couldn't allow her people to continue in their captivity, and she could no longer delay in fulfilling her pledge to Caratacus to safely deliver his queen and daughter to the land of the Brigantes.

When they finished their meal, Tacitus dismissed his servants and showed her the kitchen, where she would prepare her herbal teas in the morn. But she didn't want to think of the following day. Because that was the day she would say goodbye to Tacitus forever.

He avoided all mention of her unauthorized visit to the prisoners or the way she had taken the opium. Instead, he appeared fascinated by the magic of her herbs. And, against the unwritten laws of her people, she found herself telling him of the ways a woman could assist or prevent conception. She trailed the tip of her finger along the table in the center of the room. "Is such knowledge denied to the women of Rome?"

"It's not something I've ever considered." He sounded as though he confessed to a great sin. "If such knowledge was freely available, perhaps it would have saved my adoptive mother great heartache."

His adoptive mother? She trawled frantically through the conversations they had shared. He'd mentioned his mother several times. It had never occurred to her that she had traveled onto the next stage of her journey.

"I'm sorry for your loss." How long ago had it occurred? No wonder he sounded so tortured when he spoke of his mother's wish for his future career. And yet...her thoughts tumbled, uncertain. He had always spoken of her as if she was still in the mortal realm.

Tacitus frowned, seemingly baffled. "My loss?"

Nimue fought the urge to squirm. She had the feeling she completely misunderstood his words but had no idea in what way. "Of your birth mother," she clarified, as heat washed through her. "It's—hard to accept." Such an understatement. Even with the passage of fourteen full moons since her own mother's murder, the wound remained raw in her heart.

Tacitus' frown faded, but his intense gaze didn't waver. "My birth mother still lives, Nimue." His voice was gentle, as if he realized her confusion but his words merely confused her further. How could he possess an adoptive mother if his blood mother still survived?

"I don't understand." The admission hurt, but not as much as it would have a quarter moon ago. "When you spoke to me before of your mother, of whom were you referring?"

He smiled, but it was a pensive smile and she couldn't help but cradle his jaw in her hand, or caress the corner of his lips with her thumb. She didn't like to see her Roman sad.

How far she had fallen in so short a time.

"I spoke to you of them both." He took her braid and allowed the heavy rope to slide along his fingers. "My birth mother, whose gods I worship in her name and my noble Roman mother, whose forbearance often shames me." He heaved a sigh and wound her braid around his fist. "Their ambitions for me are identical. A mirror image of my esteemed father's."

Mesmerized both by his entrancing violet eyes and the insight to his life, Nimue swayed closer until their bodies all but touched. A possible answer to his domestic arrangements fluttered through her mind.

Sometimes, despite every endeavor, a woman failed to conceive a dearly wished for babe. In those cases, her sister or close relation might offer the sanctuary of her own womb. It was a precious gift and not lightly given and in such cases the babe did, most assuredly, possess the love of two mothers at the same time.

"Your adoptive mother was barren," she said, sure she was right. "And your birth mother gave her and your father the greatest gift of all. You."

If she expected him to be impressed by her deduction, she was mistaken. A shadow passed over his face, as though by laying out the facts so baldly she had somehow defiled him.

"Something like that." There was a trace of bitterness in his voice. Before she could probe further he tugged her closer, her hair still wrapped around his fist. "What happened to your mother, Nimue?"

His question was so unexpected she gaped up at him. How did he know something had happened to her mother? She had never so much as breathed a word about her mother to him.

"Was she killed during the invasion?" He was frowning again and there was a note of regret in his voice, as if he knew the answer already. And only then did she remember her words to him when she'd thought his birth mother had continued her journey.

Her Roman was too astute when it came to her. The knowledge didn't irk her, as it would if anyone else had shown such insight, but she didn't want to dwell on that uncomfortable fact.

"Yes." It was a simple answer for an event so traumatic she

could barely bring herself to think of it. She hoped he wouldn't press the issue, and after a brooding look that caused her heart to squeeze in her breast, Tacitus gave a barely perceptible nod and wrapped his free arm around her in silent comfort.

Her tense muscles relaxed and she breathed in deep, relishing his masculine scent and the way his touch caused spirals of arousal to dance through her blood. She wound her arm around his tunic-clad waist and closed her eyes. She had to remember who she was and where her loyalty lay. But it didn't ease the ache in her heart or the tightness in her throat. Tacitus' heart thudded against her breasts, a bittersweet blend of comfort, desire and ultimate despair. How was it possible that one man could mean so much to her, when barely a quarter moon ago they hadn't even met?

His race no longer mattered. She would never admit that aloud but it didn't matter. Her confession seared her soul, condemned her for all time—and still she did not care.

"What are you thinking, Nimue?" His hand cradled the back of her head and held her close as if he feared she might otherwise escape.

She looked up at him. Tried, one last time, to see him as she had the first time they'd met. But it was futile. Because even that first time by the mountain stream she had seen him as more than merely her enemy.

"I'm thinking," her voice was husky. She tried to clear her clogged throat, but it would not be cleared, "that I'm going to rip this Roman tunic from your body and have you at my mercy."

He laughed, and the intoxicating sound ignited the embers glowing in her blood.

"I greatly anticipate being at your mercy."

"As you should, Roman." She tugged at his robe and finally slung the linen to the floor. Tacitus stood before her in all his naked glory, his tawny flesh taut, muscles flexed and with a lascivious smile on his face that caused her knees to tremble as if this was the first time she had seen an unclothed male.

"Do you like what you see, Celt?"

Her gaze dropped and she watched, fascinated, as his erection thickened before her eyes. "I have never seen anything better."

Her words visibly aroused him further and he reached for her but she sidestepped his grasp. "You may look, but not touch."

"You ask the impossible."

Yes, she asked for the impossible but it was locked inside her heart and there it would remain. Because the foolish wish she harbored, that they might somehow forge a future together, was nothing more than that.

A foolish wish. And treacherous. Again she shoved her errant thoughts to the darkest corner of her mind. She wouldn't spoil this night with hopes that could never be.

"You'll be well rewarded for your patience." She offered him a provocative smile and slowly peeled the linen from her body. Tacitus watched every movement, mesmerized. "Do you like what *you* see, Roman?"

His gaze dragged across her body and flames licked her skin as though he physically scorched her with merely a look. Then his eyes meshed with hers, captured her as easily as he had captured her on the day they'd met.

"I have never seen anything better." His husky voice, with a trace of amusement at how he used her own words against her, enchanted her and she kicked the gown aside as she moved toward him.

CHAPTER 26

Once again Tacitus reached for her. Once again she avoided his touch. "Do you find it hard to follow orders?"

"Not usually. But my orders aren't usually issued in my own kitchens by a naked seductress."

She began to unbraid her hair, her gaze locked with his, willing victims of a dark bewitchment. "Has no woman ever given you orders, Tacitus?" She shook her loosened hair over her shoulders and hid a smile at the raw desire that flared in Tacitus' eyes.

"No." She saw the way he clenched his fists, fighting the need to reach for her yet again. "Does it please you to know you're the first?"

"Very much." She rested the tips of her fingers on his broad shoulders, their bodies all but touching. How hard it was to keep that whisper of distance between them. "It means you'll never forget me."

Of course he would never forget her. When she left with the prisoners, he would hate her for abusing his trust. But how desperately she wanted him to remember her with warmth and, perhaps, regret that they had never stood a chance.

He lowered his head so their lips brushed in a tantalizing caress. "Nimue, I believe I could never forget you even if I wanted to."

She trailed her fingers along his biceps, delighting in the granite-hard strength of his muscles, and ignored the dull ache in her shoulder. Her injury wouldn't stop her from enjoying this night, or prevent her from doing her duty tomorrow.

"I want this night to live on in your memory for all time."

His focus sharpened, as if he glimpsed the true meaning behind her heartfelt whisper and panic punched low in her gut. She didn't want anything to spoil this moment. Certainly not his suspicion.

She feathered a kiss across his lips as her palms molded his sculpted biceps. Her nipples grazed the hard planes of his chest, a torturous delight, and Tacitus' moan sent tremors skittering over her naked flesh.

"How much longer am I under your command?" The raw edge to his question was deliciously arousing, and she nibbled kisses along the length of his jaw and down his throat, where his pulse hammered against her exploring lips.

"Until I tell you otherwise." She slanted a glance up at him. He offered her a tortured grin in return. And did not touch.

She slid her fingers over his and then sucked his nipple into her mouth. He gave a strangled groan and his fingers gripped hers, and she smiled as her teeth nipped his sensitive flesh.

"Celtic enchantress." He ground the words between his teeth and she couldn't tell if he meant them as a compliment or a curse. Not that it mattered. All that mattered was that she burned a memory into Tacitus' mind. So that when the sting of her betrayal had faded into the distant past, he would recall these moments with her, and remember her with something other than derision.

Slowly, provocatively, she worked her way down his warrior hard body, exploring every ridge and contour with the tip of her tongue and graze of her teeth. Her nails scraped along his back and he jerked toward her but his fists remained clenched at his thighs.

She sank to her knees and looked up at him, feminine power thudding through her blood at the look of enslavement on Tacitus' face. "Your self-control is admirable, Roman." Her voice was breathless and her gaze slid down to his glorious erection. She wasn't so sure of her own control. "I have no need of enchantment."

"You enchant with every word you utter. With every look you give me." His voice was hoarse. "I've never met another woman like you, Nimue."

Her fingers dug into his taut buttocks at the thought that he might ever meet *another woman*. A woman he came back to every eve. A woman he shared his meals with, laughed with.

Trusted.

In the eyes of Rome, she was Tacitus' slave but she knew full well that he didn't consider her such. She was a Celt, and her people had been conquered. That was an irrefutable fact. But he treated her as if she was, as much as a woman ever could be to a Roman, his equal.

"And I have never met another man like you." She wrapped her arms around his thigh and pressed her body against his leg. Her sex throbbed with unfulfilled need but her need would have to wait. "I know I never will." Such confession would never have passed her lips in normal circumstances, but these were far from normal. And although tomorrow he might believe she had done nothing but lie to him, perhaps one day he would realize that in this matter she had spoken only the truth.

Slowly she raked her fingernails along the back of his thigh and down his calf. His fingers tangled in her hair, forcing her to look up at him.

"Gods, Nimue. What are you doing?" His eyes were glazed with lust and a frown marred his brow as though he couldn't imagine why a woman would be on her knees before him unless she was taking him into her mouth.

"Driving you to distraction." She slid the tip of her tongue across his knee and fought the urge to giggle at the look of astonishment on his face. Then she bit him and savored his taste before dragging her fingernails up from his ankle and over the taut muscle of his calf.

"You're seducing my *leg*." He sounded scandalized, but it didn't disguise the desire thundering through every word. "Is this a barbaric Celtic love ritual?"

Her foolish heart catapulted at his mention of love. But it was just a word, the same as barbaric was just a word, and he didn't mean anything by it.

"No, it's my own ritual. Has no other woman ever made love to your leg before?"

His fingers tightened in her hair and she relished the sparks of pain that danced across her scalp. Almost as much as she relished the look of amazement on his face.

"No woman has ever done the things you have to me. You could be a maiden of Aphrodite herself."

She molded her body around him, her thighs entrapping his calf, and delighted in the scrape of his hair against her belly and breasts. "And is Aphrodite your goddess of sensual pleasure?"

His fingers massaged her head in a seductive rhythm that sent shudders of desire along her spine. "She is the Greek goddess of love." His voice was raw with need but he didn't haul her to her feet or throw her onto her back. Although she acknowledged she wouldn't mind if he did either, the fact that he didn't caused her chest to contract with a strange pain. "My mother is Greek." The words were tortured, as though he confessed to something outrageous. Yet she already knew his mother wasn't Roman. Otherwise he would worship the gods of Rome.

But he clearly thought it important. And because he'd shared something with her, she wanted to share something with him.

"My father is from Gaul." It had always distressed her that her despised father's lineage meant she was not a pureblood of Cymru but oddly, now that she knew Tacitus was not a pureblood Roman, her tainted heritage no longer seemed so devastating. "But I worship the gods of my foremothers."

His smile was fractured. "Does your father still live?" He sounded as though it took great effort for him to ask the question. As if his thoughts inhabited another sphere entirely.

She slid her hand up his leg. Tantalizingly close to his impressive erection. She discovered she couldn't tear her fascinated gaze away. "I don't know." And she didn't care whether her cursed father was alive or dead. In this moment, all she cared about was bringing Tacitus to his knees. The image was alluring.

She abandoned his thigh and brushed her knuckles along the length of his cock. With every featherlight touch, his girth increased and her mouth watered with anticipation.

"I take back what I said about this being a Celtic love ritual." Tacitus' fingers, buried in her hair, were painful against her head. "It's a form of torture. What secrets are you searching for, Nimue?"

"I seek nothing from you." Her fingers trailed across his taut sac and his groan vibrated through his body and sent tremors racing along her arm and across her breasts. She struggled to recall his question, could barely form the words to reply. "That you don't willingly want to give."

"Do you know what I want to give you right at this moment?" His voice was rough, as rough as his fingers in her hair and she gave a breathless laugh.

"You're still under my command, Roman." She cradled his heavy balls in the palm of her hand, loving their texture, loving the tension she could feel radiating from Tacitus' rigid stance.

Intoxicated by his raw, masculine scent, she lowered her head and licked her delicious prize.

He tasted of every forbidden fantasy she had ever imagined. He tasted of Tacitus.

She closed her eyes and gently sucked him into her mouth and his guttural curse spiraled through her senses. Without conscious thought, she wrapped her hand around his hot shaft, and the knowledge that he was at her mercy thrilled her soul.

Slowly she released him from her mouth, her teeth scraping his taut sac, and then teased the tip of her tongue across his hard balls to the root of his cock. She looked up at him as she trailed her tongue along his rigid length, and the look of pleasured agony on his face was breathtaking. She had never imagined kneeling at a man's feet before. Yet not only was she on her knees before this Roman—she reveled in the juxtaposition of power and submission that caused her nipples to harden and cream to trickle from her pussy.

He swore violently in Latin, words she barely understood. Without warning, his fingers dug into her biceps, his grasp hard and possessive. He hauled her up, and his cock burned a path across her breasts and belly. She flattened her hands against his chest, breathless and aroused but determined to finish what she'd started.

"I didn't give you leave to manhandle me, Roman."

His grin was feral. "Consider this a mutiny, Celt. I'm the one in command now."

"Is that so?" She tried to sound fierce but his entrancing eyes, dark with passion, were too distracting. It was hard to remember what they were even talking about. "What punishment should I levy against you for such a crime?"

He wrapped one arm around her and pinned her to his body. His erection dug into her flesh, hot and unyielding and her clit throbbed with need. He leaned into her, forcing her backward, and she felt him swipe the contents from the table behind her.

"I look forward to my punishment." His hand, splayed around her waist, was hard and possessive. "In the meantime, I intend to enjoy yours."

His words ignited what remained of her sanity and she gripped his shoulders to keep her balance. "My punishment?" Illicit tremors rocked her. "You would not dare punish me, Roman—"

Her words caught in her throat as Tacitus flashed her a smile that surely Taranis, the god of thunder and lightning, would envy for its destructive intent.

He swung her about and forced her over the table. She staggered and glared up at him. His smile sizzled and his palm, pressed between her shoulder blades, rendered her immobile.

"You will find I dare many things, Celt." He leaned over her back, his body encompassing her in a mantle of masculine strength and she wriggled her bottom against his hard thighs. It served only to heighten the need spiraling through her pussy and a frustrated moan razed her throat.

He laughed, as though her evident discomfort pleased him. Curse the man. Her fingernails dug into the table and scored the timber but it did nothing to ease the thunder in her blood.

She felt him ease back, his hand running along the length of her spine in a caress designed to enflame. She could push herself upright now if she wished. But she remained as she was, sprawled across the table like a pleasure slave.

"Your obedience is welcome." Tacitus' voice was uneven but she heard the thread of amusement. "Although your continued silence is somewhat unnerving."

Her breasts and the side of her face were flattened against the table, and she could only partially see Tacitus from the corner of her eye. But she knew he was looking at her, splayed across the table, naked and vulnerable and Goddess knew, ready for whatever he planned to give her.

"Would you have me scream for mercy?" Her words were

breathless. Her chest tight and her heart thundered with erratic abandon.

He didn't answer. But his hands molded the curve of her waist and the flare of her hips. And then with slow deliberation he palmed her bottom.

Nimue hitched in a ragged gasp. In her mind's eye, she saw Tacitus as he looked at her. His hands spreading her arse cheeks, exposing her to his intimate exploration. Lightning flashed through her belly, ricocheted along her wet cleft and flickered with delicious need in the tight bud of her clit. She squirmed helplessly, her hands fisting on the table. *How much longer can I bear this?* But Tacitus continued to look at her in silence until the scream she'd threatened hovered with perilous intent in her throat.

His finger slid between her spread thighs and teased the wet folds of her sex. A desperate moan filled the room and she scarcely cared that it came from her. "*Tacitus.*" It was a plea and she twisted her head around as much as she could so she could see his face properly. His focus was intent between her legs, and his finger slid farther and caressed her throbbing clit.

"Yes." His voice was savage and she had no idea what he meant. "Scream for mercy, Nimue. Scream for *me*."

Wild abandonment seared through her and she caught his intense gaze. "Make me."

Her taunt had the desired effect. He gripped her hips, jerked her toward him and for one glorious moment his erection jammed against her backside. He caressed her hip and thigh and teased her bottom with the tips of his fingers, and she squirmed helplessly beneath him.

Her clit throbbed with need, her pussy trembled with anticipation. She felt him grip his cock and cream trickled from her cleft onto her thighs. The head of his rigid shaft nudged her wet entrance and her moan echoed around the room.

With one hard thrust, he filled her and the air rushed from

her lungs. She couldn't breathe, couldn't think, could only feel the way he stretched her, claimed her, *made her his*.

She closed her eyes, fisted her hands and reveled in the way Tacitus slammed into her. Hard, rhythmic, the friction against her sensitized clit all but unbearable as he pounded against her exposed bottom.

His hands roamed over her back and shoulders, tangled in her hair and clasped her throat. Ribbons of fire ignited wherever he touched. She writhed beneath him, incapable of coherent thought, incapable of processing anything but the pleasure his hands and fingers and cock wrought on her nipples, breasts and inside her quivering pussy.

"Do you surrender?" His uneven words rasped against her ear. "Beg for mercy and give yourself to me?"

How couldn't he know that she was already his? The thought drifted through her mind, weaved through the lust and passion and the truth of it seeped into her soul.

Of course she was his. She would forever be his.

"I will never," she panted, "surrender to Rome."

He rained kisses across her shoulder, along her throat. His teeth nipped her flesh, and then licked each pinprick of pain with the tip of his tongue. She could die of such pleasurable torture.

"To Hades with the Eagle." He sucked on her flesh, and a strangled moan vibrated throughout her body, quivering her swollen clit, erect nipples and every tender particle of skin she possessed. "Surrender to me, Nimue. *Be mine.*"

His words fueled the maelstrom of desire consuming her reason. There was no Cymru, no Rome; no deadly mission that would forever rip Tacitus from her arms. There was only now, this ethereal forever.

The last remnant of sanity shattered. "Yes." It was a hoarse gasp that flayed her throat. The scent of sex and foreign spices filled her senses as she convulsed around his pounding cock. A scream shattered the lust-drenched air. Her scream of surrender, of betrayal, of a love that could never be. *"Tacitus."*

CHAPTER 27

Wrapped in the cloak Tacitus had acquired for her, Nimue stood at the door of his quarters and watched him march across the wide Roman road that ran through the center of the fortification. A deep ache lodged in her heart as she committed this last sight of him to memory.

He didn't glance back at her. She hadn't expected him to. A Roman didn't do such things in public. But how she wished that he had.

She missed his smile and his bewitching eyes already.

Slowly she closed the door and for a moment rested her forehead against the timber as a wave of dizziness washed through her. This morn, she would once again claim the mantle of her heritage and act as the warrior she was.

Her interlude as the plaything of a Roman officer was over. She had no right to feel so torn about her path. She'd had no right to fall in love with her enemy, her captor, the man who embodied everything she had always despised most in the world.

She straightened, and for a moment felt as ancient as if she had witnessed a hundred summers instead of merely twenty-two.

After this day, she would never see Tacitus again. If they ever met in the future, she would be his deadly enemy and this time he wouldn't be blinded by her apparent fragility or the fact she was a woman. He would see her for what she was. And he would crucify her for it.

A shudder racked her body as she turned and made her way to the room he called the kitchen. Whether she succeeded or failed in her mission—and failure wasn't an option—Tacitus would never again welcome her into his arms. But oh, great Arianrhod of the Silver Wheel of Birth, Death and Rebirth, she would give anything—do anything—if only there could be a way for her and Tacitus to be together when all this was over.

~

As she waited for her herbs to steep so she could make the womb-cleansing tea for herself and the other captive women, she prepared a second brew containing the sleep-inducing herbs. Her plan was simple. Before she spoke to the women, she would offer the alternate brew to the guard. If he declined, it would be an annoyance but she had a backup in place.

Surreptitiously she glanced around the kitchen. Tacitus' orders to his servants that she be allowed free rein in his kitchen were clearly being observed, but she was being ignored as if she didn't exist. Another time that fact might have irked her, but now it gave her nothing but relief.

Stealthily she placed one of Tacitus' brooches, or fibula as he called them, onto the table. It was made of silver and was decorated with precious gems, and guilt ate through her at how readily he had given it to her this morn when she'd admired it. Gritting her teeth, she inserted a third, potent, combination of the sleeping drugs into the shallow groove of the brooch where the pin would normally rest. Usually a more lethal concoction was used with darts but since she didn't have the necessary means to make a blowpipe this would have to do. For while she could easily knock the seamstress unconscious, she couldn't afford to draw attention to herself in hand-to-hand combat with a fully trained legionary. She would have to rely on her speed, and the legionary's ignorance of her purpose, in order to stab the sleeping drugs into his bloodstream.

Carefully she slipped her weapon into a small leather pouch and tied it at her waist. Another quick glance around the kitchen confirmed that her actions had raised no suspicions. She poured herself a cup of the cleansing tea and filled a long-necked jug with the rest of the liquid.

With a sigh, she picked up her cup and raised it to her lips. And then she froze as an eerie shiver trickled along the back of her neck. Why did this feel wrong? The chill invaded the pit of her stomach as a dreadful thought occurred to her. Had she made a mistake with the ingredients or the special balance required?

Surely not. She'd made this many times in the past and the recipe was ingrained in her mind, along with every other remedy she had ever learned over the years. Although she'd never taken it herself before now, she was absolutely certain she had made no error.

So why can't I bring myself to drink it?

She was approaching the fertile quarter of her moon cycle. Although the chance she'd conceived last night wasn't high, neither was it impossible. To prevent even the smallest chance that Tacitus' seed might bear fruit she owed it to her people and her Goddess to drink this tea.

Yet she remained motionless, as her stomach roiled with sudden nausea as a treacherous thought slid through her mind. Did she actively want to ensure that she didn't conceive Tacitus' child?

Could she truly curse her unborn babe to such a despised heritage?

Except she didn't despise Tacitus. And the notion of having his child didn't disgust her.

Far from it.

Before the thought finished forming, she swiftly poured the liquid back into the jug. Heart pounding, she sealed the top and waited long, agonizing moments before she could finish preparing the sleeping brew. Without another glance around the kitchen, as though the possibility of catching a servant's eye might declare her guilt to all of Rome, she returned to the bedchamber.

Disjointed thoughts hammered through her mind. She refused to contemplate any of them. Instead she once again unlocked Tacitus' casket, except this time the guilt that ate through her was a physical entity with jaws that clawed through her soul and left her bleeding.

She clenched her fists, took a deep breath and reminded herself why she was doing this. Tacitus would see it as a betrayal, but she wasn't betraying him. She'd give her life to save him if she had to, but that was not her choice.

Her choice had been made and her honor pledged before she'd ever met him.

He would never see her as a warrior. It would never occur to him that she would willingly put her life in danger in order to carry out her orders. And yet he would expect nothing less had she been a man.

Would such knowledge cause him to think less of her, rather than more?

She didn't know. She would never know. Perhaps that was just as well.

Her medicine bag was still buried beneath the linen and she dropped the pouches she had filled with Marcellus' herbs into it. Swiftly, she closed the lid of the chest and swung her cloak around her shoulders, concealing her bag.

For a moment, she hesitated as she looked around the room

and instantly knew it was a mistake. She couldn't stop to contemplate or reminisce. There was no time and she couldn't afford the luxury of regret for something that could never be.

All she could do was act. Only when her mission was complete would she allow herself to think of personal matters.

Of Tacitus.

NIMUE HAD ALMOST REACHED THE PRISONERS' quarters when disaster struck. Tacitus' commander rounded a corner, caught sight of her, and began to march in her direction.

Panic gripped her. If he decided to drag her off she knew nobody would stop him—certainly not the officer by his side. Tacitus had assured her she was safe from his commander's clutches. But Tacitus wasn't here.

"Nimue." He halted directly in front of her and although he left adequate space between them, his suffocating presence loomed over her. "I understand you're on the way to visit the captives."

The overwhelming urge to leap to her people's defense burned through her, but she battled to douse it. Rising to the commander's bait would do her no favors. She wanted to be as unobtrusive as possible, not create a scene.

"Charitable as well as beautiful," the officer said, and it was only then she realized it was the same officer who'd spoken to her the other day. Tacitus' cousin.

"An admirable trait in one whose people have been conquered."

Injustice spiked through her chest and she glared up at the commander, who was staring at her as if he possessed the power to penetrate her skull and read her true thoughts. Scathing words scorched her tongue and she struggled to keep them there and not escape her lips. The commander's eyes narrowed slightly, seemingly well aware of her internal battle and the strangest conviction gripped her that he expected her to protest.

Despite the fact that by so doing she risked her life.

"I wonder that my esteemed cousin allows you to wander the garrison without protection." The officer dismissed the seamstress's presence with barely a glance. "*I* would never allow you to put yourself at such risk."

The commander's penetrating gaze finally slid from her face and lingered on the piles of clothes and jugs that she and the seamstress held. For one horrifying moment, Nimue had the icy certainty that he knew exactly what she planned to do.

"I doubt," the commander said at last, "that the Celt is at any risk within this garrison, Tribune."

How much longer did he intend to delay her? At any other time she would have simply stalked off, but she couldn't risk angering him in case he decided to haul her off for some barbaric punishment.

Something behind her caught the commander's attention and he beckoned. She refused to glance over her shoulder on principle. Not that it mattered, since within moments the Gaul, Gervas, who had informed her of her slave status, came into view.

The commander turned back to her. "You've picked your moment well, Nimue. The captives, including Caratacus' queen and daughter, are being sold to the slave traders at midday. Thanks to you, they will now all be cleanly attired."

Fury at his callous words merged with relief that she was not yet too late to save them all, and she barely registered the sharp glance the officer shot his commander. Finally satisfied by their bizarre exchange the commander indicated that she was free to go and without a word, she did.

Arianrhod surely used her blessings to smooth the path for Nimue. The legionary on guard, a different one from the previous day, could barely tear his gaze from her and accepted her offer of a drink without the slightest trace of suspicion.

"The commander and the tribune said you'd be coming by," he said, ramrod straight but holding her cup in his hand. She offered him a smile that clearly befuddled his mind as he grinned back, seeing her as no potential threat whatsoever.

Only as he unlocked the door of the prisoners' quarters did his comment fully penetrate. She knew that Tacitus had been going to warn the guard of her visit and she understood that he needed to inform his commander, but why would the commander also mention it to the legionary?

Just as she was about to enter the building, the Gaul whom the commander had hailed paused by the legionary's side and looked at her. Heat flooded through her and she prayed desperately it wouldn't spread to her face and declare her guilt for all to see.

Goddess, was he going to stand and watch her? She doubted that he'd fall for her false smile and didn't even bother to try. But she couldn't let him thwart her plans when they were so close to execution.

"Would you care for some herbal tea?"

He glanced at the jug, then at the legionary and then back at her. His expression gave nothing away and yet she knew that, unlike the Romans she'd encountered, he saw past her face and figure and pretty words.

"No." His response was uncompromising. "I don't drink while on duty." With that he turned and marched onward, and she let out a relieved sigh.

"Miserable Gallian bastard," the legionary said, his stance no longer quite as rigid. The seamstress sniffed, whether in agreement or disapproval Nimue couldn't guess, and continued to sip her tea.

Once again Nimue entered the building. This time when the women approached there was far less hostility. "We didn't expect to see you again," the woman who had spoken to her the previous day said. "Did your Roman beat you for coming to see us?"

"No." Nimue looked down at the jug she held so the woman couldn't see the truth in her eyes. She would never understand how Nimue felt about her Roman. Nimue would never expect her to. But neither could she bear for Tacitus to be so unjustly accused. "He would never beat me. Not all Romans are the same."

She'd despised Romans long before they'd invaded her homeland. How could she so easily dismiss years of ingrained contempt? But Tacitus was nothing like she had imagined her enemy to be. With him, at least, she would acknowledge that her sweeping prejudice against his race was unfair.

"Yes, they are," the woman said and Nimue knew nothing would change her mind. Knew that it was not even her place to try to change the woman's mind. All she had to do was ensure her safety.

"We don't have much time." She didn't miss the way the woman's eyes narrowed at her sudden change of subject. "Here, take these gowns and put them over your own." She handed the clothes to a second woman who took them but didn't appear to know what to then do with them. "The slave traders will be here soon. This is the only chance you have for freedom."

"You're rescuing us?" The first woman stared at her in disbelief. "We'll never make it. Roman scum are everywhere."

"You will make it." From the corner of her eye she saw the others had started to pull on the clean gowns over their own. "The market isn't far. It will be easy enough to mingle with the local populace. The important thing to remember is not to draw attention so don't all move together in one group."

"And then what?" asked one of the women, as she helped a young girl into a clean gown.

"Then we will return to the enclave of Caratacus where I'll repair the sacred circle. When the Source of Annwyn conceals us from Roman eyes, there will be time to heal and gather resources." She glanced over her shoulder, but the legionary was leaning against the open door, yawning widely, and showed no interest in what she was saying. "In moments the legionary will slide into unconsciousness. When he does you must make haste." She gave brief instructions on how to reach the bustling market within the fortification's walls. If they could get there undetected then their chance for escape was high. "Take this." She handed the woman the jug, and explained the purpose of the contents. "Don't wait for me," she said. "I'll follow with the Briton queen and her daughter and meet you at the sacred enclave."

Satisfied that the woman would ensure her orders were carried out, Nimue checked on her victims. The seamstress had slumped to the ground and was snoring softly and the legionary, still upright against the wall, was no longer sensible to his surroundings. After ensuring the way was clear, she turned back and jerked her head at the woman who began the stealthy exodus.

Nimue slid her earring free and hoped the door to the queen's prison was as simple to unlock as Tacitus' casket. She curbed her impulse to run and instead strolled toward the building, shocked by the lack of security. It was especially surprising given the Romans' military record and yet, when she considered it, their oversight to guard their prisoners adequately wasn't surprising at all.

Who, after all, would try to rescue a dozen native women and children from the heart of their formidable fortification?

They would never suspect *she* would be so daring. It wasn't as if she was a *man*.

She gripped her earring and slid it into the lock, and attempted to derive satisfaction from the notion that the Romans so underestimated the warriors of Cymru. But all she could see in her mind's eye was the look on Tacitus' face when he discovered what she'd done.

The lock gave way and after another quick glance over her shoulder, she opened the door.

"Do not be afraid," she whispered as she stepped into the darkened room. And then the words lodged in her throat and her heart slammed against her ribs in horror as, instead of the queen facing her, it was the commander.

CHAPTER 28

Flee. The panicked command pounded in her head but within the space of a heartbeat, she discarded the notion. If she ran, she risked drawing attention to the women and children who, Goddess willing, would by now be mingling with the morning market crowds.

And even if she ran in the opposite direction, how far could she get in the middle of the enemy's camp, with their commander on her trail?

"Nimue." The commander's voice was low as his intense gaze burned into her. "My instinct wasn't wrong."

Dagger-sharp terror ripped through her but she remained motionless and willed herself not to show by the slightest tremble how deeply she feared facing Roman torture.

He didn't know her true plans. To him she was simply a weak woman in both mind and body. He couldn't possibly suspect that she had opened the door in order to help the queen and her daughter escape.

Yet if all he imagined was that she intended to bring fresh clothes then why was he standing in the middle of the room, hands clasped behind his back, as if he had been specifically waiting for her?

Of course he had been waiting for her. And the true reason why he waited smashed into her with the force of a landslide.

It had nothing to do with him suspecting her of an ulterior motive.

She edged back a step, cursing the fact that she didn't have her dagger. At least then she could inflict serious injury on him before he attempted to rape her. Yet even as that dreaded thought crossed her mind, discordance vibrated along her senses. For despite the way the commander's presence dominated the small room he didn't make any threatening gesture toward her.

Perhaps she was wrong. Perhaps he hadn't had the queen moved from this room merely to get Nimue alone. Perhaps, after all, there was a perfectly logical reason why he'd locked himself in and waited for her to...

Rescue him.

"Don't run." His voice was still low, conversational even, yet threaded through with pure command. "You won't get far."

Ice formed in the pit of her stomach and leaked into her veins. She straightened her already rigid spine, forced herself to maintain eye contact. She wouldn't give these Roman barbarians the satisfaction of running, of being hunted down like a wild creature. She was an acolyte of the Moon Goddess Arianrhod and the pride of her people rested within her.

She would not let them down, the way she had let the Briton queen down.

"I have no intention of running." Her voice was cold, regal but instead of anger at her disrespectful tone, she witnessed a flash of admiration in the commander's green eyes.

"I didn't imagine for one moment that you would." Finally he took a step toward her, but didn't attempt to grab her. "A woman who would risk the wrath of the Eagle by releasing valuable prisoners wouldn't run from her fate like a coward."

He knew. The words pounded through her mind in an erratic tattoo and dread curled like a serpent around her heart. He might want to fuck her, but the reason she was in this situation was because he'd guessed what she truly was. Why else would he think she had planned to mount a rescue? Why else would he taunt her with the knowledge that Druids didn't run from their fate but faced it head on?

She swallowed, her throat dry as dust. He could speculate as much as he liked. She would never admit to her heritage or spill the secrets she held sacred.

"I came here only to give the Briton queen and her daughter clean clothes." How could he argue with the evidence in her arms? It was impossible that he already knew of the others' escape, although it wouldn't be long before one of his subordinates informed him of the fact. "You said the slave traders wouldn't arrive until midday."

"Yes." His gaze roved over her face and she fought the urge to squirm. He looked at her like he wished to devour her and yet the strangest conviction gripped her that his interest was no longer sexual. "I had to force your hand, Nimue. I had to discover if you really were who I believe you to be."

Her stomach liquefied with nerves and a fleeting, brutal image of her mother's last agonized moments flashed through her mind. In the end it didn't matter if she admitted to being a Druid or not. It was enough that the commander suspected her. He could do whatever he wished and no one would prevent him.

She angled her jaw at him. If he thought she would beg for her life, grovel at his feet for mercy, then he was pitifully mistaken. "You've already sold the queen."

"No. Gervas ensured that she and the girl are safe elsewhere. And they aren't destined to be sold, Nimue. Their fate awaits them in Rome, by the Emperor's decree. Do you really think I could allow you to free such valuable assets? Slaves are one thing. The queen and daughter of Caratacus are another."

Despite herself she felt her face burn. Was he telling her that he'd known of her plans all along? That he considered the loss of the women and children negligible? She knew the ways of Rome were different to her own, but no leader would willingly allow a member of the enemy to free captives of war.

Yet wasn't that exactly what the commander was saying?

She tried one last time to protest ignorance. "I'm merely a woman, a slave. Why would you think I'd risk my life to save a foreign queen?"

"The door was locked." That was all he said. That was all he needed to say to let her know that she could deny her involvement until her dying breath and it would make no difference. "Yet that was no deterrent."

Despite the frenzied staccato of her heart and the rushing of her blood in her ears, she was acutely aware that no legionaries had descended to prevent her escape. But why hadn't the commander issued such orders in advance? Did he intend to drag her through the fortification himself?

"Nimue." He took another step toward her and beneath the cover of the clothes she held, Nimue stealthily opened the pouch that contained the poisoned brooch. She knew her chance of escaping was slender but at least she would go down fighting. "How did you come by your silver torque?"

His question was so unexpected, so utterly bizarre, that she forgot about her makeshift weapon and stared at him in disbelief. "My torque?" she echoed. Why did he care about such a thing? If he desired it, there was nothing to prevent him from taking it from her once she was fully within his power.

"It's very unusual." His gaze was no longer fixed on her face. He stared at her throat as if the silver jewelry captivated him. "I've seen only one other like it, many years ago."

Her fingers slackened around the clothes; her hands were clammy, chest tight. Her torque was unique. There was no other like it. *He's lying.*

He took another step toward her, his gaze still focused on her throat. "When I was a young officer stationed in Gallia."

"No." The denial seared her throat and she staggered back a step, her stomach churning with distress. "You couldn't have. You're mistaken."

"She had hair the color of honey and gold." His voice was pensive, as though he'd slipped into the past and was reliving another life. The clothes fell from Nimue's limp grasp and despite how she tried to fight it she was plunged back in time, to the night of her initiation.

This was the happiest day of her life. The proudest moment she had yet experienced. But then her mother had drawn her aside and had whispered a secret that shattered the moment and tarnished its beauty and wonder forevermore.

"You're old enough to know the truth of your father's heritage," her mother had said. All Nimue knew of her father was he came from Gaul and although her mother had always refused to tell her any more about him Nimue knew, in her heart, he was a Druid of great power and renown. Thrilled at the prospect of finally discovering more about him she'd hugged her mother, eager to hear the secrets of her shadowed heritage. *"He was a Roman officer, stationed in Gaul. I loved him with all my heart..."*

But she hadn't heard any more. Hadn't been able to process anything but *he was a Roman officer.* The words haunted her then, and had haunted her all her life. *A Roman officer.* She was the spawn of her people's deadliest enemy, and it was a secret her mother had shared only with her. A secret they both would take to the Otherworld.

"She was in Gallia visiting distant kin," the commander said and Nimue's throat closed as panic clawed through her body. "But her home was here, in Cambria."

"I don't—" Her voice was hoarse and she floundered, the words paralyzing her throat, stupefying her brain. Because there were no words. Because he was wrong.

"How old are you, Nimue?"

The need to conceal her true age pounded through her mind. *Twenty-one summers. Twenty-three.* She could tell him anything, anything but the truth. But denial blocked her throat and her chest constricted with a pain so all-encompassing she feared her heart would cease to beat.

"It's been twenty-three years since I last saw her." The commander's intense gaze meshed with hers and a detached corner of her mind noted their clear green depths. She knew those eyes. They looked back at her every time she saw her reflection in a still pool. In that moment she knew it didn't matter what she said. The commander knew, as surely as she did herself, whose child she was. "When you put the torque on the other day it was as if the gods themselves granted me a revelation. I knew who you had to be, Nimue. There's not a day that's passed in these twenty-three years that I haven't thought of her."

His words had the power to break the stranglehold on her vocal cords and a bitter laugh flayed her throat. "Why would you think of her? She wasn't a *Roman*." She coated the hated word with as much venom as she could. "She was a Celt from Cymru, a land your filthy Emperor had yet to conquer."

He didn't strike her for her insult against his loathed Emperor. How she wished he would so that she could sink her fingernails into him and shred the skin from his aristocratic face.

"I know what she is," he said, and a chill trickled along her spine at what he implied. "I always knew what she was, Nimue. It made no difference."

If he knew her mother had been a Druid, then from the moment he'd suspected who Nimue was he would have also known that she belonged to that ruling class too. Yet despite there being an automatic death sentence for any Druid discovered within Roman occupied lands the commander had allowed her to live.

"Pray don't try to tell me that you *loved* my mother." She'd wanted derision to drip from every word, but instead a despicable tremble weaved through them. She'd despaired at the way she'd so easily fallen in love with Tacitus, a Roman; a race she had never admired but after her initiation her dislike had spiked into acidic loathing. Yet how could she not love him? She was a part of his heritage. And she was, after all, merely following in her own mother's footsteps.

"Why? Is that so hard to believe? She challenged me at every turn. As do you."

The restriction in Nimue's chest eased, but instead of giving relief her heart rate accelerated and it became increasingly hard to breathe. But she hitched in a shallow gasp and jabbed her finger in the commander's chest.

"If you loved her so much then why did you leave her? Why did you never seek out your daughter?" *Great Goddess Arianrhod, please let me not have said that aloud.* She hated her Roman blood. She'd never wanted to know her father. And she certainly had never wondered, in the blackness of night, what he was really like or why he'd never wanted to know her.

His jaw tensed. It appeared her accusation hit a raw nerve. "I didn't leave her. I asked her to stay. Would have compromised my career for her if that's what she wanted. She left me, Nimue. And she didn't tell me that she had conceived my child."

No. This couldn't be right. This couldn't be happening. She had spent too long being angry with her mother, had lost too many moon-times to silences and harsh whispers. Eventually the passage of time soothed the sharp edge of shock and she'd forgiven her mother and had transferred all her sense of betrayal to her absent father.

Who hadn't even been aware of her existence.

"What difference would it have made?" She flung the question at him as she struggled not to slump against the wall, wrap her arms around her waist, collapse onto the floor. "Why would a Roman wish to claim the child of a...a Celt?" They both knew she meant *Druid*. But even between them, she would not allow the word to pass her lips.

His nostrils flared, as if she had insulted his honor. "It would have made a difference. I would never have abandoned the child of the woman I loved."

"Your pledges of undying devotion come too late." Her chest hurt with the force of her heartbeat, and she still couldn't breathe properly. She was lightheaded, akin to the sensation when she ascended into trance, but there was no sense of peace and joy in her soul. "They mean nothing to me, do you hear? Nothing."

As if she watched the scene from above she saw him grip her arms, obviously concerned she might fall. But she felt nothing, only the heavy thump of her heart and pound of her blood. Even her vision was dimming, as though storm clouds concealed the sun.

"It's not too late." His urgent words penetrated the fog in her mind but they didn't make sense. "I can erase all record of your capture and enslavement, Nimue. You'll be free to return home. But grant me one small favor. Tell me where your mother is."

The dizziness vanished; the sense of unreality dissolved. She gasped in air, and tried to pull free but his grip on her tightened. "My mother?" Bone-deep sorrow flooded through her and twisted around her aching heart. "You want me to tell you about my *mother*?"

"Yes." His face was so close to hers she could see golden flecks in his eyes. Could see, also, the truth of his words when he declared his love. Somehow that inflamed her fury, magnified her grief.

"Are you sure you want to know?" She fired the question into his face, and derived morbid satisfaction from the wariness that suddenly clouded his eyes. "Are you sure you can stomach it, Roman, knowing what your precious countrymen did to her?"

CHAPTER 29

Tacitus tried to ignore the insidious voice in the back of his mind that insisted he check on the slaves. He knew Nimue would be there. He'd informed the legionary on guard and his commander of the fact so there would be no misunderstanding either of Nimue's motives or that she was there with his permission.

There was no need to check on the slaves. Nimue was only giving them clean clothes and one of her teas. What did he imagine she might do armed with only a pile of gowns? Yet he kept seeing the determined gleam in her eyes when she'd asked his permission to give them to the slaves.

He was under no illusion that even if he'd denied permission, she would have found a way to countermand his orders.

It wasn't that knowledge that disturbed him.

He rounded the corner and caught sight of the prisoners' block. And instantly saw his seamstress slumped on the ground, apparently deep in slumber.

There was no sign of Nimue.

Instinctively he glanced around the surrounding area but it was deserted. Black rage seared through his chest, a suffocating fog that filled his lungs and tightened his throat. Nimue had betrayed him.

He reached the sleeping woman and glowered at her. A cup—one he recognized from his own kitchen—rested in her slack grasp. He jerked his gaze upward and saw the legionary propped against the wall. His eyes were closed.

Tacitus cursed violently under his breath and dropped into a crouch. "Wake up." He accompanied the order with a swift shake of the woman's shoulders. "Where's Nimue?"

The woman stirred, muttered and opened one glazed eye. The rage coalesced in the pit of his gut, a savage, writhing fury he could barely contain. Nimue had used her herbs to drug them both. Herbs she had gathered right under his nose.

"Get up." He forced the command between his teeth, and hauled the woman to her feet. "Get back to my quarters and don't breathe a word of this to anyone." He picked up the discarded amphorae and tipped the incriminating contents into the ground before thrusting it into her arms. "Do you understand?"

She blinked, caught sight of his face and visibly blanched. "Yes, sir," she whispered, bowing her head before she stumbled off.

Tacitus reined in his urge to smash his fist in the insensible legionary's face and instead shoved open the door to the prisoners' quarters. It was empty. He knew it would be empty but still another scorching flame of betrayal seared through his chest.

Nimue had released the prisoners but it wasn't that fact that hammered through his brain or razed his senses. It was the knowledge that she had taken his trust, trampled it beneath her feet and escaped him at the first opportunity.

He marched around the corner, hands fisted, teeth clenched. She wouldn't have gone without Caratacus' queen and daughter. He no longer needed to hide from the truth that had been obvious from the moment he and Nimue had met.

She was no ordinary Celtic noblewoman. If she had been, she

wouldn't have been alone by that mountain stream. She wouldn't have stood her ground, holding a dagger, unless she had been trained in self-defense. Nor was she simply a gifted healer who'd been traveling with the Britannia queen.

She was a Druid. Why else would she risk death by staging such a daring rescue of her people? How could he have allowed her delicate beauty to blind him to what she truly was?

Bitterly he acknowledged the truth. It hadn't. He'd chosen to remain in ignorance because the consequences, had he faced his suspicions, had been unthinkable.

Now he would pay the price for that self-illusion.

It was too much to hope that she was in the adjoining building preparing the queen for escape, and yet still he hoped. The alternative—the Legion hunting her down—was too horrific to imagine.

"Tell me where your mother is." The commander's voice, muted yet with an oddly desperate tone, stopped Tacitus dead in his tracks. Was his commander in the queen's prison?

"My mother?"

The familiar voice caused his heart to jackknife. Against the odds, Nimue was still there. But the savage relief that spiked through him was instantly shattered. She was in there—with his commander.

"You want me to tell you about my *mother*?" The incredulity in her voice hammered through his brain, melding with his own. Why in Hades was his commander asking Nimue about her mother?

"Yes."

Gods, he didn't know where the commander was going with this conversation, but it didn't bode well for Nimue. He couldn't imagine how she and his commander had ended up together but one certainty pounded through his mind.

So far, his commander was in ignorance of Nimue's involvement in the slaves' escape. If he knew, then he certainly wouldn't be questioning her about her maternal heritage. And then a torch flared in his mind and his chest tightened. There was only one reason why his commander should ask such a question and that was if he suspected her bloodline.

Tacitus reached the door. Saw Nimue in the commander's arms.

"Are you sure you want to know?" There was a savage note in her voice. "Are you sure you can stomach it, Roman, knowing what your precious countrymen did to her?"

"Fuck, Nimue." The words burst from him as he grabbed her arms and ripped her from his commander. Did she have a death wish? Was she completely insane?

"For five days they kept her. Tortured her. Tried to break her body and spirit—"

He shook her in horror, for once uncaring about her injured shoulder. "Nimue, be silent—"

"Those bastard Romans raped her, beat her with chains and leather—"

Tacitus' stomach roiled and for a moment he glanced at the commander, a section of his mind wondering at his continued silence; wondering why an order not to render her unconscious hadn't been issued his way.

But his commander wasn't looking at him. His gaze was riveted on Nimue, seemingly bewitched, and there was a sickly pallor to his skin.

"And then they lashed her naked and broken body on a cross. *Crucified her* because she wouldn't betray her people for your cowardly Emperor—"

Tacitus dragged her forcibly back against his body and wrapped his hand over her mouth. She was shaking as if she had a fever, and his fury at her treachery seeped from his veins in sickened disgust.

No wonder she hated Rome. No wonder she'd attempted to escape at the first opportunity. But he didn't have time to comfort her, even if such a feat could be possible. He had to somehow placate his commander. Convince him Nimue was out of her mind, not in control of her tongue. Inspiration struck. He would say she had been drugged and couldn't be held accountable for her actions.

"Sir—"

His commander looked at him and the rest of his words jolted from his mind. In the space of moments the older man had aged before Tacitus' eyes, and a shudder inched along his spine. Was this some strange Druid magic of Nimue's?

"Caratacus' queen and daughter are being sent to Rome tomorrow." Despite his ashen appearance, his commander's voice was the same as it had always been. "Ensure Nimue is kept under control, Tribune. Her safety cannot be guaranteed if you allow her free rein."

He'd already made that decision. Nimue would be confined to his quarters now and it had nothing to do with her safety and everything to do with…

For a moment his thoughts halted, uncertain. Was it truly only his pride she had wounded?

"Yes, sir." At this moment nothing else mattered but getting Nimue away from his commander. If his superior officer suspected she was a Druid, he wouldn't have allowed her to remain with Tacitus. They were too valuable; and after all information had been extracted from them they were publicly executed as a warning and reminder of the might of the Roman Empire.

As he dragged an uncooperative Nimue from the building, the pit of his stomach churned at the thought of her being crucified. She stumbled against him and he released his restraining hold across her mouth. She hitched in a ragged breath, and the vulnerability of that small, broken sound stabbed through his heart.

She was a Druid. It was his duty to report his suspicions. His loyalty to his Emperor, to Rome and his family honor dictated nothing less.

He gripped her arm and marched her toward his quarters, avoiding the deserted slaves' building. Nimue was a native of the most hated people of his Emperor. He knew it and he would deny the truth of her heritage with his dying breath.

She pulled up suddenly and he rounded on her, rage at his conflicted loyalties pounding through his blood. But she wasn't glaring at him, wasn't trying to escape. Instead she merely swayed on her feet and her pale face and oddly blank eyes caused another wave of cursed protectiveness to smash through him.

Was he destined to battle what was considered the norm for his society for the rest of his life? He'd always thought there could be nothing worse than the familial conflicts that plagued his conscience.

He had been wrong.

"Forgive me," she said in an oddly dignified voice. "I am going to be ill." Then she slipped from his loosened grasp, fell to her knees and was violently sick.

∽

FOR TWO DAYS Tacitus had managed to avoid a conversation with Nimue. He left before she awoke in the morning and returned late at night after she'd gone to bed. Then he woke her, kissing her treacherous lips, invading her willing mouth and pussy until she writhed with orgasmic pleasure beneath him. She never turned away. Never pushed him back. She wanted his body as desperately as he wanted hers. But it was never enough. Because never a word passed between them.

He couldn't trust himself to speak to her. Couldn't trust what she might confess in return. He hadn't been able to confiscate her embroidered bag, despite the fact that she possessed it only proved, yet again, how she'd gone behind his back. But how could he take it from her when she had stood before him, silent, vulnerable, *broken*?

He'd taken her collection of herbs though. And it had given him no pleasure to burn them but how could he trust her not to one night drug him with them?

"There's a storm coming." His commander's voice penetrated his tortured thoughts and he hauled himself back to the present. Despite the uproar when it was discovered the Cambrian slaves had escaped, his commander hadn't demanded that Nimue be interrogated. The legionary on guard had been held fully responsible and the man's honor hadn't allowed him to attempt to shift the blame to a mere woman. A slave, no less.

But it was strange that the commander apparently made no connection with Nimue. Tacitus still didn't know how they had both ended up in the queen's room.

Nimue's name was the last thing he intended to bring up with his commander. And he wasn't speaking at all to Nimue.

But it was slowly eating him alive.

"Sir." The reply was automatic. He had no idea whether a storm was brewing or not. As far as he could tell, it had been a perfectly normal summer for this primitive province. Chilly and unpredictable.

They stood outside the commander's quarters and the older man, hands clasped behind his back, stared up into the dusky twilight sky. Tacitus quickly looked away again. Since the confrontation with Nimue, his commander had been far less gregarious than usual. Blandus had passed comment on his uncle's changed attitude just that afternoon and Tacitus had brushed it aside. But it confirmed one thing. His commander hadn't confided anything about Nimue to his nephew.

"Haven't you noticed, Tacitus?" Still the commander stared into the sky apparently fascinated by the blackness. "There's been no sign of the moon since we crushed Caratacus. The Celts' gods do not rest easy."

Tacitus had an instant vision of the exquisite engravings on Nimue's silver jewelry and the embroidery of her bag. They showed the passage of the moon. He knew she worshipped Arianrhod, the Celt goddess of the moon. Against his better judgment, he followed his commander's gaze. The sky loomed, dark and ominous, without a single pinprick of distant light.

"In time they too will succumb to the gods of Rome." It was an automatic answer; one he didn't fully believe in. How could he, when he favored the gods of Greece over the gods of his forefathers?

The commander was silent for so long Tacitus thought the conversation over, and silent relief washed through him. He didn't want to think about the Celtic gods or the Celtic priests and priestesses who communed with them. Yet it seemed everything reminded him of Nimue.

"Will they?" The commander turned his brooding gaze to Tacitus. "Should they?"

Unease prickled the outer edges of his mind. Was his commander uttering a rhetorical question?

"Go back to your Celt." It was a command and Tacitus stiffened, every sense on full alert. "Enjoy her while you can, Tacitus. And when the time comes, remember your pledge. Bring her to me and I'll pay whatever you demand—for her manumission."

CHAPTER 30

*O*nce again, Nimue ate the eve's meal by herself. It was served to her in a frosty silence but she couldn't blame Tacitus' servants for their attitude. Not after what she'd done to one of their own. The seamstress hadn't come near her since that morn, two days ago.

She pushed her half-eaten meal away. Tacitus had barely come near her since he'd dragged her away from his commander. *My father.* She still couldn't think of him in that way without her stomach knotting and breath strangling her throat. In her heart she knew it wasn't a coincidence. They had been destined to meet by the gods. But whose gods? Hers?

Or his?

She sat on the edge of Tacitus' casket and attempted to regulate her breathing. She'd wondered how he'd react when he discovered her betrayal. She had never imagined witnessing it firsthand.

The reality was far worse than anything her mind had conjured. He hadn't yelled at her. Beaten or berated her. If he had, she might have convinced herself that she didn't love him. But if Tacitus had been the kind of man to whip or brutalize her, then she would never have fallen in love with him in the first place.

Nimue had prayed, *begged*, that somehow she could see Tacitus again when her mission was over. And her wish had been granted. She had seen Tacitus again. And failed, with spectacular disgrace, in her pledge to save the Briton queen and her daughter from slavery.

For two days, she'd wallowed in self-recrimination at her failure. For two days, she had reeled between shock and reluctant fascination at the discovery of her father. For two torturous days and nights, she had battled the hopeless realization of how deeply she'd fallen for her Roman captor.

She couldn't—*wouldn't*—continue this way. She had no idea what Tacitus intended to do with her. When he took her in the dead of night, he never said a word, although her foolish heart imagined that his touch and his lips told her everything she secretly desired.

He had taken from her the means to prevent conception and yet he always ensured he used his Roman condom. As if even now, when she knew how deeply he despised her, he still afforded her enough consideration to respect her wishes that she didn't want to conceive his child.

She brushed the tips of her fingertips across her belly. Arianrhod had turned her back on her, but her Moon Goddess had prevented her from taking the womb cleansing tea two morns ago for a reason.

Despite all their precautions, she had conceived his babe. It had been foretold in her vision; blessed by Arianrhod. And although only days ago such an outcome would have devastated Nimue, now the prospect of having Tacitus' child filled her with a maelstrom of primal love, protectiveness and an overwhelming sense of awe.

Was this how her mother had felt when she knew she had conceived Nimue? Twenty-three summers ago the Romans had not yet invaded Britain, but Gaul had already succumbed to the Eagle. The Romans wouldn't have been her mother's deadly enemy the same way they were hers. But even so, they were foreign barbarians and the threat of the Legions crossing the narrow sea into Britain was always an acknowledged threat.

Why hadn't her mother told her Roman lover that she was expecting his babe? Could Nimue do that to Tacitus? Didn't he deserve to know they had created a child together?

She knew he did.

Nimue straightened her spine. Even though she had failed to save Caratacus' queen, she had saved a dozen of her people from a similar fate. No rumor had reached her that they had been recaptured. She could only hope they had reached the relative safety of the enclave.

She'd spent enough time berating her failures. She had to re-strategize. Make alternate plans for escape.

Not only for her unborn child, whom she would never allow to be born under the slur of *slave*. But because she had to return to the enclave and complete the circle so her people were protected.

And the Romans destroyed?

How dearly she had once wished to unravel the mystery of the powerful Source of Annwyn. To continue the work of the great High Druid, Aeron, in his plans to eliminate the enemy from her land. But she not only possessed the blood of her enemy. She had fallen in love with one too.

She spread her fingers across her thighs and tried to calm her galloping thoughts. Was there a way to protect her people without decimating the Legion? Could Gwydion, Warrior Magician and god of Illusion be swayed in Arianrhod's ultimate desire? Would he intervene with his sister goddess and grant Nimue a concession for returning the last shard of bluestone to the enclave, for conducting the sacred rituals required?

The lamplight flickered, although no breeze stirred the air, and unnatural shadows lengthened across the far wall. Mesmerized, Nimue watched the shadows swirl into the unmistakable outline of a man—a god. A god whose eyes glowed like fire; a god who reached out his hand, palm up, acquiescing her request.

The door swung open and the shadows vanished back into the dark corners. Nimue stared up at Tacitus as he stood in the doorway, his scarlet cloak billowing around him. Awe filled her at the power of the mighty god. He had not only condescended to save the one she loved from the coming destruction. He had reinforced the strength of his power by sending Tacitus to her now.

∼

Tacitus braced himself against the enchanting look Nimue cast his way. Her beautiful green eyes showed no trace of deception and, dressed in the manner of a Roman noblewoman, any man could be forgiven for thinking her a fragile creature in need of protection.

She *was* in need of protection. But not because she was incapable of looking after herself. He glared at her, willed himself to see beyond her delicate features and aura of vulnerability to the Druid he knew her to be.

Druids were bloodthirsty barbarians who sacrificed babes on the altars of their heathen gods. They incited fear and madness among their followers and were behind the uprisings against the Empire.

But all he saw when he looked at Nimue was the woman who haunted his waking hours and beguiled his dreams with the aid of an infatuated Morpheus.

He kicked the door shut. "Why?" The word tore from his throat, unbidden. He wasn't even sure what he was asking.

She stood and faced him, as regal as an empress or a barbaric foreign queen. He tried to imagine her wielding a dagger over a helpless child to appease her goddess—and couldn't.

"Would you do anything less for your people, Tacitus?"

Why did she have to throw logic in his face? Why couldn't she fall to her knees and weep with despair like another woman would, or beg for his forgiveness and tell him that she'd never had any intention of leaving him without saying a word?

He ground his teeth at such fantasy. And bitterly acknowledged that if Nimue was such a woman, they wouldn't be in this position in the first place.

"What were you doing with the commander?" That overheard conversation had plagued his mind countless times, but he still couldn't fathom why they had been in that room together or how they had been talking of Nimue's mother. Most of all he couldn't fathom why the commander hadn't exposed Nimue's heritage. It was inconceivable that he hadn't made the connection between the crucifixion of a Celtic noblewoman and the likelihood that she'd also been a Druid.

For a moment, he didn't think she was going to answer him. Then she drew in a deep breath, as if coming to a decision. "He was waiting in there for me."

Tacitus had suspected as much, but if that was so, it pointed to the fact that the commander had somehow been aware of Nimue's intentions. And that made no sense at all. Surely his commander didn't want Nimue in his bed enough to compromise his integrity?

The way I'm prepared to compromise mine?

He wanted to grip her shoulders, shake her, demand to know *why was he waiting for you?* But he feared that she would tell him. Once the words were spoken aloud how could he continue to ignore the truth?

Yet he knew that he would.

"Tacitus." She took a step toward him and he forced himself to remain as he was and not drag her into his arms. Why did he still find her so irresistible? His lust for her hadn't eased. It increased every time he took her. Every time he thought of her.

He wanted to despise her; discard and forget her and knew he never could.

"What?" His voice was harsh but she didn't flinch. She never flinched. His mind flashed back to the scene with his commander when Nimue had trembled violently in his arms. She'd witnessed the crucifixion of her mother. Had likely escaped the same fate by sheer good fortune. Why would she flinch when a hated Roman raised his voice to her?

"What's going to happen to us?"

Her question threw him. She hadn't asked what was going to happen to her, which he'd expected. But when did Nimue ever do or say what he expected of her?

"Us?" Derision soaked the word but it was a derision aimed at his own despicable need to keep Nimue in his life. "There is no us, Nimue. What gave you that idea? You belong to me and that's the end of it."

If only that was the end of it. Yet even now, after everything she'd done, the knowledge that in the eyes of Rome she was nothing more than his slave tore his guts.

But even that faded into insignificance when he faced the bitter truth. If he wanted to keep her, that was how she would have to remain. Because she would never willingly stay with him as his concubine.

The truth was stark, brutal and flayed his sense of honor. In the end, when it truly mattered, he was no better than his father.

For a brief moment he thought he saw raw anguish in her eyes as if his dismissal of what they had between them genuinely wounded her. But what did they have between them?

Nothing but lust and sex. The intimate touches, the laughing glances and stimulating banter they'd shared before her betrayal had gone. He despised the fact that he missed it all; that he craved to once again be shocked and challenged and enchanted by her unorthodox conversation.

"No." Her voice was soft but it wasn't the voice of a woman

cowed or beaten by circumstance. For that at least he could thank whichever gods were responsible. "It's not the end of it, Tacitus. No matter how dearly you wish it could be."

Still she defied him. He tried to crush the admiration that snaked through him for her courage, and failed. Because she had always shown courage and it was one of the aspects about her that so ensnared him.

Curse her Druid blood. He wanted to reclaim what they had once shared, but it was impossible. If he gave her the slightest taste of freedom, she would vanish like mist in the morning.

"I wish for nothing more than you learn your place, Nimue." Rage and despair at where they now stood pounded through his blood, thundered through his mind. No other woman had ever weaved such a mystical spell around him. Her heritage meant death but he didn't care about her heritage. He wanted her. And he wanted her to choose to stay with him because she couldn't stand the thought of existing without him.

But the only way to make her stay was to keep her enslaved.

How low he had sunk in so short a time. All his life he'd prided himself on denying his father's way of life. Tacitus didn't buy slaves for sexual gratification. The prospect revolted him. Yet he stood before Nimue and couldn't stomach the idea of letting her go.

He was truly his father's son. The knowledge sickened him, but still he would keep her. He would keep her until she forgot about her need to escape, her desire for revenge. He would keep her until Olympus itself crumbled to dust.

"Tacitus—"

"I have no intention of releasing you. You can't be trusted outside my quarters and therefore you will not venture outside my quarters." He glared at her, daring her to disagree, willing her to say *I'm sorry*.

Silence crackled between them, their gazes locked in a mute

battle of wills. Finally she tilted her jaw at him, a proud gesture that he recognized, and pain stabbed through his heart.

"Perhaps you'll allow me to venture outside your quarters if you accompany me."

He had the sudden vision of them riding across the Cambrian countryside, unencumbered by the chains of their pasts or the dark clouds of their present. It was dangerously seductive.

"I doubt it."

He watched blood heat her cheeks but she didn't look angry at his refusal to succumb to her Druid-inspired charms. She looked hurt.

"Perhaps in time you'll change your mind." She sounded as though she struggled to keep her voice calm, and he clenched his fists in an effort to prevent himself from reaching for her and dragging her into his arms. Did he have no self-control when it came to Nimue? "I give you my word, on the names of my beloved foremothers, that I wouldn't attempt to escape from you."

"Why should your word mean anything to me?" She had once before given him her word. And she had broken it.

But she hadn't pledged her honor on the names of her beloved foremothers. Did he really believe that made so much difference?

Again, silence stretched between them, and an unaccountable trickle of unease stirred deep in his gut. Why did she look at him as though there was something she wanted to tell him? Why didn't she simply say what was on her mind? She had never thought twice of doing so…before.

The tip of her tongue peeked between her lips but with that same sense of unease he was certain she didn't do it to be provocative. There was a strangely haunted air about her that hadn't been present just moments ago, and he recalled what she'd said to him when they had first arrived back at the garrison.

She wasn't used to being confined inside for extended lengths of time. Was it possible she might truly lose her mind if he denied her freedom?

"I pledged my word to the Briton king, Caratacus, to protect his queen and daughter before I ever met you." She continued to gaze at him and he knew what she was saying. But he didn't want to hear it. "As a warrior, my oath is my bond, Tacitus. I had to release my people and, although I failed to save the queen, I didn't do any of it with the intention of abusing your trust in me."

"And yet you did abuse my trust."

"You would have done the same in my place."

He stared at her, momentarily speechless. Did she really think their positions could ever be comparable?

She called herself a warrior, but simply because she knew how to wield a dagger and possessed bravery to the point of self-sacrifice didn't qualify her as such in his mind. Gods, next she would tell him that she'd been part of the battle itself.

He knew it had been the Druids who'd led the uprisings against the Legions when they'd first marched into Cambria. But they were male Druids. And any woman who followed her man into battle had to be built like a man herself. How else could she survive?

"What I would have done is irrelevant." He swung off his cloak so he had an excuse to break eye contact. They might no longer share the level of intimacy he craved, but it appeared Nimue was still capable of challenging his long-held beliefs with her conversation. "I'm a Roman Tribune. My loyalty lies with my Emperor, with Rome and with my family honor."

The words sounded hollow to his ears. Because by keeping Nimue from harm he had irrevocably betrayed all such loyalties.

"We're not so different, you and I." Her softly spoken words hammered through his mind but he refused to acknowledge them. She was a woman, not a warrior. Her loyalties were, by virtue of her sex, different from a man's.

Black guilt gnawed through his heart. For his actions in

protecting Nimue from his Emperor's decree, did he still possess the right to call himself a warrior?

"Tacitus." She curled her fingers around his wrist, and her touch sent desperate need splintering through his blood. He turned to her and once again became lost in her beautiful eyes. "Can you put this behind us? Could you not learn to trust me again, in time?"

If she continued to look at him with her deceptively innocent eyes then gods help him. He'd agree to anything that poured from her lying mouth. He pulled free from her grasp before he was tempted to lose himself in the scented sanctuary of her arms.

Except he was lost already.

He turned his back. In time, he feared he would forgive her for anything and everything. But now was not the moment to let her know just how far he had fallen under her Druid spell.

"If not for me," her quiet voice, filled with such sadness it made his chest ache, halted his planned exit, "then for the sake of our unborn child."

CHAPTER 31

Nimue saw Tacitus stiffen at her words, and nerves tangled low in her stomach. She gripped her fingers together and waited for him to say something. Anything. But he remained utterly still, as if he had turned to stone, and the nerves multiplied, filling her stomach and heart and closing her throat.

Nothing had gone as she had imagined. When Tacitus had appeared, she'd thought it was a sign he'd forgiven her. She thought she would be able to persuade him into granting her a measure of freedom—dependent upon him accompanying her.

That was of utmost importance. That he accompany her when she left the fortification. Hadn't Arianrhod, through her brother god Gwydion, bestowed her blessing on her wish that Tacitus be spared from the coming devastation?

But even the most beloved Goddess gave nothing easily. And so she'd had no choice but to share her most sacred of secrets. The secret she'd intended to tell him when they were safe in the enclave.

Finally he turned to face her. Any small hope she'd harbored that he'd greet her news with pleasure withered. Horror etched his features as though she'd just admitted to murdering his precious Emperor.

"How can you be—?" He choked, unable to even say the word. His glance slid to her belly as if seeking confirmation. "I used protection."

She dug her fingernails into the palms of her hands and focused on that pain in the vain hope it would help diminish the pain eating through her heart. "It seems Arianrhod had other ideas."

He exhaled, and appeared riveted to the spot. "How can you be sure? It's too soon to know for certain. You're mistaken."

Even though every word pierced her with the knowledge of how deeply he wanted nothing to do with their child, one thing shone through the darkness. He hadn't questioned her on her certainty that he was the father.

"I know, Tacitus." She pressed one hand against her belly and a part of her died at the way Tacitus flinched at her action. "I'm an acolyte of the Moon Goddess herself. How could I be mistaken in something like this?"

"My child." His tortured gaze clashed with hers. "Conceived on a slave."

Another time his words would have stoked her fury, burned her pride. But the look of anguish in his eyes, the self-disgust in his voice, caused only a deep sense of grief in the core of her soul.

"I don't have to be a slave," she whispered, *to be yours*, but those words remained locked tight in her heart.

"Fuck." He paced the room, as if Belatucadros, god of destruction, rained fire at his heels. "If you'd agreed to my request, you would already be my concubine." He swung around and faced her. "I swore on my mother's heritage I would never force a child on an unwilling woman."

Doubt whispered in the back of Nimue's mind at his words. They weren't the words she'd expected from him. Was his horror at the situation not because the thought of siring a child with her repelled him, but because he thought *she* must hate the circumstances?

"Tacitus." Once again she reached for him but he stiffened as though her touch was unwelcome. She hesitated for a moment, then gripped his arm regardless. He didn't jerk away. "I wasn't unwilling."

He looked as if her confession shredded his soul. It didn't make sense. What else could she say to make him understand that she no longer loathed the thought of having his child?

"How the gods delight in exacting their vengeance." His words were bitter, and although he looked at her, Nimue had the feeling he didn't see her at all. "The blood of Rome triumphs once again."

Unease snaked through her at the wild look in his eyes. "I don't know what you mean."

He didn't seem to hear her. "How I despised my father for what he did to my mother. What choice did she have? Yet now I find I'm no better, despite my lofty pledges."

Self-disgust dripped from every word and Nimue stared at him as disjointed fragments of all their conversations tumbled through her mind.

She'd jumped to conclusions at his disclosure that he possessed two mothers. Tacitus had never truly clarified what he'd meant. Now she thought about it, his reaction to her assumption had been oddly…muted.

Her stomach churned as another possibility reared its unsavory head. Surely not. Tacitus belonged to the upper echelons of Roman society. She didn't know a great deal about the patrician class but she knew enough. Romans didn't embrace those they considered their inferiors into their jealously guarded noble ranks.

Yet the thought plagued her mind as Tacitus' tortured gaze scorched her face.

My mother is Greek. When he'd told her that, she had imagined his mother to be a high-ranking Greek lady, related somehow to Tacitus' Roman-born mother.

What choice did she have?

Skeletal fingers raked over her flesh as she saw beyond his words to the anguish beneath. To the underlying reasons why he was so conflicted whenever he mentioned his parentage to her.

"Your mother," she whispered. "Your Greek mother, Tacitus. Why did she not have a choice?"

He gripped her arms and jerked her toward him. "Slaves don't have the choice to say no, do they, Nimue?" His words were savage but despair filled his eyes. "They're at the mercy of their masters' whims. They don't even have the right to keep their child if their master decrees otherwise."

Pain engulfed her heart as finally she understood. His birth mother hadn't given him up at all. He had been taken from her and given to his father's Roman wife. "I'm so sorry." It was hard to speak through the lump that choked her throat and the words were muffled. But he heard her and looked at her, as though he didn't understand; as if she spoke a barbaric tongue that he had never before encountered.

"I would have done anything to prevent this outcome." He sounded so wretched her heart squeezed with pain.

He'd misunderstood her words.

"No, Tacitus." It was important he realized that, unlike his mother, she did have a choice. That she had knowingly made a choice. "I could have prevented this. But I chose not to take my womb cleansing tea. Arianrhod intervened—but only because she knew how much I wanted this."

How surreal that she said such things to him, a Roman. And how humbling for her Druid pride to know that she meant every word.

He looked at her as though he couldn't process the depth of her confession. "I've dishonored my mother and my sisters. I swore on their names a child of mine would never be stigmatized in such a way."

Nimue pulled free of his grip and grasped his jaw in one hand, forcing him to look at her instead of looking through her. "No child of *mine* will ever be stigmatized, either." Did he think she would allow their child to be thought of as a slave by all of Rome? "You aren't, after all."

He gave a bitter laugh, but instead of thrusting her aside, he covered her hand with his, and pressed her palm against the roughness of his jaw. "My father was desperate to sire a son. I have seventeen older half-sisters, all conceived with various slaves. In their eighth month he granted their manumission, in the hope the child would be a boy. He had no intention of his only son being born into slavery."

"Your father took all the babies away from their birth mothers?" She tried to keep the horror from her voice because she didn't want Tacitus to think she judged him. But the tortured look that flashed across his face made it clear that she hadn't succeeded.

"He had no interest in daughters, Nimue. They may have been born free but he didn't acknowledge them as his own. They're merely the bastards of his freedwomen. But they're still my sisters."

Repressed anger vibrated through every word and she stared at him, transfixed. His culture placed little value on females. Yet despite the actions of his father, she knew Tacitus would never turn his back on his child, simply because it wasn't a son.

Hadn't the commander said he would never abandon the child of the woman he loved? Why did she think of her father now? Was it because she knew, in her heart, that her mother had seen the same noble qualities in her Roman officer that Nimue saw in Tacitus?

"The Emperor granted permission for my father to adopt me. I lived in luxury while my sisters toiled as servants. My father could never understand why I insisted on recognizing our blood link."

She had the savage urge to plunge her dagger through Tacitus' father's arrogant heart. "It's clear you don't take after your father at all in such matters."

Not only did she mean the words with every fiber of her being, she meant them to comfort Tacitus. But he jerked back from her, as if her words scalded, and a wild light gleamed in his eyes.

"You're wrong." His gazed raked over her, burning her skin. "We're more alike than I ever imagined. You'll only stay if you're not allowed to leave. What choice is that, Nimue?"

Before she could even fully process his caustic question he snatched up his cloak, swung it around his shoulders and marched from the room.

CHAPTER 32

Nimue jerked awake as the door swung open. Tacitus stood there, his foreign armor gleaming in the light from the lamp that he held, his cloak adding to the dramatic effect. For a moment she wondered if she still dreamed of her Roman lover, but as he entered the room and the light chased shadows back into the corners, she knew that this was no dream.

She pushed herself upright on the bed that he hadn't shared with her during the night. Or was it still nighttime? Disoriented she raked her tangled hair off her face and frowned at him. After he'd left her last night, she'd followed him, only to watch him stride outside and disappear deeper into the fortification. And the legionary on guard made it clear that his orders to ensure she remained inside hadn't changed.

"Get dressed." His voice was pitched low, but it was a command nevertheless. For a moment, she continued to stare at him in bemusement and then the meaning of this odd nocturnal communion blazed through her.

Heart pounding she pulled on the gown she'd worn the previous day, slung her empty medicine bag over her shoulder and wrapped her cloak around her. Tacitus watched her in silence. His expression gave nothing away.

Blessed Arianrhod, thank you. Nimue sent endless prayers to her beloved Goddess as she once again clutched the pouch that held the shard of bluestone and followed Tacitus outside into the dusky early morn. All the half-formed plans she'd made during the night, to try to persuade him to accompany her to the secret enclave, faded back into the shadows. While she'd endlessly worried, her Goddess had weaved her magic around Tacitus, irrevocably entwining their destinies together.

He took her hand and led her toward a horse that waited on the wide Roman road that bisected the fortification. The legionary by the horse stepped back, and raised his arm in the traditional sign of respect she had come to recognize. Tacitus merely jerked his head in response and helped her onto the horse. Then he adjusted a strangely shaped pack that was slung over his shoulder before he swung up behind her.

Without a word, he urged his mount forward. She gripped her fingers together as they neared the great gates of the fortification but she needn't have worried. They passed through without the slightest problem and she released a relieved breath.

"How far from here are your people?" His voice was clipped and she looked over her shoulder, but it was too dark to discern his expression. For a moment, unease rippled through her mind and she glanced at the pink-streaked sky. Although dawn had not yet broken, the starry wheel had fallen. Yet even as the thought formed, an unassailable certainty gripped her.

Once again, the Moon Goddess had not reigned in the nighttime skies. Was it because Nimue had failed in her original mission? Was this a facet of Arianrhod's displeasure?

But wasn't Nimue following her Goddess' orders now? Why then did Arianrhod continue to conceal her radiance from her people?

She pulled her mind back to the present. To Tacitus' question.

"We'll be close when the sun reaches the zenith." She pointed in the direction they needed to travel and ignored the tiny flicker of alarm that edged her consciousness. Tacitus would never betray the location of her people. But in any case, the concern was irrelevant. Tacitus wouldn't be returning to his fortification. She, with the help of her elusive Goddess, would make sure of that.

He redirected his horse and dug in his heels. His strong arms encased her but only through necessity. He didn't wind one arm around her waist or give any indication that he'd accepted Arianrhod had bound their futures together.

As the sun rose on the eastern horizon, casting a golden glow across the land she loved, the unease within her heart expanded. She was close to fulfilling the first part of Arianrhod's plan by returning the shard of bluestone and completing the sacred circle. The magic of the bluestones would ensure her people's safety from the might of the Eagle—but this time the gods intended more. Gwydion had conveyed the message. She knew devastation would follow. Knew also, in her heart, that should she succeed then great knowledge of the Spiral of Annwyn, the Source of Universal Life, would be hers to embrace.

Unthinking, she reached out and speared her fingers through Tacitus' as he held the reins. Her hand looked so small on top of his. And yet the future of his Legion rested in her palm.

She should feel triumphant. Victory was within her sights. Soon, not only would she be able to claim vengeance for her people, she would also, finally, avenge her mother's murder.

By murdering the man her mother had loved with all her heart.

"Are you cold?" Tacitus' voice against her ear caused her to shiver again. But she wasn't cold. It seemed the soul of her mother clasped her hands, a silent condemnation for what Nimue proposed to do.

"No." Her voice was hoarse as the full implications of what might happen hammered through her heart. Could she take responsibility for the death of her mother's beloved? For the death of *her own father?*

"Do you need to rest?"

For a brief moment, she squeezed her eyes shut. From the first time she'd met him, Tacitus had always been mindful of her comfort. Even now when they fled for their lives—for surely if he was caught abandoning his Legion he'd be executed—his first concern was for her.

"It's better if we keep going." She tightened her fingers around his, willed him to relinquish his grip on the reins and crush her in his arms. But he remained rigid, as if her touch didn't affect him at all.

"Let me know if you need to stop for a while." He sounded distant, as though he spoke to a stranger, and yet his actions in taking her to her people belied his chilly exterior.

As the sun rose in the sky, Nimue's deeply held desire to learn all the secrets of the magic bluestones wavered further. Was such knowledge worth the death of so many Romans? They weren't all evil as she had so long believed. Marcellus was a healer. Did he deserve to die?

A few times, she attempted to engage Tacitus in conversation but his responses were stilted and in the end she gave up. She understood. He was conflicted at deserting his people. It would take time for him to see that he'd had no choice.

∼

ANTICIPATION TINGLED through Nimue's senses as they walked deeper into the forest, Tacitus leading his horse by the reins. The tangled undergrowth snagged her ankles and up ahead she saw a familiar pair of great oak trees.

They had arrived.

She curled her fingers around Tacitus' biceps and he looked down at her. Even in the muted light that filtered through the forest canopy, she could see the entrancing violet of his eyes. Would their child have his father's eyes?

"Are they here?"

"Very near." They'd stopped walking and her voice was hushed. She glanced around, but could see no sign of hidden ambush. It was imperative she find her people quickly so she could explain that Tacitus was with them, by decree of Arianrhod. "We just need to go beyond the—"

"I imagined you'd return to your village." Tacitus glared at the surrounding forest as if it offended him. "How can you be certain anyone is here, Nimue? I can't leave you here alone."

"Alone?" Her voice was sharp. Even if, by some mischance, her people hadn't made it back to the enclave she wouldn't be alone. Tacitus would be with her. "We won't be alone. It's far safer here than in any of the surrounding villages." And it would be safer still once she'd completed the sacred rituals and replaced the shard of bluestone she'd stolen.

Her mind shied away from what would happen after she'd restored the circle of bluestones around the enclave. Perhaps, now that she was free, Arianrhod would grace her with her presence, and Nimue could beg for a further favor.

Tacitus gritted his teeth as though her assurances both tested his endurance and tormented his soul. He cast another black look around the forest before he pulled the pack from his shoulder and ripped it open.

"You'll need these." His voice was gruff as he pulled her dagger from the pack and handed it to her. She took it and a fierce joy raced through her at the familiar weight of it in her hand. How she'd missed its comforting presence at her hip. "And this." He sounded as if the words choked him as he pulled her bow free. "The arrows are gone."

Reverently she took her bow and traced one finger along its elegant edge. "Thank you." She'd never expected to see either of her weapons again. "Don't worry about the lack of arrows. I can easily replenish my stock."

He looked as if the thought of her crafting her own arrows made him ill. "Take this." He pushed something sharp into her hand and she frowned at the silver brooch encrusted with emeralds. It was one she'd never seen before. "My family name is engraved on the back of this fibula. If you ever need me, for whatever reason, send this to me and I'll find you."

The warmth that had filled her with the return of her weapons instantly evaporated. She looked at him, saw the tension etched on his face and radiating from his body, and denial slammed through her.

"But you're coming with me." It was an imperious command and she slung her bow over her shoulder so that she could grab his hand. "There will be no need for me to find you because we'll be together."

He jerked back from her touch. "How can we be together? We come from different worlds. In my world, you're a slave. This is the only way I can set you free."

Denial prickled along her flesh. This wasn't how it was meant to be.

"You can't go back." The words condemned her but she didn't care if he found them suspicious. *He couldn't return.* "Your place is by my side. You know this."

A strange, tortured smile twisted his lips. "Even if you'd agreed to become my concubine, in your eyes you and our child would never be free. Yet that's the best I can offer you." He pulled from her grasp and stepped back. "Stay safe, Nimue. Tell our child that I wish I could have known him."

"But—" Horrified at how her plans were turning to ash before her eyes, she watched Tacitus turn his back. "You can't leave." She sounded desperate. She didn't care. How could she stop him? By throwing her dagger and felling him to his knees? What good would that be? She darted after him and grasped his cloak. "My Goddess has tied our destinies together."

He paused and looked at her. Her heart ached. How could he walk away from her? Was this the last time she'd ever look at his face? Into his eyes?

"Your goddess of the moon." It wasn't a question. "It's not me she wants. It's you. All the time I've enslaved you, the skies have been dark. But I'm not doing this for a faceless goddess I know nothing about. I do this for you. If I took you back to Rome, your status would destroy you from the inside out." For a brief, heartbreaking moment he cradled her face between his hands. "I won't be responsible for crushing your spirit, Nimue, the way my father so carelessly crushed the spirits of my two beloved mothers."

He released her but she could still feel the imprint of his fingers on her face as he once again turned away. Fragmented denials screamed through her mind. *You're nothing like your father.* But the words remained locked inside, pounding against her skull, thundering through her veins.

She had asked him to stay. And he had refused. For a terrifying instant, she saw herself on her knees, begging him not to go, imploring him to choose her and their child.

Pride stiffened her spine. She was a Druid and it didn't matter if her heart was breaking or her soul weeping. She wouldn't have Tacitus' last memory of her as a weak woman clinging to his boots. Then he glanced over his shoulder and their gazes meshed.

Her resolve wavered. What did her pride matter if it meant Tacitus would stay? But the words lodged in her throat, her knees refused to buckle and the pride of her foremothers forbade the tears to fall.

He would leave her as he had found her. A warrior of Cymru.

CHAPTER 33

It was late afternoon before Tacitus returned to the garrison. Despite having left a message for his commander, he knew his exemplary military record would now be blighted for having taken the day off without leave. The knowledge made no impact on him at all.

He strode toward the commander's quarters, refusing to think of anything but the absolute present. Because if he let his guard down, the last image he had of Nimue, her beautiful green eyes glittering with unshed tears, haunted every shadowy corner of his mind.

"Enter." The commander's curt tone matched his expression when Tacitus pushed open the door.

Tacitus saluted but the older man continued to glare at him. There was no point in delaying tactics. The commander would discover what he'd done sooner or later.

"I request the manumission of Nimue."

Only as the words left his mouth did he realize that on the last occasion his commander had spoken to him of Nimue, manumission was the word that had been used. He had no idea why his commander desired Nimue's manumission and it didn't matter. She was beyond his reach now.

Shock flashed across the older man's face, but within a heartbeat he had regained his previous dark glare. "Granted. Bring her to me."

"I require her formal manumission first." He had no intention of angering his commander by telling him Nimue was no longer in the garrison. Not before she'd been formally freed.

For a moment he thought he had gone too far. The commander's eyes narrowed as though he considered Tacitus' words a direct threat to his authority. But then, just as swiftly, his expression lost its hostility.

"That can be arranged. No one need know that she wasn't present at the official signing of the documents." He pulled sheets of papyrus across his desk. "What's your price for this, Tacitus?"

His gut knotted. It was degrading enough that he had bought Nimue. He wouldn't further soil his soul by selling her. "She is beyond price."

The commander shot him a look that he couldn't decipher. As if he had read too much into that statement. Fuck, why had he said anything at all? He just wanted this over so that he could get on with his life.

A life without Nimue.

"You care for her." The commander's voice was oddly gruff. "I will remember that, Tribune."

Tacitus glared at the older man as he returned to his documents. He had no wish for the commander to assume he knew anything about Tacitus' feelings for Nimue. And what in Hades did he mean by he would remember it?

The only thing the commander was likely to remember about this encounter was that Tacitus had illegally freed a slave. But once the documents were signed, there was little that could be done about it.

Finally, the commander handed him the documents and

Tacitus scrutinized them before making them official. He straightened, and looked his commander in the eye. He had no intention of lying, but neither did he particularly want to raise his commander's ire unnecessarily.

"I'll arrange for Nimue to be returned to her people."

The commander stood. "I'll accompany you. I look forward to seeing her reaction to such news."

Two thoughts hammered through Tacitus' head. First, he would have to tell the commander that Nimue was already with her people. And second—there was something very odd about the commander's entire attitude when it came to Nimue.

He straightened his already rigid spine. "She is no longer under Roman control."

Tension crackled in the air as the commander stared at him. Finally he exhaled a measured breath, clearly battling for some degree of control.

"Where is she, Tribune?"

"Back where she belongs."

The commander's jaw clenched. "You let her go?"

"Yes, sir." If the commander chose to make an example of Tacitus, he would require the influence of his powerful family to prevent dire consequences. How ironic that his father should be the one to assist in Tacitus' only time of need, considering the actions that had led him here.

To Hades with it. He'd rather be disgraced than call on his father for nepotistic intervention.

"You let her go." The commander slammed his hands onto his desk and leaned forward. He looked furious yet there was a strange undertone of awe in his voice. "Despite how you feel about her?"

Curse all the gods in existence. Why was his commander fixated on the thought that Nimue meant something to Tacitus? Was it truly so obvious?

"Rome would destroy her."

His commander looked at him as though he'd never seen him before. As if he had just experienced a terrible revelation from the gods themselves. Slowly he sat down and once again, it appeared that he aged before Tacitus' very eyes.

"Yes." His voice was hollow and there was a glazed look in his eyes. "Rome destroyed her. As she always claimed it would."

Who was the commander speaking of? Unease mounted and when finally the older man jerked his head in dismissal, relief washed through Tacitus and he made good his escape.

∽

NIMUE STOOD in the center of the small glade in the forest. A circle of massive bluestones surrounded the edge of the glade and an earth-covered dolmen had been constructed countless generations ago. It had been used for sacred rituals during the time Caratacus and his rebels had hidden from the Romans, and an elusive sense of otherworldly power swirled in the air.

She stared up into the night sky, but only blackness loomed. Not even a glimmer of silver pierced the canopy of cloud. Yet there hadn't been a single cloud during the day and there was no scent of rain.

The women and children who had been captured by the Romans had arrived safely in the enclave. Several others, from various tribes, had also found their way back from the battleground and they'd all greeted her as their savior.

Tomorrow was the full moon. It was the night she was to perform the sacred rituals to restore the magical protection to the enclave. It didn't matter that she hadn't the first idea what she was supposed to do. She knew that, when the time came, the knowledge would be hers.

Would the skies finally clear? Would Arianrhod, in all her shining magnificence, once again grace the night?

Her Goddess hadn't come to her since Nimue had returned to

the enclave, despite how fervently she'd prayed. Was it because Arianrhod knew that Nimue's heart was no longer committed to ridding Cymru of the enemy? Because she knew her acolyte had already *given* her heart to the enemy?

∼

THE FOLLOWING MORN, as Nimue purified her body in preparation for the coming night, the dark sense of malignancy that had haunted her for the last two days magnified. Her stomach churned, her palms were sweaty and it wasn't her imagination—the forest was unnaturally silent. It didn't feel as if freedom beckoned on the horizon. It felt like a terrifying abyss threatened to destroy everything she had ever known.

Or was that simply her crippling guilt attempting to rationalize how close she was to betraying her Goddess, her heritage and her people?

With shaky fingers, she undid one of her small leather pouches and took out the brooch Tacitus had given her. Even looking at it caused her heart to ache and she curled her fingers around it, unheeding of how the jewelry dug into her flesh.

Tacitus, my love. She pressed her clenched fist against her naked breasts and saw, in her mind's eye, her Roman's face in the moment before he'd turned from her forever.

How could she have let him go? Would agreeing to be his concubine have been so very dreadful? Yet how could she desert her people, the land of her birth, when they needed her most?

Even if the terrible conviction that gripped her—that the promised devastation was *wrong*—didn't feel as if it sprung solely from her own conflicted loyalties?

But if that conviction was not entirely hers, *then whose was it?*

CHAPTER 34

"Glad to return to Rome." Blandus scowled at the legionaries who were training on the field beyond the garrison. Tacitus grunted in response. Rome no longer held the appeal it had before the battle with Caratacus.

Before he'd met Nimue.

"The Senate," Blandus continued, "is a far more civilized battlefield than those we encounter in these far-flung provinces. The facilities here are appalling. I've never endured such primitive conditions."

The facilities were barbaric when compared to what they were used to in Rome. In less than three months, Tacitus' tour of duty would be over and his political career admirably advanced. With the fall of Caratacus, his military record glowed. He could pursue law, his long-held ambition.

Or he could remain in the Legions.

The thought pierced through his mind, as clear and sharp as if he had spoken the words aloud. For a moment he froze, disoriented by the power of the thought and the solid certainty that it wasn't only a viable alternative…

But his only alternative.

In Rome, as his concubine, Nimue would wilt. But if he remained in the military and took posts throughout Britannia and Gallia, Nimue could remain in a more familiar environment.

Still under the yoke of Rome. But at least she wouldn't be stigmatized the way she would if he took her home.

He'd already asked her to be his concubine. She had refused. Why did he think her answer would be any different now, simply because his plans for his future had changed?

But he knew the answer already. It was because this time Nimue truly did have a choice. Because this time he'd ask her not when she was enslaved; he would ask her now that she was a free woman.

~

Dusk settled, drifting through the forest, malicious fingers of darkness unrelieved by a shimmer of silver from the skies. Even now, on this night, Arianrhod denied light to her people.

A polished stone altar stood some distance from the dolmen. A fire burned in the center of the glade and from the light of the flames, Nimue watched the women, children and the handful of men who'd returned to the sanctuary daub ancient symbols onto their skin.

Torches blazed at the four corners of the altar and Nimue pulled one from the ground. She knew exactly where the shard of bluestone she'd stolen needed to be placed, and yet an overwhelming compunction compelled her to ensure she knew the way.

As she left the glade, she couldn't fathom what she was doing. Did she intend to go through with the ritual tonight? Her Goddess refused to hear her pleas and Arianrhod would never forgive her for such betrayal. She would be struck down without mercy. Could she willingly sacrifice the life of her unborn child for the lives of Tacitus and her father?

She pushed through the encroaching forest as despair seeped from her heart and corroded her soul. The life of her babe for the life of her lover. How could she live, knowing she was the one who had killed Tacitus? Yet how could she sentence his child to eternal torment for having defied a direct imperative from her Goddess?

Something small and dark hurtled by her head and she gasped, fell to a crouch, her eyes straining to see beyond the flickering pool of light from her torch. Disbelief shuddered through her as the fleeting shadow imprinted into her brain.

A young owl.

Even as the thought formed, she heard a sickening thud and without thinking she rushed forward toward the sound. An ash tree loomed from the shadows and she stopped dead, momentarily paralyzed by the appearance of Gwydion in one of his majestic manifestations.

The god had heard her treacherous thoughts. He had come in his sister-goddess' stead to exact vengeance.

Above the terrified pounding of her heart, she heard a rustle in the undergrowth. Her torch dipped and there, at the base of the ash tree, lay the injured owl.

And slithering toward it, the dark spear shape on its head clearly visible, was an adder.

"No." She thrust the torch at the snake and instead of instantly vanishing back into the undergrowth it turned to her, fangs gleaming in the flickering light. Rage pumped through Nimue and, unheeding of the connection between god and tree and creature, she thrust the torch again until it abandoned its prey and disappeared.

Nimue fell to her knees, plunged the tapered end of the torch into the ground and carefully scooped the owl into her hands. Its fragile heartbeat and unnatural stillness sent a new wave of terror thundering through her blood.

How could an owl, the manifestation of Arianrhod, die at the hands of her own brother?

Save them all. The feminine whisper that weaved through Nimue's mind was not powerful, as it had been during the last vision she'd experienced. But ethereal fingers trailed along her arms as, this time, understanding of the cryptic words unfurled.

Arianrhod did not speak only of the women and children who'd been captured by the Romans. She spoke of all the people of Cymru, both native *and invader.*

The owlet's eyes opened and in the flickering torchlight she saw the crescent moon gleam in the bird's glassy stare. Mesmerized she watched as the crescent dimmed, became less defined; disappeared. And as the light died, so too did the owl's heart.

"Blessed Arianrhod." Her whisper echoed through the trees and the undergrowth stirred although there was no breeze. The elusive presence of her Goddess surrounded her, a fragile brush against her flesh, a mystical caress deep within her soul. Love flooded through her and warmth seeped into her veins, filled her heart and cocooned her womb. Arianrhod had come to her at last.

Just as swiftly, darkness descended and ice speared through her breast. The terror returned but it was savage, unformed, and she glanced wildly around the shadowed forest in search of answers to unknown questions.

It couldn't be true. But despite her panicked denials, the last few moments hammered through her head in a constant refrain.

She had watched Gwydion destroy Arianrhod. Her goddess hadn't sent her brother god in her stead to visit Nimue during the last few days because she was angry with her acolyte. She had not sent Gwydion at all. And the only reason she'd failed to answer Nimue's prayers was because, somehow, Gwydion had prevented it.

It had been Gwydion who'd wanted her to take the opium. Only when she was under its influence could he penetrate her mind and manipulate her to his will. By taking the drug, she'd made it harder for Arianrhod to reach her. But still her Goddess had protected her. On the night before she and Tacitus had reached the fortification, she'd been consumed by the imperative to take the opium. Only the sight and haunting sound of an owl had prevented her from searching for the drug. Arianrhod had fought, in the only way she could, to keep her acolyte's mind clear of Gwydion's influence.

Nimue had wanted to discover how the High Druid Aeron had manipulated the Source of Annwyn to his will. She'd been so certain that Aeron was a martyr, a hero to all the people of Cymru. That he had been following the will of the gods when he'd created the first magical enclave and attempted to cleanse Cymru of the invaders.

But it was not her Goddess' will that she resurrect the magic of the bluestones. *It was Gwydion's.* It had always been only Gwydion's will. And he would destroy everything in his path, immortal, native and invader, in order to claim the mystical power that was the birthright of the Moon Goddess.

Only here, deep in the forest for this one tangible moment, had Arianrhod been able to manifest a physical vision. A warning of what might be if Nimue did not act.

Her Goddess offered no guarantee that Nimue would survive the outcome. But she knew she had no choice. Gwydion, master god of Illusion, could not be allowed to succeed in his fratricidal ambitions.

CHAPTER 35

Despite the lingering twilight, Tacitus knew he was close to where he'd last seen Nimue. Just up ahead were the two great oaks. How he would then find her when she could be anywhere at all within the forest, was another matter. Yet he was convinced he would succeed.

The gods were with him. Whether they were the gods of his mother or his father's heritage, he wasn't certain, but why else would his commander have given him leave to bring Nimue back?

Sword in hand he led his horse along the nonexistent forest path. The light was fading and yet again clouds obscured the moon. The sensation of being followed had eased as he entered the forest but returned now with a vengeance. He felt unseen eyes watch his progress and the hairs on the back of his neck rose, but all he saw were shadows.

A rush of air ahead caused him to freeze, senses alert, but even as his brain recognized the sound as that of an arrow a body tumbled from the oak in front of him to land with a heavy thud at his feet.

He saw an arrow protruding from the man's throat, a dagger

in his hand. Tacitus swung round, sword at the ready for any other would-be assassin, but the forest remained silent.

Who in Hades was the archer? To strike a target in this light, in these conditions was astounding. That the warrior hadn't been aiming for Tacitus, even more so.

"It is I, Nimue." Her voice whispered through the twilight as her slender figure approached. Relief, desire, *thankfulness* rushed through him at how easily he'd found her. That she was well and obviously under her people's protection. He looked beyond her, for the warrior who'd accompanied her, but nothing else stirred. She reached his side and pressed her palm against his jaw. A touch he'd never thought to experience again. He covered her hand with his. She felt so fragile beneath his fingers. He would never let her go again. "You returned to me, Tacitus."

"We have much to discuss." And discussing their future in the middle of a forest when assassins lurked behind every tree, was not ideal. "I couldn't wait any longer."

She gave a brief nod, as if his unexpected appearance made utter sense to her. "We must be quick." She knelt by the fallen man and his instinct to pull her away, to shield her from death, vanished when he saw her began to methodically strip the body. "Hurry. Change your clothes. You can't come into the enclave dressed as a Roman tribune."

He stared at her. He understood her words and yet they made no sense. "Why should I wish to enter the enclave? I've come to take you back so that we can talk."

She glanced up at him, and for the first time he noticed strange shadows cast about her face, although he couldn't imagine from where they came.

"Yes. We will talk. But first there's something I have to do. I can't leave yet, Tacitus. Cymru hovers on the precipice of eternal darkness."

She spoke in riddles, as the Oracles did in Rome. He didn't want to make the comparison yet it was impossible not to.

Here in the forests of Cambria, in this strange half-light between day and night, Nimue exuded a presence of authority, the authority that came with being chosen by the gods.

She clearly had no intention of leaving with him straightaway. Since his whole purpose in speaking to her was based on the fact she was now a free woman able to make her own choices, the enticing image of sweeping her into his arms, onto his horse and away from the forest was not a feasible option.

He gritted his teeth and ripped off his cloak. "Where is the archer?" He glared in the direction from which Nimue had appeared but still could see nothing. The thought of being watched by a stranger while he took on the disguise of a Cambrian peasant wasn't something he relished.

She paused in her task and looked up at him. "I came alone. My Goddess warned me you were in danger. Another heartbeat and I would've been too late to save you."

The Wings of Mors trailed the length of his arms in a caress of death. Speechless he stared at her and only now saw the bow slung across her shoulder. The bow he'd returned to her earlier.

The bow he had never really envisaged her using with such shocking skill.

"You." He cleared his throat and cast a swift glance at the fallen man. The warrior who had been poised to kill Tacitus; who would have killed him had Nimue not stopped him with such breathtaking accuracy. "You did this?"

Nimue stood and took a step back. He could no longer see her face but he could feel the tension vibrating in the air between them. "I'm a warrior, Tacitus. Yes, I did this to prevent him from killing you. Would you do less for me?"

"That's not—" He bit off his words and clenched his teeth. Of course he would kill any man who tried to harm Nimue. But she was a *woman*. She needed to be protected and shielded from the brutality of war. It wasn't her place to rescue *him*.

"I'm sorry my actions displease you." There was an odd

formality in her tone and bizarrely it reminded him of when she'd been ill after freeing the slaves. Except what did she mean? He wasn't displeased. He couldn't grasp how he felt about it, except that nothing in his life had prepared him for being saved from certain death by...

A woman.

"But know this." In the deepening shadows he saw her straighten and his chest tightened with pride. She looked so fragile, his Nimue, and yet she possessed a strength he'd rarely encountered. "I don't regret it. And I would do it again in a heartbeat if the alternative was your death."

He reached for her and took her hand. She didn't fall into his arms. He hadn't expected her to. A dozen responses collided in his mind but there was only one thing he needed to tell her.

"Then as fellow warriors we are in accord, Nimue. I would defy my Emperor himself to ensure you lived." He already had. But her soft laugh, and the way she squeezed his fingers, told him that his decision to relinquish a career in Rome was no sacrifice at all.

~

She led him deeper into the forest, her step unerring. The rough clothes didn't fit properly and although he'd refused to give up his sword he was naked without his armor. But he would endure a great deal more if it ensured that Nimue would eventually listen to his proposal with respect.

A flickering light glowed up ahead. As they approached, he saw it was a torch rammed into the ground. Nimue wrenched it up and turned to face him, and his heart slammed against his ribs.

He knew she was no longer wearing a Roman gown, but now the light illuminated her he saw the strange, barbaric markings on her face and arms. Her hair was braided and she looked like a wild savage, except he knew the vision was an illusion.

Because, Cambrian or not, *Druid* or not, Nimue was as refined, as knowledgeable and as intelligent as any patrician male of his acquaintance.

She thrust the torch at him and then pulled out a small pot from her bag. "I need to paint your face." She sounded apologetic but it didn't stop her from dipping her finger into the pot. "It will stop any suspicious glance. And Tacitus, there's something you must promise me."

"That depends what it is." Gods, what primitive ritual had he walked into? He no longer believed the rumors he'd heard about Druid sacrifices, but unease still knotted his gut.

"If I fail this night, you must promise to save yourself." With the tip of her finger she daubed the cold paint across his cheekbones. "If Gwydion, the god of Illusion, succeeds in claiming Arianrhod's destiny for his own then he'll destroy everything. Celt and Roman—it makes no difference in his quest for power."

He had no idea what she meant, but one thing was certain. He had no intention of allowing her to continue with what she had planned.

"Let another do this." He gripped her arm and glared into her face. "You don't need to put yourself in danger. The gods always fight for power between themselves. Nothing we do will ever change that."

She didn't try to pull away. Perhaps it was a trick of the flickering light from the torch, but for a moment sorrow wreathed her face. "I can't let my beloved Moon Goddess fade into the shadows." Her voice was gentle, as if she explained something to a child. "Gwydion would subjugate her utterly, and destroy all traces of her precious knowledge. Her wisdom must be preserved for balance to prevail."

Despite the warmth from the torch, shivers scuttled over his arms. Once again she sounded like an Oracle, channeling obscure prophesies from egomaniacal gods. He could easily end this now. It would take little effort to forcibly take Nimue back to the garrison where she would be safe from the manipulations of her goddess.

And any hope of a future together, the kind of future he wanted, would be irrevocably shattered.

"My lady." The masculine voice came from the shadows and Tacitus swung around, instinctively reaching for his sword. Nimue grasped his hand and moved in front of him.

"I am ready." She sounded like an empress. *She sounded like a priestess.* He wouldn't stop her from doing what she considered her duty. But he wouldn't stand by and allow her to be sacrificed on the altar of barbaric gods and goddesses who cared only for their own immortal posterity.

CHAPTER 36

Standing in the shadows behind Nimue as she stood before a primitive stone altar, Tacitus remained rigid as the Celts danced with apparent abandon in the small clearing. Pungent incense smoldered at various points on the altar and a strange blue fire, contained within a shallow bowl, burned in the center of the altar.

It was nothing like the civilized temples of Rome and yet the primal thud of the drums touched a raw nerve deep in the core of his being.

But it was Nimue who held his riveted attention. She'd loosened her hair and in the eerie blue light, the markings on her face made her look breathtakingly savage. With utmost concentration, she focused on the unnatural fire, chanting in a language he'd never heard before, a language that sent a trickle of primal awe along his spine.

It was easy to imagine, in this ancient Cambrian forest, that she spoke an archaic tongue known only to the gods and their chosen ones.

A wind sprung up from nowhere, swirling forest debris around ankles and thighs. His fingers curled around the hilt of his sword although he knew it was a useless reaction. A god, even a heathen god, could not be slayed by mortal weapon.

The darkness around the perimeter of the glade, where imposing monoliths loomed, coalesced. Tacitus narrowed his eyes. Were the flames playing tricks? But the great shadow lengthened until it towered over the treetops. A black nothingness in the massive shape of a man.

A god.

If he hadn't been paralyzed by the sight, Tacitus might have joined the Celts as they collapsed onto the ground, prostrate before the immortal being. But he wasn't of Cambria. He was of Rome and the only gods he knelt before were those who had shaped his childhood.

Mouth dry, he watched the great shadow glide across the clearing toward Nimue. She hadn't fallen to her knees. She remained ramrod straight and even above the cacophony of the wind he could hear her mystical chant.

She picked up something from the altar. It looked like her precious shard of bluestone. Mesmerized, Tacitus watched her hold out her hands above the flickering blue flames. And then, before he realized her intent, she sliced open her wrist with the sharp stone, and her blood dripped into the bowl.

He cursed violently and jerked forward. It felt as if iron bands restrained him and he grunted with effort. What in Hades was she doing?

"Gwydion." Her voice rose above the infuriated pounding of his heart. "Warrior God. Greatest of the Enchanters. I see through your false illusions."

She plunged her hand, holding the stone, into the bowl. The god-creature roared, a sound of bone-crushing fury, as the flames encompassed her. Instantly each monolith surrounding the glade cracked like thunder, split like lightning and spewed luminous violet flames into the skies.

"Nimue." He staggered from the enchantment that held him at

the same moment that the malignant god fell onto the collapsed figure of Nimue. Raw terror propelled Tacitus forward and he wound his arms around Nimue's waist and dragged her from the altar, dragged her from the jaws of vengeance. She was unconscious, blood covered her arm and the hand that had held the bluestone looked gray.

Vile blackness engulfed him. He could feel Nimue being sucked from his grasp. He couldn't release her to draw his sword. What use was his sword anyway?

"Heathen idol." He spat the words into the night, the only weapons he possessed. "Your time has passed. *You are nothing.*"

Thunder rumbled across the sky and the thick clouds parted, revealing a dazzling display of stars. The black shadow howled, lost shape, became nebulous and was then swept away in the swirling wind that circled the glade. From the corner of his eye, he saw the panic struck Celts flee from the clearing but he didn't care about the Celts. He only cared about the woman in his arms who hadn't moved since she had defied her god.

"Nimue, wake up." He crouched over her and pushed her hair off her face with a hand that shook. What would he do if she never woke up? "You can't leave me." The words hurt his throat, his chest, *his heart*.

Her eyes opened and she looked at him as if he was all that mattered in her world. He wanted to crush her in his arms, wrap her in a protective cocoon and never let her out of his sight. A foolish fantasy. His life with Nimue would never follow such a predictable pattern.

He wouldn't want it to.

She began to smile as he lowered his head toward her. Just to taste her lips. Just to reassure himself that she was still in the world of mortals. That her vindictive god hadn't won.

A strong hand clamped on his shoulder and thrust him back. Tacitus swung around, one arm still supporting Nimue, and the acidic words died on his tongue. His commander stood by his side, his gaze riveted on Nimue.

His commander? His brain couldn't comprehend what his eyes told him. He watched as the older man sank to his knees and gripped Nimue's uninjured hand. What the fuck was he doing? Had it been his *commander's* presence he'd felt following him from the garrison?

"Nimue." The commander's voice held a tone that Tacitus had never heard before. If it was not so ridiculous, the commander sounded as shaken as Tacitus felt. "Don't go. Don't leave me as she did. Let me give you what she would never accept."

"Get your hands off her." Unheeding of what his actions might cost his career, Tacitus knocked the commander's hand from Nimue's. "She's no longer a slave. She is no longer beholden to any man." Not even to him.

Nimue struggled to sit up, and he held her securely against his chest. His commander didn't attempt to interfere.

"Arianrhod is free." Her voice was hoarse but her smile was as radiant as the sun. "Your belief in me caused the last chains imprisoning her to crumble. My Goddess deems you a worthy warrior, Tacitus, despite your Roman blood."

"Stay with me." The words sounded harsh, sounded like an order. Obscurely he realized the commander had asked the same of her. He had to explain what he meant but had no wish to discuss it in front of the older man.

"Yes." Her response was so soft he wondered if he'd misheard. Of course he'd misheard. Nimue would never agree to anything so swiftly. Certainly not something like this.

"Wait." He sounded desperate. Gods, his career was over. His commander would see to that. No man spoke to a woman in such a manner. At least they certainly didn't in front of their commanding officer. "Let me explain."

"No." She pressed a finger against his lips. "I want to be with you, Tacitus. I know I could find my people. But it won't be the same. Because my heart is with you."

All the arguments he'd prepared in an attempt to persuade her to stay with him vanished. "You won't regret this decision. You'll be accorded all due respect as befits your status." He wanted to kiss her, to reassure her that all would be well. But he was acutely aware of the silent figure of his commander by his side. "You'll be my wife in all but name."

A strange look came over her face and bizarrely she looked at the commander. Surely the light dazzled his eyes, because why would she look at his commander with compassion?

"Wouldn't your noble patricians ostracize you for that? It's one thing to keep a concubine. Surely it's another to keep a foreigner, an enemy of your Emperor, in such an elevated status?"

Still she gazed at his commander. He had the strangest sensation that an unspoken message passed between them, but that was impossible. The events of the night were addling his brain.

"No one would question your status. But that is irrelevant. I'll pursue my career in the Legions. Then you won't have to face the hypocrisy of Rome."

She looked at him in what appeared to be horror. "But what of your desire to study law? You can't give that up. I know how much that means to you—"

"Enough." The commander barely raised his voice but fury thundered through the word regardless. "We need never have returned to Rome. She knew I didn't care about taking my place in the Senate. I would have given up everything for her. But she wanted nothing but a meaningless liaison."

Tacitus stared at his commander as ice trickled along his flesh. Yet again the older man spoke to Nimue in words that didn't quite make sense. Who was he talking about? And why would he say such things to Nimue in any case?

"You're wrong," Nimue whispered. "She once told me she

loved you with all her heart. I don't know why she left but it wasn't because you meant nothing to her."

Tacitus tore his gaze from his commander and stared at Nimue. Her attention was fixed on the older man, and with a dread fascination, Tacitus once again looked at his commander. Something stabbed through his chest and the world tipped.

The first time he'd met Nimue there had been something familiar about her. He hadn't known what, just that he'd had the strangest certainty that they'd met before.

They never had. But he knew why she looked familiar to him. It was because she possessed the same eyes as her father.

His commander.

"Shit." The word slid out, unbidden. Nimue was the daughter of a high-ranking patrician. The blood of Rome flowed in her veins. Jagged thoughts ripped through his mind. If his commander acknowledged her as his daughter there was a good chance the Emperor would approve a marriage between Tacitus and Nimue.

But what were the chances of that? It wasn't as if Nimue was a son.

"Do you have something to say, Tribune?" The commander rounded on him. "Or are you simply pissed that your magnanimous plans of using *my daughter* as your concubine are crumbling before your eyes?"

For a torturous moment, the vision of his seventeen half-sisters flashed through his mind. Noble blood ran through their veins, just as much as it did his. But in the eyes of Rome they were merely the bastards of freed slaves.

"At least I'll acknowledge to the entire world that any child of Nimue's is my child also. Son or daughter I would be proud to claim as mine."

The commander heaved himself to his feet and glowered down at Tacitus. "I intend to acknowledge my daughter. And as her father I also intend to ensure she has everything that her status deserves."

Nimue made a sound in the back of her throat and staggered to her feet. Tacitus kept his arm around her. She didn't attempt to pull away although she did shoot him an exasperated glance.

"Your concern is touching." She glanced at the commander —*her father*—then back at him. "But I have status of my own and don't require the approval of Rome to do as I wish with my life."

"Nevertheless, as my daughter, as my only child, you will receive it." The way the commander looked at her, he obviously expected a fight. "Whether you choose to live in Rome or her provinces you *will* be accorded the respect due to your rank."

Finally the words penetrated the seething thoughts pounding through Tacitus' brain. The commander intended to recognize Nimue?

Nimue gave an odd smile, clearly touched by the commander's orders. "If it means that much to you, then I accept. As long as you understand I'll never be an obedient Roman daughter at the mercy of her father's whims."

"I would expect nothing less from the daughter of your mother."

Nimue's smile faded. "The people I freed—the people here this night. Will you pursue them?"

The commander's jaw tightened before he let out a measured breath. "The escaped slaves will not be found. And nothing happened here tonight."

Stunned, Tacitus stared at his commander. He had committed treason with his words, just as much as Tacitus had by refusing to voice his suspicions about Nimue. Slowly he turned to look at the woman who stood between them. The woman who united them in their betrayal against their Emperor's decree.

Protocol demanded that his father choose Tacitus' bride. That Tacitus sought approval from his prospective bride's father before the woman herself was consulted.

To Hades with protocol. Once the commander officially adopted her, Nimue would be a Roman citizen. His father would be only too pleased to see an alliance between the two families. As for his commander, Tacitus had the suspicion he would do anything to ensure his daughter's happiness.

The only obstacle, as far as he could see, was Nimue herself. She'd finally agreed to be his concubine. But he wanted so much more than that. He realized that he always had.

But what did she want?

He took her injured hand, and her skin felt dry like autumn leaves. He'd never imagined asking a woman such a question in the dead of night in the middle of a forest in a far flung province of the Empire. And yet, despite the looming presence of her father, the surroundings were perfect to ask Nimue the most important question of his life.

But the words were the hardest ones he'd ever spoken. "Will you do me the honor of becoming my wife?"

She looked up at him, his beautiful savage, and it was hard to breathe.

"Why?"

A section of his mind acknowledged the grunt of laughter from the commander, but he couldn't tear his gaze from Nimue's upturned face. *Why?* How could she ask him such a thing?

"Because you're mine." He glared at her and realized that was only half the reason. "And I am yours."

She laid the palm of her uninjured hand against his heart. "You know I'm a Druid." Her voice was soft. "I can't change who I am. And I wouldn't, even if I could."

Finally the words were spoken aloud. It didn't make any difference. "I would have you no other way."

She leaned in toward him until their bodies all but touched, until their breath mingled and he could see surrender in her eyes. "Why, Tacitus?"

He should have known she would never surrender. Not until

he offered her everything that he was. The words choked his throat but he forced them out regardless. "Because I love you."

Her smile illuminated his soul and banished the dark corners in his heart forever. "Then I'm honored to take you as my husband, Tacitus." She brushed her lips against his. "I love you, my brave Roman warrior." And the look in her eyes wasn't surrender at all. It was the promise of eternity.

∽

Nimue held Tacitus' arm as they left the forest. He was once again dressed as a Roman tribune and she had never seen such a magnificent warrior. On her other side strode her father, the man she'd hated for almost half her life, who had caused her self-respect to corrode since the night of her initiation. The man she was now prepared to acknowledge as her blood kin, because now she saw the truth. Her mother hadn't betrayed her people. She had fallen in love and her warrior had been worthy.

A large owl swept by, so close Nimue felt the rush of feathers against her cheek. She gasped, followed its path as it soared into the sky and then stared, transfixed. The full moon, in all her shining glory, graced the clear night sky. And in stark silhouette against the backdrop of silver flew the owl, its wings outspread.

Arianrhod's legacy would live on.

∽

ALSO BY CHRISTINA PHILLIPS

Tainted

The Druid Chronicles Book 4

A dangerous love Rome will never allow...

Driven by the knowledge he failed to protect his king, Druid warrior Gawain abandons his gods and vows to destroy the Roman invaders by any means possible.

Nothing and no one is more important than protecting his fellow Druids from the enemy until he meets the beautiful Roman patrician, Antonia. She is everything he's never wanted in a woman, yet she fascinates him like no other. Despite the danger of discovery he embarks on an illicit liaison with her, determined to uncover the reason for the infinite sorrow that haunts her eyes.

Newly arrived in Britannia from Rome, Antonia is inexplicably drawn to the cold, tough Celt. His touch stirs a passion she long thought died at the hands of her brutal former husband and his unexpected tenderness thaws her frozen heart. But she hides a deadly secret that could be her undoing, and knows her growing feelings for him can lead nowhere. Yet when a shadow from her past threatens her future Antonia is torn between the Empire of her birth and betraying Gawain, the man she's grown to love.

~

If you would like to know when my next book is available, you can sign up for my Newsletter at my website, and receive **Catalyst**, the prequel short story in my new paranormal romance series, *Realm of Flame and Shadow*, for free.

Christinaphillips.com

ACKNOWLEDGMENTS

As always, a big thank-you to my CPs Amanda Ashby and Sara Hantz. I don't know how you guys put up with me but I'm very glad you do!
And Caleb, weapons expert extraordinaire. You went above and beyond the call of duty in answering my questions—thank you!
A special thank you to Anna Campbell and Kylie Griffin for all your help and support over the years. You ladies are awesome.
And of course, to my husband Mark who never complains whenever I disappear into the first century, and our fabulous children who think it's normal to have a mother who spends half her time in other worlds. Thank you, with all my heart.

ABOUT THE AUTHOR

Christina Phillips is an ex-pat Brit who now lives in sunny Western Australia with her high school sweetheart and their family. She enjoys writing paranormal, historical fantasy and contemporary romance where the stories sizzle and the heroine brings her hero to his knees.

She is addicted to good coffee, expensive chocolate and bad boy heroes. She is also owned by three gorgeous cats who are convinced the universe revolves around their needs. They are not wrong.

AUTHOR'S NOTE

During the first century AD, the languages used in Britain were Brythonic by the native tribal peoples and Latin by the Roman invaders. In *The Druid Chronicles* I've used words not in common usage in the English language until the 1500s and later, on the reasoning these people had words of similar meaning in their own languages at that time.

It was likely the Romans who called the ancient peoples of Europe and Britain Celts. They would have called themselves by their own tribal names. For clarity, I have taken the liberty of using the term "Celt" in reference to the ancient tribal peoples of Cymru as a whole.

Printed in Great Britain
by Amazon